I0536177

ROSE WULF

Evernight Publishing

www.evernightpublishing.com

Copyright© 2016

Rose Wulf

Editor: Amanda Jean

Cover Artist: Jay Aheer

ISBN: 978-1-77233-872-0

ALL RIGHTS RESERVED

WARNING: The unauthorized reproduction or distribution of this copyrighted work is illegal. No part of this book may be used or reproduced electronically or in print without written permission, except in the case of brief quotations embodied in reviews.

This is a work of fiction. All names, characters, and places are fictitious. Any resemblance to actual events, locales, organizations, or persons, living or dead, is entirely coincidental.

ROSE WULF

DEDICATION

This book is dedicated to my Evernight Family. So many of you have stepped up to offer words of encouragement, praise, and even friendship. You have truly touched my heart. Your support helped me find the strength to revise this book, and the rest, after the fiasco of the series being taken down last year. So it's in large part thanks to you that I can present this new and improved story to the world.

Thank you, Evernight Publishing, staff and fellow authors alike. It's a joy to be a part of this family each and every day.

ROSE WULF

WET

Elemental Series, 1

Rose Wulf

Copyright © 2016

Chapter One

"Hawke, Blake."

Brooke barely had time to think, *What a name,* before the guy sitting in the desk beside hers pushed to his feet. Subsequently, that provided her with another perfect opportunity to ogle him. He was a good four inches past six feet tall, with dark, slightly shaggy hair and a strong yet angular profile above a lean and toned body. Hell, she'd dated a guy on the swim team a couple of years earlier who'd be jealous of that body.

"Here," Blake Hawke called obediently, his thumbs hooking into his jeans pockets. And he even had Brooke's favorite kind of voice—she thought of it as 'light masculine'. Definitely male, but not so deep or gravelly that he sounded like he was growling all the time. 'Lighter' just meant she could as easily hear him laughing, or talking with a smile.

She was so lost in her mental cataloguing, she nearly missed the name of Blake's assigned partner. Which, naturally, was hers.

"Munroe, Brooke."

Doing her best not to stare at the balding man in the front of the room, or to let on that she'd been supremely distracted, Brooke rushed to her feet to announce her presence. Fortunately, he merely nodded, made a mark on his roll sheet, and moved on. Brooke resettled, releasing a silent breath, and nearly jumped out of her skin when Blake Hawke leaned toward her.

"At least we don't have to move," he whispered, that smile she'd been thinking about projected in his voice.

Brooke turned to offer her own smile as it dawned on her what he meant. Her name had been called immediately after his. And since their professor was using the first day of the new semester to assign partners, that meant Blake Hawke was her new partner. They'd be working together *all* semester. And that made her smile easier.

****

"So," Blake began on Wednesday morning, "are we supposed to exchange life stories or something?" He had one dark eyebrow cocked over his shining blue eyes to match his tone, and his lips were kicked up at the corners with mild amusement.

Brooke shrugged. "Something like that, I guess."

It was the second day of class and, after spending the first pairing off his students, their professor had declared that it was time to get to know each other. He'd even taken the liberty of turning pairs of desks to face each other, so that the students were broken into their pairs as soon as they sat down. Which was fine for Brooke. She could handle a whole hour staring at Blake's smooth face and gorgeous blue eyes. Though those eyes would surely make it hard to hear what he was saying.

Blake shifted, leaning back in his seat and angling himself so that he could stretch one long leg out without kicking her—or anybody else. "All right, then … you want to go first?"

After taking a deep breath, Brooke said, "I suppose I can. I'm twenty-two, this is my third year here, and I'm only taking this class because it qualifies as a substitution for another one that I need." She paused, realizing too late what it sounded like when she said it that way, and quickly added, "Not that I won't take it seriously, I promise!"

Blake chuckled. "No worries, I understand. I'm only taking it because it's required."

She smiled, laughing quietly, and nodded. "Fair enough." She tried to figure out what more she should say and belatedly decided he might need to have a half-decent idea of her schedule. "I'm actually only taking two other classes, but I work a lot at a diner over in Darien, so I definitely need to plan ahead if we have to meet outside of class." *Or when.* With group projects it was *always* a when.

With only the faintest of grins, Blake inclined his head. "That's fine. I actually live in Darien, so that could work for me."

"I do, too," Brooke admitted. "It's a heck of a lot cheaper, and quieter." Darien was a small coastal town about thirty minutes directly west of the university. But with the university also being several hundred feet higher in elevation, as well as on the edge of another, bigger city, Darien may as well have been in another world.

"Definitely," Blake agreed with a laugh.

There was an extended moment of awkward silence between them, and then finally Brooke said, "I don't actually know what else I should say… Is there, like, something you wanted to know?" And was there a way she could sneak in 'are you single' without tipping her hand? *No.* Not only would it be awkward if he had someone in his life, but they had a whole semester to work together. Their professor had already made it clear he pretty much didn't allow partner-swapping.

Blake shrugged. "I can't really think of anything. I'll tell you a little about me, and we can just go from there if you want?"

She smiled now and nodded. "Works for me."

"Well, like you I'm twenty-two, but this is my last semester. I'm taking a few more classes, and I work part-time as a lifeguard at the beach in Darien."

The minute the word 'lifeguard' left his lips, Brooke's imagination was off and running. She could just picture him jogging down a sandy beach on a beautiful day, barefoot and bare-chested, donning the requisite fire-engine-red swim trunks of a lifeguard, his dark hair ruffling in the wind. And even though her imagination insisted that red wasn't necessarily the best color for his skin tone, the image was striking. Mouthwatering. He'd be damn near irresistible if lifeguards were allowed to wear blue—which she was sure of, because he'd worn the same blue overcoat to school now both days.

"I'm sure we can coordinate our work schedules when we need to," Blake continued, unknowingly jarring Brooke from her distracting thoughts. "My supervisor's pretty reasonable, especially this time of year."

Suddenly, the picture in Brooke's mind shifted until Blake was running along a snow-covered beach, and she realized she was being incredibly ridiculous. Swallowing back her awkward laughter, she said, "Yeah, I bet January's not the best time of year for beach traffic."

His grin was back in force. "Yeah, not so much. Most of us are really only on call right now."

As their conversation again fell silent, Brooke's eyes drifted around the room and she caught a glimpse of another pair exchanging scraps of paper. *Oh, right!*

Turning her attention back to Blake, she said, "I suppose we should exchange information, too."

Brooke looked up from the organizer she'd subsequently extracted from her school bag to see Blake unlocking a sleek, shiny black smartphone. She couldn't help but feel a pang of envy. His phone might as well have come straight from a commercial, while hers was old, chipped, scratched, and just all around out of date. But she brushed it off, knowing she was behind on the technological times. Technology was expensive.

It didn't take them long to exchange the necessary information. And then it was time to resume making small talk, because their professor had made it clear he wasn't letting them out early.

****

Brooke looked over, still tying her apron around her waist, when her supervisor, who doubled as one of their bartenders, poked her head into the room. "Hey, Paula," she called.

The older woman smiled. "Hey. Wanted to let you know, you got a couple cuties at three. They just sat down."

"All right, I'll be out in a second," Brooke promised. Paula was nearly out the door before she added, "And don't you dare go all Cupid on me!" Laughter was the other woman's only response before the door swung shut once more.

In under a minute, Brooke had managed to get all of her things thrown into the appropriate pockets and was making her way to her first table of the night. It was an odd time of day, and so the majority of customers were currently staking claims on barstools, which made it easy for her to spot the 'cuties' at her table. They were sitting calmly and talking, one leaning forward with an elbow propped on the table, and the other leaning back with his arm half-hanging off of the chair. Both were dark-haired, probably tall, and fairly well muscled from what she could see.

Then she was standing before the table, professional smile easily in place, and launching into what she figured must be the world's most over-used line. "Hey there, my name's Brooke. You boys know what you want?"

Both men had turned their full attention to her the moment she had appeared, and she realized that they both had nearly identical bright blue eyes. Eyes that reminded her of Blake. The man to her left smiled semi-flirtatiously, his eyes twinkling, and said, "I haven't seen you here before, Brooke. You new?"

"I'm new to the dinner shift," Brooke offered, opting to play along for the moment. It wasn't like she had other customers to worry about just yet.

"Well, that explains everything," he replied, still grinning. "Except for why I haven't seen you around town."

Brooke allowed a small laugh to slip past her lips as she said, "Trust me, you're not the first to bring that up. It's just hard to find a lot of free time between work and school."

He scoffed, pulling his arm from the chairback in order to wave dismissively as he said, "Ah, school. I don't miss it."

"Wish I knew the feeling," Brooke admitted. A middle-aged couple had just stepped through the doors, so she knew she had to wrap up their conversation. Pulling her tablet from her apron pocket, she asked, "So, what can I get for you tonight?"

The flirtatious one easily took the hint and proceeded to order his meal, and then she turned her attention to the other man, who had yet to speak. While neither man looked at all weak or lanky, the second man appeared noticeably stronger than his companion. It was in his broad-shouldered, strong-jawed build as much as it was in his expression. And he had a voice to match, she discovered when he calmly ordered almost the exact same meal.

When she was done, Brooke flipped to another page and then easily maneuvered the tables and booths until she could greet the couple who had just taken a seat. They had claimed a booth in the middle of the restaurant, along the window-wall. It was the same booth they usually occupied when they came in.

"Good evening, Mrs. Buchannon, Mr. Buchannon," Brooke greeted sweetly. The Buchannons were practically local royalty, and though Brooke had only been living in town for the better part of two years, even she was friendly with them. They were incredibly wealthy, and incredibly generous. She had never met a resident of Darien who could speak a bad word about them.

Katherine Buchannon smiled up at her. "Oh, hello, Brooke! Are you working the dinner shift now?"

Brooke laughed and nodded. "Yeah, I had to switch it up this semester, since I got stuck with early classes."

"And how is school going?" Maxwell Buchannon asked curiously, his tone indicating genuine interest.

"It's going." Brooke gave a frustrated laugh and brief shake of her head.

"Are you close to graduating yet?" Katherine asked as she brushed a runaway wisp of faded blonde hair out of her eyes.

"Not close enough. At this rate, I've probably got a year left after this semester."

"Well," Maxwell began encouragingly, "continue keeping the faith, then, and you'll do fine. It'll all be worth it in the end."

Brooke smiled. "I certainly hope so. But enough about me. What are you in the mood for tonight?"

****

"I am so jealous," Georgia Clarke declared as she stepped up beside Brooke in the back room a short while later. Georgia was Brooke's favorite coworker, and probably her only good friend. She was about an inch shorter than Brooke, nearly three years older, and had a whole lot more hair than Brooke ever would—at least in volume.

Cocking an eyebrow at her, Brooke asked, "Why are you jealous, exactly?"

Georgia lifted a perfectly manicured hand and absently twirled a strand of her red hair. It was a dark, maroon shade of red, but when Brooke had met her (nearly a year and a half before), her hair had been blonde. She wasn't entirely sure that had been her real color, either. "You have two of the Hawke brothers at table three, that's why," Georgia declared with a fake pout. It might have had better effect, Brooke decided, if not for the gleam of mischief in her light green eyes.

Brooke was halfway through rolling her eyes when Georgia's words clicked in her head. "Wait, what? Hawke brothers?"

Now Georgia paused, her hair falling from her loose grasp, and in a strangely shocked voice, she asked, "You mean you've been living here for nearly two years and you've never met or at least heard about them?"

"Obviously not. But I met a Blake Hawke on Monday. He's in my first class. We're partnered up for the semester."

Georgia's grin was instantaneous, and she planted her hands on her hips. "You lucky girl! Although Blake isn't my favorite of the bunch, but they're all gorgeous."

"So they're, what, triplets?" Brooke ignored Georgia's comment for the sake of her sanity. She didn't know their exact ages, but the two at her table had looked to be fairly close to her own age, and she knew Blake was twenty-two, just like her.

Georgia was laughing, and she lifted one hand to drop it on Brooke's shoulder. "Oh, no, sweetie," she said, her tone teasing. "They're *quads*. The two at the table are Dean and Logan, and in addition to Blake, they have another brother named Nate."

"Quads?" Brooke repeated, shocked. *Wait,* she thought, giving herself a mental headshake, *why does it even matter? So what if Blake has three nearly identical brothers?* There was something seriously wrong with her head.

Brooke was yanked out of her internal critique by a nudge from her friend. "I think that's their food on the bar," she said. "Go make friends. Maybe they'll put in a good word for you with Blake."

This time, Brooke did roll her eyes as she started forward. "I'm not even going to mention it," she replied, already moving toward the freshly prepared food. Behind her, Georgia laughed.

Chapter Two

"How was your first week of school?" Lillian Hawke asked as she handed a bottle of water to her first-born.

"I've had worse, I suppose. I'm just glad I'm finally in the home stretch."

It was late Saturday afternoon, and since it was also the last Saturday of the month, the Hawke family was gathering for their traditional family dinner. Blake, like usual, was the first of his brothers to arrive, and since his father and younger sister were at the store, he had a few minutes alone with his mother.

Lillian crossed her slack-covered legs as she settled comfortably on her favorite chair. She rubbed at an invisible spot along the cuff of her beige, long-sleeved blouse. "Before you know it, it'll be over and you'll be wondering what on earth you're going to do with yourself next."

Blake grinned around the bottle he'd been about to take a drink from and pulled it down long enough to ask, "You mean like Nate?"

His mother shook her head faintly, a smile tugging at her lips. "Precisely." In the silence that followed her reply, as Blake took a long swallow of his water, the distant, familiar rumble of a motorcycle could be heard pulling up to the house. "It sounds like your brother's here."

"I'm surprised," Blake admitted, setting his bottle on the coffee table in front of him. "Nate's usually late." Muffled voices floated to them a moment later, indicating that the roar of Nate's motorcycle had most likely covered the sound of another impending vehicle. "Sounds like Dad and Angie are home, too."

Lillian pushed to her feet, and Blake easily followed suit, hanging back and letting her lead the way down the hall.

"—get anything good?" Nate was asking as the trio stepped into the house a minute later.

"When was the last time we ate something that wasn't good?" Christopher Hawke, their father, laughed as he shut the door behind them.

Nate shrugged out of his leather jacket and hung it on the coat rack in the entry way before moving and tugging at one of the bags in his sister's hands. "Let me see," he said.

Angela shifted away from Nate at the same time as she held out the bag in her other hand. "The stuff for tonight's dinner is in this bag, not that one, Snoopy."

"Wait," Nate replied, "I thought I saw brownie mix in that bag. Give it back."

"Nope." Angela deftly dodged her brother's outstretched hand and maneuvering around him. "Eric's birthday is coming up. I'm going to make him brownies."

Blake joined the conversation with a teasing grin. "You can't start baking for a man until you're married to him, Angie. Sorry."

Angela rolled her eyes. "Keep dreaming, Blake." To her mother, she said, "Is it okay if I keep this stuff in the kitchen for a couple of days?"

"Of course," Lillian said with a smile.

As Angela skirted around her family and disappeared down the hall, Nate crossed his arms over his chest and declared, "I still don't know how I feel about that guy."

Lillian rolled her eyes at her son's comment and gestured to the hallway. "Eric's a fine young man, Nate. You and your brothers need to try not to scare him off."

"Your mother's right," Christopher added, falling into step behind his sons.

Blake raised an eyebrow at him over his shoulder. "You, too?"

Christopher laughed. "I see him more often than you do, remember?"

Blake shifted his gaze, meeting his brother's eyes, before they both sighed and shook their heads. Hesitantly, Blake asked, "He's not coming to dinner, is he?"

It was Angela who answered him, having caught up with them as they returned to the living room. "Of course he is. He should be here in a few minutes, so you'd better be nice or you're off my Christmas list, got it?"

"Gee, Angie," Nate began teasingly. He moved toward her and looped an arm around her shoulders. "Christmas is so far away, I'm sure I could wiggle my way back into your good graces by then."

Angela narrowed her eyes in a futile gesture and shoved Nate off her. "Oh no, I have a memory like a steel trap, I wouldn't forget." The front door opened before Nate could retort, and Angela used the opportunity to dart around him and claim a spot on the couch.

"We're in here!" Christopher called from the loveseat.

Two sets of footsteps indicated that both of the remaining Hawke siblings had arrived, and then Dean and Logan were walking into view. Dean smirked and moved to the couch, dropping a hand on his sister's hair and deliberately ruffling it. "How's my favorite sister?"

"The same as yesterday," Angela replied, reaching up as soon as her head was released in order to fix her hair. Looking past her nearest brother, she added, "Hey, Logan."

Logan moved around Dean and claimed a seat beside Angela as he said, "Hey."

"So what's for dinner?" Dean asked, stepping back a foot and shoving his hands in his pockets.

"Angie's boyfriend," Blake replied with a laugh.

Dean ignored his sister's pointed glare. "That's unfortunate. I prefer brunettes."

"Boys," Lillian called pointedly from her chair.

Christopher interrupted her would-be lecture, saying, "Ah, let them get it out of their systems now. Maybe that way they'll behave when he gets here."

"Wait," Dean said. "What's-his-name's actually coming for dinner?"

"Yes," Angela and Lillian replied simultaneously.

At Dean's irritated look, Nate nodded and said, "Yeah, that's how I feel."

"And his name is Eric," Angela added, turning her attention directly to Dean. "Please don't be an ass."

"Angela," Lillian scolded with a frown.

Dean held his hands up in surrender. "Okay, okay, fine, I'll try to behave."

The words were barely out of his mouth when the doorbell rang, announcing the arrival of their guest.

Angela stood up immediately. "I'll get it. Compose yourselves, will you, please?" She disappeared down the hall without waiting for their response.

Christopher looked to his three still-standing sons and gestured to the remaining seats. "You might want to consider sitting, or your sister will probably accuse you of trying to intimidate her boyfriend again."

"I'll stand," Dean insisted.

Blake shook his head and moved behind Dean, putting his hand to Dean's shoulders and shoving. "Come on, sit down already. You'll only upset her."

Obediently, Dean allowed Blake to steer him towards the couch, and Nate silently sat on Blake's other side. The seat Angela had previously occupied was still open, as well as the seat beside their father and the one remaining chair. And then Angela led her boyfriend of just over a year into the large living room.

Eric Matthews walked comfortably beside the youngest member of the Hawke family, hands casually in his pockets and eyes aimed forward. His dirty-blond hair was styled as it always was, with a little too much gel and thin, combed spikes. The soon-to-be-eighteen-year-old's posture matched the expression in his eyes. He was comfortable beside Angela, and did not fear her older brothers.

"It's so good you could join us, Eric," Lillian said with a smile, standing and moving forward to greet him.

Eric embraced her quickly. "Thank you for having me, Mrs. Hawke."

"Please, make yourself comfortable," Lillian continued, gesturing wide before turning back to her chair. "Christopher was just about to start dinner."

Christopher pushed to his feet easily, recognizing the hint, and smiled as well. "Hope you like meat, because that's what we're having. I was thinking a good old-fashioned steak dinner sounded like just the right thing."

"That sounds delicious," Eric assured his host with an inclination of his head.

"Come on." Angela took her boyfriend's hand and guided him toward the newly vacated loveseat as Christopher stepped out of the room.

Once everyone was settled, Lillian swept her eyes around the room before asking, "Now then, what's new with everyone?"

****

Blake met up with his brothers again the following afternoon at Earl's Diner. For once, he was the last to arrive, so he simply smiled at the girl behind the register before moving toward the booth they'd snagged. When he reached them, he raised an eyebrow at Dean, who was sitting in the center of their side, and said, "You're going to have to slide over, bro."

Dean grinned back at him and shook his head. "Nah, since you were late, we figured you should have to sit on the floor."

Resisting the urge to smack his brother upside the head, Blake replied, "You make me sit on the floor once, I'll make you sit on the floor every single time you're late from now on."

As Dean quickly slid to the inside of the booth, Nate laughed. "He got you there, Dean."

"Shut up." Dean rolled his eyes.

Blake was barely settled in his seat when someone he hadn't expected to see until the following morning was suddenly standing beside their table.

"Well, hello there," Brooke declared with a smile as she lowered her writing tablet.

The brothers all looked over, and Blake couldn't help but return the smile. "Hey," he said. "It's only natural we run into each other now that we've already met, right?"

"Makes sense to me," Brooke agreed.

"Hold up," Nate interrupted, leaning forward and glancing between them. "How come I've never met you?" he asked as his gaze settled on Brooke.

With a shrug, she replied, "Maybe because you don't come in often enough? If it's any consolation, I've only seen those two once before today."

Jumping into the conversation, Dean said, "And really, the more important question here is: how do you two know each other?"

Raising an eyebrow at his sibling, Blake explained, "We have a class together."

Nate almost looked disappointed. "That's so … ordinary."

Brooke laughed softly at their exchange. "Yep, just about as ordinary as you come. Now then, not that I don't love your company, but I'm afraid I need to know what to feed you."

She completely missed the shared smirks the brothers exchanged before Blake obligingly ordered his lunch.

Brooke had walked off, headed to the back to put their order in, when Dean smirked and declared, "Please tell me you haven't called dibs yet."

The other three turned raised eyebrows to him, and Blake slowly asked, "What?"

"Oh, come on," Dean said pointedly. "Don't tell me you haven't noticed. She looks like she'd be fun."

Nate's head hit his hands and Logan released a deep sigh, closing his eyes and shaking his head.

Blake narrowed his eyes on his brother and said firmly, "No."

It was Dean's turn to cock an eyebrow. "So you *have* called dibs?"

"I haven't called anything," Blake said. "But she's my partner for the semester, so I'm telling you to leave her alone."

Attempting to lighten the mood, Nate looked back to Dean and said, "Yeah, besides, she's blonde. Didn't you just say last night that you prefer brunettes?"

Dean grinned. "That was last night, Nate. It's a new day."

"He's got a point, Blake," Logan declared with a mocking smirk. When Blake silently raised an eyebrow, Logan said, "He'll have forgotten all about your classmate by tomorrow."

Dean rolled his eyes as his brothers laughed good-naturedly.

****

Brooke watched the Hawke brothers leave a short while later, pursing her lips in thought. When they were walking side-by-side like they were, it was easy to see both the similarities and the differences between them. They were exactly the same height—tall, over six feet at least—and they had the same dark brown hair and bright blue eyes.

But while Blake's features were a little more angular, Logan's were strong and broad. And Nate and Dean's were somewhere in between—not as angular as Blake's, but not as broad as Logan's. While Logan was the definition of broad-shouldered and probably a dream come true for any football coach in America, both Blake and Nate were more towards lean and narrow-shouldered. Like swimmers. Dean was more broad-shouldered than the two of them, but even he wasn't in the same league as Logan.

And if she'd thought Blake's hair was slightly shaggy (probably just in need of a haircut), then Nate's was definitely shaggy. Blake's was long enough to blow in a breeze, just a little, as it danced over his forehead and covered the tops of his ears, even teasing the line of his jacket collar where it met his neck. Nate's hair, however, nearly covered his ears, and definitely overlapped his jacket collar. Dean's hair was more like what she imagined Blake's would be like if he got that haircut and spiked it just a little. And Logan's was the shortest out of all of them—just long enough to assure the world that it was there, and show off what color it was.

Despite the fact that they were all sexy, Brooke found herself focusing mostly on Blake. Comparing his own brothers to him.

They didn't stack up.

When the brothers reached the doorway, Blake held it open until the others had slipped through, and then he turned, meeting her gaze one last time and smiling.

Brooke's face heated instantly, and she lifted one hand in an awkward wave as he stepped through the door. She couldn't believe he'd caught her staring.

****

"Brooke!" Georgia declared later that evening as she popped her head into the back room. "Could you do me a huge favor? The food's ready for five, but the people sitting at two are giving me a hard time, and I can't serve it *and* handle two."

"Sure, sure." Brooke was already re-tying her apron around her waist. "Go deal with two, and I'll grab the food."

"Great, thanks!" Georgia beamed before quickly disappearing.

Brooke took a second to make sure she was still presentable, as she had been getting ready to go home, and then stepped out of the changing room and headed for the kitchen. She found the food easily and swept it onto a tray before expertly maneuvering her way out of the kitchen and towards the main room.

She was halfway to her destination before she recognized the people whose food she was carrying. Emma Matthews and her younger brother, Eric. Emma was one of Georgia's friends from high school, and since they were still fairly close, Brooke was on good terms with her as well.

"Hey there," Brooke greeted with an honest smile as she lowered the tray. "Georgia's a little busy, so I'm helping her out."

Emma returned her smile. "Hi, Brooke. I don't think I've seen you in a little while. How are you?"

"I'm doing all right," Brooke replied. She picked up the larger of the plates and paused. "Who's got the appetite?"

Emma laughed and pointed at her brother. "He says his appetite's growing with age."

Eric grinned as the plate was set before him. "It is, I swear."

"Funny," Brooke teased as she lifted the other plate and set it in front of Emma, "I've heard exactly the opposite."

"Then I must be getting younger on the inside," Eric replied.

"Yeah," Emma said, rolling her eyes. "Because you're old enough to have to worry about your age."

"I'll be eighteen in a couple of weeks," he reminded her even as he stabbed his fork into his food.

"Oh, wow," Brooke said after she'd shifted the tray to hold it sideways against her body. Other hand on her hip now, she added, "You know, he's right. He's getting ancient. I mean, what would it be like to be eighteen?"

"I can't even imagine," Emma laughed.

Around a mouthful of rice, Eric grumbled, "I hate to break it to you, but you're not nearly as funny as you think."

Emma cringed, leaned across the table, and flicked her brother's forehead. "What happened to your manners?"

When Eric only grinned tauntingly at his sister, Brooke looked over at Emma and said, "I cannot express how happy I am that I didn't get saddled with a younger brother."

Eric looked up at her then and, with a completely straight face, said, "I don't know what you're talking about. I'm an angel."

Brooke smirked. "For future reference, that claim will work a lot better after you file those horns down." Emma and her brother both laughed lightly, and after a moment Brooke added, "It's been great to see you, but I'm technically off the clock, so I probably shouldn't be dawdling."

Emma waved one hand in a shooing gesture. "Of course, of course. Go home already!"

Brooke bade them good-night and once again made her way to the back of the diner. When she was done transitioning back from Brooke-the-Waitress to Brooke-the-Woman, she slipped her purse over her shoulder and stepped out of the back room. She was barely parallel with the entrance to the kitchen when she was waylaid by Paula.

"And what are you still doing here, young lady?" Paula demanded in a strangely motherly tone.

Smiling, Brooke adjusted her purse and explained, "Georgia needed a little help, so I ran the food out to Emma and her brother."

"That was very nice of you," Paula complimented her. "Tomorrow's your early day, right?"

Brooke nodded. "I have to be in the classroom by eight o'clock sharp. Which means up at six, maybe six-fifteen."

Paula frowned. "The college isn't *that* far from town."

"No, but the parking is horrible after seven-thirty," Brooke stated.

Paula shook her head exasperatedly. "I praise your motivation, sweetheart. If it were me, I'd have quit by now. That's too much trouble."

Brooke laughed sympathetically. "Tell me about it! But I really have to run, Paula. I have another chapter I have to read tonight."

"Well, what are you waiting for? Don't let me keep you!" Paula insisted, taking Brooke by the shoulder and physically guiding her toward the sitting area. "I better not see you in here before tomorrow night, understand?"

"Good-night, Paula," Brooke replied with a wave before she turned and continued on her way.

The people at table two, who had been causing Georgia problems, were gone already, which meant that the only table occupied besides five was a booth far in the back. Brooke didn't know the old man in the booth, and for a beat she wondered why he was sitting by himself, but she moved on just as quickly. She looked back towards the Matthews siblings to smile at them again, but they weren't looking in her direction.

Shrugging it off, she went to continue forward and nearly bumped into a chair. Mentally shaking her head at herself, she angled to walk wide of the threatening piece of wood, and unexpectedly found herself in ear-shot of Emma and Eric's conversation.

"—much longer, anyway?" Eric was grumbling, sounding for all the world like a frustrated child on a road-trip. "I'm sick of waiting."

Emma's voice was lower, as if she were over-aware of her surroundings, when she said, "That's his decision, Eric. Just do what you're told and be patient."

"But it's been—"

Emma suddenly interrupted him when she realized that Brooke was nearby, though Brooke hadn't been watching them, and she loudly called, "Oh, good-night, Brooke!"

Brooke turned to smile awkwardly at them and replied, "Good-night." But as she turned forward once more, she couldn't help but think that that had been entirely too strange. *Or maybe Emma was just tired of listening to her brother's whining,* she told herself. Either way, it wasn't any of her business.

Chapter Three

It was raining heavily Monday morning. Brooke, like everyone else, felt and looked not unlike a drowned rat as she sank into her seat before class. Shoes squeaked irritatingly along the linoleum floor, and most of the conversations Brooke could hear were not unlike her own thoughts. Who wanted to deal with rain at eight in the morning?

To say she was confused when Blake eased into the seat beside hers with an easy smile and an undeniable vibrancy in his eyes would be an understatement. Not only did he *not* look like the requisite drowned rat, he actually seemed to be in a better mood than he'd been in the last time she'd seen him. *I thought he said he wasn't a morning person?*

"Good morning," Blake said, smile still in place, as he easily pulled out his notebook and set it on the desk. Today their desks were facing forward, though still in pairs, so it was probably safe to assume they'd need the notebooks.

"There's hardly anything good about it," Brooke grumbled as she draped her sopping-wet raincoat over the back of her chair.

"Don't like the rain?" Blake asked conversationally even as he shrugged out of his own coat.

"I like the rain just fine," Brooke corrected him. "Just not when I have to be out in it, and especially not when I have to be out in it so early in the morning."

Blake chuckled and, as their professor moved toward the front of the room, whispered, "I suppose that's understandable."

At this point, Brooke desperately wanted to ask him why he was in such a good mood, because she was sure she remembered him saying he wasn't a morning person. Not to mention, even if he was, who was in a *good* mood when it was pouring outside? And he was absolutely in a better mood than anyone else in the room at that moment. But, as her luck would have it, the professor chose that very moment to begin class, meaning her inquiry would have to wait.

****

Her luck hadn't improved by the time her final class was done for the day. She stood at the lip of the overhang, barely a dozen yards from the main parking lot, and stared up at the sky. The temperature had dropped, but the rain had not stopped, and now the lightest of snow was falling from the sky. It wasn't cold enough yet for the snow to stick on the ground, for which Brooke was grateful. She absolutely hated driving in the snow. In fact, she suddenly recalled, that was one of the reasons she'd moved to Darien—it never snowed there. *It's amazing what a difference thirty minutes makes,* she reflected.

"You have seen snow before, right?" Blake asked as he came to a stop beside her, hands in his pockets and trusty backpack slung over one shoulder.

Brooke jumped visibly, as she hadn't realized he'd been standing there, and turned to look at him. Her retort died in her throat, however, when she realized something else. His hood was down.

Blake looked over at her and raised an eyebrow. "You okay?"

"Are you crazy? Or do you *want* to get sick?" Brooke asked incredulously, completely ignoring both of his questions. Before he could do more than give her a confused look, she added, "Why in the world is your hood down?"

He stared at her for a long beat, blinking slowly, before his lips twitched just slightly. "I'm not crazy, I won't get sick, and I don't like hoods. I like to feel the rain."

Holding one arm out for emphasis, Brooke exclaimed, "That's not rain, it's snow!"

Blake shrugged calmly. "Snow is just frozen rain. And this is practically more sleet than real snow, anyway."

Brooke gaped at him for a long moment before pulling her arm back beneath the overhang and shaking her head. "Snow, rain, sleet, whatever. You're not supposed *let* yourself get soaked in it."

Blake's lips twitched, threatening another grin. "Come on, the snow's not going to stop just because you're standing here. I'll walk you to your car."

Not knowing what to say to that, or even if she should, Brooke nodded mutely and watched as he casually stepped out into the snow. For a moment, she just stared, watching with strange fascination, as the fragile white flakes dusted his dark hair and the top of his dark blue rain coat. She shook herself out of it and took a deep breath before following him.

"You'll have to lead the way," Blake pointed out as they stepped off of the sidewalk and into the parking lot.

Pretending she had already thought of that, Brooke easily stepped ahead of him. "You know, you don't have to walk me to my car. What if you're all the way on the opposite side of the parking lot?"

A teasing grin apparent in his voice, Blake replied, "Then I guess I'll be spending a little more time in the snow."

"Or I could drive you to your car," Brooke offered guiltily. She was, at the moment, questioning his sanity, but he was being nice enough to walk her to her car, so really it was the least she could do.

"That's very nice of you," Blake began, "but you don't have to. Like I said, I enjoy this kind of weather."

"Well, that explains your good mood this morning," Brooke declared before she could think better of it.

"What do you mean?" He moved a bit closer to her.

"Just that you were, I don't know, glowing or something when you got to class earlier," Brooke replied awkwardly. That really hadn't come out the way she had wanted it to, but it wasn't exactly wrong, either, so she didn't bother to correct herself.

"Glowing, huh?" Blake repeated with a tone that indicated curious amusement.

She had the distinct impression he wasn't actually going to elaborate at all, and even as her lips curved into a frown, she found herself wondering what she had really expected him to say. *He likes the rain,* she reminded herself. *What more does he* need *to say?*

And then she realized she had nearly walked past her own car.

Abruptly turning, she pulled her keys from her pocket and stepped up to her silver Honda Civic. "This is me," she declared as she unlocked the car. Turning a smile up to her escort, she added, "Thanks. Are you sure you don't want that ride?"

Blake's grin was automatic, and he shook his head as he said, "You're welcome, and absolutely." Jerking a thumb at the somehow-still-shiny, dark-blue newer-model Mustang in the parking space behind her Civic, he added, "That's me right there."

The jealousy she'd felt when she'd first seen his phone flared to life again when her eyes settled on the sports car. She'd always wanted a Mustang. "Well, that's fortuitous. Guess I'll see you on Wednesday, then?"

Shoving his hands back into his pockets, Blake replied, "At the latest." Then he turned and began calmly walking towards his car.

As much as she wanted to stand around and ogle the car—and the man—she really wanted to get out of the slurry-snow, and so she yanked open her door and practically dove inside. She could've sworn she heard him chuckle as she jerked the door shut again in her effort to keep the inside of her car somewhat dry. Grumbling, she adjusted herself properly in the seat, deposited her bag in the passenger seat, and then cut a glance to her rearview mirror.

She watched as Blake beeped his car unlocked, easily opened the door, and then casually tossed his backpack inside. Then, and only then, did he angle himself inside, and it was several more seconds before he pulled the door closed. Watching him move so casually, Brooke almost thought she was hallucinating the wet weather. Never, in all her life, had she known someone who loved rain and snow *that* much.

****

Blake was ten minutes out from Darien when his cell phone rang. It was Dean's ringtone, and so he switched it easily to his earpiece and hit the appropriate button. "Hey."

"Hey yourself," Dean replied grumpily. "I need a favor."

"What kind of favor?" Blake asked skeptically. With his brother, the favor was just as likely to be some harmless errand as it was to be some outrageous request.

"I'm out of coffee, and I'm dying," Dean replied.

That explains his extra-grumpy tone, Blake reflected. "And you want me to go to the coffee shop for you?"

"No," Dean said with obvious irritation. "I want you to go to the store and pick me up a can of Folgers or something. And don't take your good mood out on me."

Blake rolled his eyes and did his best to bite back his grin. "You do it to me and you know it. But yeah, I can pick you up some coffee, as long as you don't mind waiting. I'm still a few minutes from town."

"I can handle that," Dean assured him as his microwave dinged in the background.

"Lunch?" Blake asked curiously.

"Leftover pizza," Dean replied. "It sounded good. Hey, aren't you supposed to be in class still?"

Blake could only laugh at Dean's belated realization. "Yeah, but my last professor lives in the mountains up north, and they got snowed in, so class was cancelled. You got enough of that pizza for me?"

"Sucks for them," Dean commented. "I might … but only if you don't make me pay you back for my coffee."

"Right," Blake replied as he slowed to take the necessary turn-off, "'cause you're broke. I'll be there in about fifteen."

"Sweet, later," Dean said before disconnecting.

****

"Ugh, it's roasting in here," Blake declared as he stepped into Dean's single-bedroom house.

Rolling his eyes at his sibling, Dean snatched the can of coffee from him. "What'd you expect? Anyway, I need your help with something else, too."

Blake shrugged out of his coat and hung it on the coat rack Dean kept by the door. "My help?"

Dean gestured for him to follow and began walking towards his kitchen. "I already called Logan and asked if he'd mind patchin' it up for me, but he said it has to be dry first—which is where you come in."

"Your window leaks?" Blake guessed as he came to a stop beside his brother.

"Yeah. I hadn't seen it yet when I talked to you."

Blake moved up to the window over Dean's kitchen sink, spying the steady stream of water seeping in. "Piece of cake. Did you tell Logan I was on my way?"

"Yeah, he said he'll be here soon, whatever that means."

As Dean's front door eased shut from behind them, Logan's familiar deep voice called, "It means that we don't all drive like a bat out of hell. Now where's this leak I'm patching up?"

Blake looked past Dean and lifted one hand in greeting. "In here. If you're ready, I'll dry it up for you."

Logan inclined his head, coming to a stop beside Dean. "You realize that since it's still raining, it might not stick? Unless Blake's gonna stay overnight and keep an eye on it."

Dean sighed. "All right, I have an idea. Make the area dry for me and I'll … go out and see what I can do to keep it that way." Then he turned and headed for his entry, where he pulled his slick raincoat from his closet and shrugged into it.

After Dean had slipped—hood up and pulled tight—through the door, Blake looked back at Logan again. "He always makes such a big deal out of rainy weather."

Logan shook his head. "Tell me about it. I just hope he doesn't set his house on fire."

Blake chuckled, turning his attention back to the window when he saw Dean's huddled form on the other side. "I hear you," Blake agreed. Taking a deep breath, he lifted one hand deliberately and held it out.

Logan watched as the water that had leaked in began retreating, seeping back into and then through the same miniscule crack it had entered from. His gaze lifted to the window, and, as he watched, the rain that was still steadily falling seemed to curve around Dean's body, leaving a gap of several inches. After another moment, Blake lifted his hand a little higher and offered Dean a thumbs-up.

Dean returned the gesture and then reached out, toward his wall, beneath the window.

"That's probably your cue," Blake said, stepping away from the window.

"Yeah," Logan replied, pulling the tube of caulking from his jacket. He easily applied it to the crack along the window, and then moved back. "He better not flash-fry it."

Blake laughed and said, "Maybe we should move back, just in case."

Both brothers stepped backwards until they were standing on the threshold of the kitchen, several feet from the window. When Dean lifted his eyes from his work and saw this, he aimed a glare at them and lifted one hand to flip them off. Then he stepped back as well and hunched his shoulders forward to shield himself from the rain, before moving out of sight.

Dean slipped back into the house thirty seconds later, kicking the door shut and shaking off as much of the water as he could. "It's freakin' wet out there!"

"That's the general idea behind rain," Blake pointed out with a grin.

"You know," Dean replied after he'd draped his coat beside his brother's and lifted his eyes back to

Blake, "some days I wish it could rain fire, just so you could know how I feel."

"Thank God you're not in charge of the weather, then," Blake exclaimed.

Dean sighed and looked to his other brother. "Anyway, I heated up the area enough that it should be dry by now."

Logan inclined his head. "With a little luck, it should at least last you through the storm. And maybe next time when I offer to check your house before winter sets in, you might let me."

"Yeah, yeah," Dean replied, rolling his eyes.

****

"Thanks for picking me up," Angela said as she eased into the passenger seat of Blake's Mustang. She easily tossed her backpack into the backseat, beside where his still rested, and pulled the door shut.

"It's not a problem," Blake assured her with a smile. As she snapped her seatbelt into place, his smile turned into a teasing grin. "Wouldn't want you to get sick or something having to walk home in this downpour."

Angela rolled her eyes at his joke and leaned back in the seat. "Like that even *could* happen. Really, aren't you supposed to be the sensible one?"

"I am," Blake stated with the straightest face he could manage. They were silent as he pulled away from the curb in front of her school and eased back into traffic.

It wasn't until he had aimed the Mustang toward their childhood home that Angela sighed, leaned her head against the cool window, and exclaimed, "I can't wait until I'm eighteen."

Curious at her declaration, Blake looked sideways at her with one eyebrow raised. "What makes you say that?"

"Mom and Dad bought all of you the car of your choice for your eighteenth birthday," she replied. "I want my own car, so I can stop relying on everyone else to be available when I need a ride."

Blake could easily recall the last few months of his seventeenth year, when he'd felt much the same. Only his options had been significantly smaller. With a grin, he said, "C'mon, Angie, one of us is always around. You know that."

"I know," Angela assured her brother. "Although I hate riding on the back of Nate's motorcycle. All I can ever think about is how easy it would be to fall and die."

Trying not to cringe, Blake said, "Yeah, sometimes I still can't believe Nate chose a motorcycle when he could have had just about any car he wanted. He could've just gotten a convertible. Same wind factor, right?"

Angela laughed this time and nodded. "Exactly!"

"Still," Blake continued with a grin as he turned onto their court, "at least he doesn't drive like Dean."

Angela mock-shuddered. "You do have a point."

Blake slowed as he pulled up in front of the double-garage that housed their parents' vehicles and said somberly, "On a serious note, Angie, give your car some real thought, okay?"

"Says the guy who asked for a Mustang," Angela returned, her lips and tone teasing even though he could see in her eyes that she took his words to heart. "Thanks again, Blake." She leaned over, snatched her backpack, and planted a kiss on his cheek before popping the door open. "See you later!"

Blake watched until she had closed the front door behind herself before switching his car into reverse and backing out of the driveway.

****

The rain was still falling that night when Blake stepped up to Earl's Diner for dinner. He rarely ate out by himself, and he certainly had plenty of food in his refrigerator, but the idea had hit into him as he'd been leaving Dean's to pick up his sister and nagged at him ever since. And he'd have been lying to himself if he tried pretending he'd chosen Earl's by random coincidence, too.

He reached to pull open the main door as it swung open, nearly slamming into him and forcing him to step backwards as he yanked his hand back. A man he barely recognized was holding the door wide, waiting patiently for an older man he didn't know at all. Blake moved to the side politely even as the older man lifted his eyes to Blake with a glare.

Not a word was spoken as the men made their way past him and toward the parking lot. The man whose name he probably should have known had also paused to glare at him, as if he were deliberately blocking their path.

Blake was completely dumbfounded. He knew he didn't know the older of the two, and if he did know the younger one, he didn't know him well enough to claim any level of familiarity with him. So why would they go out of their way to glare at him? It made no sense. Maybe he didn't actually know either of them; maybe they were just unfriendly strangers staying in town to wait out the storm.

Brushing it off, Blake reached out once more and pulled open the door to the diner. This time he managed to make it inside without incident, and he paused to shake off some of the rain water instead of trekking it through the establishment.

"Evening, Blake," the woman behind the register called with a smile.

Blake inclined his head. "Evening, Shelly," he returned even as he made his way to an open booth. Finding one he liked, he slid halfway down the seat and let his forearms rest lightly on the tabletop. Looking at the empty bench seat across from him, Blake decided it was weird to eat out by himself. *I should think this through a little better next time,* he decided.

"Some weather we're having, huh?" Georgia declared as she came to a stop beside him a few seconds later.

Blake turned and smiled up at her, hoping his disappointment didn't show on his face. He honestly hadn't expected to see her. "It's not so bad," he replied easily.

Georgia crinkled her nose. "You're only saying that because you can't tell what it did to my hair when I stepped outside this morning."

Blake grinned. "That's probably true."

With a grin of her own, Georgia took his order and tucked the pad back into her apron pocket before suddenly declaring, "Sorry Brooke's not here tonight. She switched with Amanda last minute."

Blake stared up at her, sure she couldn't possibly have read him that easily. But she clearly had. Suddenly feeling awkward, Blake lifted one hand to scratch at the back of his head and said, "Oh, it's fine…"

Georgia offered him a knowing smile, mumbled, "Uh-huh," and turned to check on her one and only other table.

With a muffled groan, Blake's arm fell back to the table and he hung his head. *That's humiliating. And what's worse, she'll probably tell Brooke every last detail. I am beyond pathetic.* He only wished he could argue with his conclusion as he sat and waited impatiently for his meal to arrive.

Chapter Four

It'd been two or three weeks since Blake's impulsive solo trip to Earl's Diner, and fortunately Brooke didn't seem to have heard about it. Now they'd been given a research project and just under a week to get it done, so he and Brooke had agreed to meet up at his place to knock out as much of it as possible. Brooke was due in less than ten minutes, and for the first time in his life Blake found himself scouring his kitchen, making sure it was presentable. He stopped himself before he'd taken more than two steps toward his nearest bathroom and shook his head. "I'm an adult, for crying out loud," he told himself. "My house is clean. All I need to do is go, sit down, and wait for her to get here."

He had hoped by saying the words out loud he would be able to snap himself out of it. His plan didn't work.

With a heavy sigh, Blake forced himself to turn around and half-stomped past his kitchen, toward his living room. He'd already turned on his laptop and set it on the otherwise-bare coffee table, so that it was ready and available for their research. He'd checked the ink levels of the printer in the spare-bedroom-slash-office, as well as the amount of paper in the tray. He had several bottles of water and iced tea in his fridge, in addition to some cans of Dr. Pepper and an almost-full jug of orange juice. He had everything they could possibly need for the afternoon.

He had barely begun to lower himself onto the couch when he heard a car engine in his driveway. It occurred to him that he should probably have let his brothers know that he was going to be busy, as they had a habit of just popping in, but by then he had already turned to look out the window and realized the thought was unnecessary. None of his brothers drove a Honda.

The impatience he felt as he waited for her to knock was foreign to him. Usually he was the patient one, at least compared to his brothers. But all of a sudden he really wanted to tap his foot, or fidget with his hands. Because it would be weird if he went and opened the door before she even walked up, wouldn't it?

Hesitant tapping sounded at his front door before he could give the thought any more attention.

Blake was immediately in motion, striding to the door and pulling it open with an easy smile. It was several seconds before he realized that her jacket was wet. *I've reached new levels of pathetic. It's raining and I didn't even notice.* To the woman in his doorway, he said, "Hey," and stepped aside so that she could enter.

"Hey," Brooke replied, slipping past him. "Um, what do I do with my coat? It's kind of wet."

"Oh, here." Blake held out his hand. "I'll just drape it over a chair real quick."

She shrugged out of her coat after setting her school bag on the floor and then held it out for him. "Thanks," she said. "It just started raining out of nowhere a couple blocks ago. Fortunately I had it in the backseat."

Blake had already begun moving toward his dining room, which opened to the side of his kitchen and extended from his living room, so his back was to her as he called, "That's weird. I don't remember seeing rain in the forecast until Sunday."

"When do the weathermen ever get it right?" Brooke replied with a half-laugh. Before he could reply, she asked, "So, do I just, um, sit?"

From the dining room, Blake said, "Yeah, make yourself comfortable. And if you're thirsty, I've got a little of everything in the fridge, so feel free. I figure we can order a pizza or something when we want lunch."

"Pizza sounds amazing." She was grinning sheepishly at him when he came back into the room. "And I don't want to be rude, but do you have coffee? I could go for something warm. The heater in my car's having a temper-tantrum today."

"Ouch," Blake said, returning her grin with one of his own. "Yeah, I'll get it started while you set up." He moved to his kitchen, which was open to the living room except for an island.

"You have a really nice house."

The tell-tale start of the coffee maker preceded Blake's response by several beats. "Thanks. I just got it last semester, so sometimes it still feels a little weird." By the time he was finished speaking, he was moving back to the living room, a bottle of water in hand.

Brooke was grinning again as she said, "I'll be honest, I only wish I could sympathize. My apartment is probably the size of your living room and kitchen combined, maybe, and it's definitely a whole lot older."

"I don't know about the older part, but yeah, I know it's kind of big. I'd rather grow into it than have to move again as soon as I'm not single anymore, you know?" *And how did the conversation go from weather and houses to my relationship status?* He had to fight not to shake his head at himself. "So," he continued after clearing his throat, having claimed a seat on the adjacent piece of furniture. "Should we get started?"

****

Brooke was on her third cup of coffee, and her fourth slice of pizza, when the computer screen suddenly blinked. For a moment it disappeared, and then a heartbeat later the image was back, and brighter than it had been before. But in that moment, the computer had not been the only thing that had flickered. The lights they had turned on to help compete with the heavy cloud cover outside had also disappeared, only they did not come back on.

Blake sat up straight and looked around, quickly ascertaining what had happened. "Looks like we lost the power," he declared. Only his battery-operated atomic clock, which was mounted on the wall, and his laptop were still functioning.

"That's unfortunate," Brooke commented as she looked around reflexively. Her eyes eventually settled on the window, and the storm that had blown in while they'd been working. "It's really crazy out there. I hope you don't have any old trees in your backyard."

"None that are *that* old." Blake shifted his attention to the world beyond his window. The storm was in full swing.

Even with the windows shut, it was easy to hear the howl of the wind as it ripped through the trees. There were streaks of water running sideways along the outside of the glass that Brooke could see through the slats of the blinds. So many that they obscured any real view of the outside world. But Brooke knew what a hard storm looked like.

"Honestly," she said as she watched the rain continue to pelt the window, "I hate storms like this." She could never be sure if the echoing wind was coming from outside or from deep in her memory. The chill already raising goose bumps on her arms was almost certainly from memory.

Blake must have recognized something melancholic in her voice, because he turned his attention to her. She looked away, her gaze lowered and distant as her hands clutched the rim of the plate on her lap. It was that or wrap them tightly around herself, and she didn't need a mirror or a shrink to tell her how weak that would make her look.

Blake reached out, dropped one hand on her shoulder, and gave a gentle squeeze. "Don't worry about it," he said. His voice was lowered with concern that wrapped around her like a whisper of a warm coat.

Brooke looked up at him and managed a small smile. "Sorry."

He attempted a reassuring smile and released her shoulder. "The power will probably come back on in an hour or two."

Taking in a deep breath, Brooke set the plate on the table. "Yeah, I'm sure you're right." It was just a storm. She'd endured countless wind storms since *that* one. But every thirty seconds or so the wind gusted enough to shake the walls, and Brooke couldn't quite stop herself from scooting a little closer to Blake. Truthfully, she'd been fighting that particular urge pretty much since she'd walked through the door.

Another gust of wind tore through the trees, and something crashed outside a little ways off.

Brooke jumped, startled at the unexpected loud noise. Her head whipped back around, toward the window, and she felt a twinge of relief when she couldn't immediately discern what had made the noise. But that same fact made something inside clench with worry.

Blake frowned and pushed to his feet. "That can't be good," he mumbled as he moved to his window, angling his head in an effort to see the source of the crash.

"Can you see what it was?"

"No," Blake said, stepping away from the window. He frowned for a moment in thought before turning and starting toward the door. "I'm going to go outside for a minute and see if I can't see it."

That was a bad idea, she was sure. "It was probably nothing," she insisted. When he turned a curious look toward her, she corrected, "I mean, nothing you need to worry about, anyway. You should stay inside." *Where it's safer.*

Brooke could see his argument building, and she held her breath. She'd been told she could sometimes be irrational in situations like this, but surely she had a point. And she didn't want Blake getting himself hurt. There was no need to go outside and take that risk.

At length, Blake suggested, "I'll just go to the end of the driveway, okay? You can watch me from the door if you're worried." She could tell he was trying to be pacifying because she wasn't exactly being subtle about her problem with the situation. But he didn't understand.

Brooke opened her mouth to respond, instinctively wanting to disagree, but caught herself in time and snapped her mouth back shut. *Are you an adult or an oversized infant?* So she nodded instead and warily found her feet.

They walked together to the door, and Brooke suddenly wanted to hold onto him.

Blake slipped into his raincoat and shoes simultaneously, turning a smile to her as he reached for the door.

"Wait!" Brooke exclaimed before she could really *think* about what she was doing. His hand stilled just shy of its goal, and Blake's smile faltered, concern dimming his blue eyes. Instead of waiting for his obvious question, Brooke caught the exposed collar of his shirt and tugged him into her. Before she knew what the heck had gotten into her, her lips were moving over his.

Blake froze against her for a moment before his arms came around her waist and he was kissing her back.

And whatever had possessed Brooke fell back, satisfied, as her tongue slid over his for the first time.

The kiss was over long before she was ready as her brain jumpstarted with a little help from a refreshed deluge of rain over the roof. The sound was just jolting enough to remind her of the situation, and she whispered, "Be careful."

He smiled again, easier this time, and released her as he said, "I'll be fine, I promise. You wait here."

With a heavy swallow and tingling lips, Brooke nodded and watched as Blake stepped out into the storm. It was still raging up and down the street, blowing the barely blooming leaves from the branches of the surrounding trees. Winter was going out with a bang, apparently.

Brooke watched Blake jog down his driveway, his hood immediately blown off his head. But he wasn't stumbling. He was barely even shielding his eyes, and he stopped on the inside of his drive—not in the street. She watched his head swivel to the right and linger before swinging to the left. She was too far away to see his expression, but his attention lasted longer to the left before he turned and jogged back up toward her.

"What'd you see?"

He was stripping out of his soaking raincoat even as he kicked his door shut. "Looks like the crash was a large limb from a neighbor's tree. No one was hurt, just the fence," he explained as he stepped out of his shoes.

A sigh of relief escaped her and she allowed a small smile. "That's good."

Blake grinned and teased, "I'd kiss you again, but you'd get soaked. I'd better go change real quick."

Brooke was sure her face turned pink, but she had no one to blame for it but herself. Not that she would actually *complain*. "Go change, then." As an afterthought, as he started down the hall, she asked, "Where are your candles?"

****

Brooke sat in the sand, staring at the ocean as it lapped at the beach, not really seeing the waves or hearing the crack as they crashed down. It was a little before one o'clock on Saturday afternoon, and the sky was clear. The storm that had shaken her up Thursday had all but blown itself out by the time she'd left Blake's house for work, but its effect still lingered. And that wasn't all that lingered. Since Thursday, and her impulsive kiss, she had felt like her subconscious was on a never-ending roller coaster. One minute she felt weirded out by that freak, unpredicted storm, and the next minute she swore she could taste Blake on her lips like they'd only just broken apart.

She certainly wished that were the case.

Their first kiss had been an impulse, but their second and third most definitely had not. After Blake had come back into the living room, they'd realized with the power out there wasn't much they could do in terms of making progress on their project. Or perhaps some of that quick surrender had had something to do with the kiss he'd wrapped her up in almost immediately. Either way, they'd certainly made out on the sofa like a couple of fifteen year olds taking advantage of their parents being away at work. And the body she'd felt beneath the soft fabric of his shirt… She'd be lying if she implied she didn't want to see it first-hand in the near future.

The waves crashed into the shore again, spraying salty seawater in wide arcs and dragging her roller coaster back to the frightening precipice. Why she'd chosen the beach, aside from the unlikely interruptions and fresh air, she wasn't sure. The sounds of the rolling tide reminded her an awful lot of a powerful windstorm. And lord knew she hated those.

Another shiver danced up her spine, and Brooke swallowed heavily. Yes, she *hated* those. And while Blake had certainly helped to distract her from Thursday's, it had still been a distraction. Inevitably temporary.

She only barely processed the soft sound of crunching sand beneath someone's feet before the voice she least expected to hear called out to her.

"Brooke?"

Chapter Five

Completely caught off-guard by Blake's unexpected appearance, all Brooke could think to say as she looked up was, "Hi." *Well, that was impressive.* But what else could she say? Blake stood there, just a couple of feet back, hands in his jeans pockets with a mildly curious and concerned expression on his face. He wore a lightweight blue blazer over his shirt, and his hair fluttered in waves not unlike the tide in the faint breeze. He looked so *right* on the beach, even in jeans, that her brain needed a full restart.

Blake seemed to take her response as a sort of invitation and settled himself in the sand beside her. He sat with one leg raised and bent at the knee. With an elbow propped on his knee, he faced her and asked, "Is everything okay?"

Brooke looked away from him, unsure of how to answer his question. She figured she ought to give him the stock answer and assure him she was fine, but she wasn't so inclined to lie to him. *And over what, a storm?* But her alternative was to actually answer his question, and tell him something about herself that she didn't even like to think about. Something she generally pretended had never been.

Seeming to take her silence as the answer it was, Blake shifted his own eyes forward and quietly said, "Let me rephrase that. What's wrong?"

She sighed and opened her mouth, pushing out whatever words would come. "I'm sorry about Thursday," she said. "That is, I'm sorry for freaking out over the storm…" What was wrong with her? She didn't want him thinking she regretted their kiss!

Blake started and looked back over to her. "You're still upset about that? It's not like you need to apologize for anything."

Eyes downcast now, Brooke replied, "The truth is … a part of me is terrified of windstorms like that."

Blake's tone indicated that he could tell there was more to her story when he gently asked, "Can you … talk about it?"

Brooke was silent for a long minute, her gaze returning to the ocean reflexively, as she contemplated her answer. She could, it was true. It was also true that she didn't necessarily want to. But it was the least she could do, she figured, since he had already seen a glimpse of the results.

"When I was little," she began, still looking forward, "my parents left me home with a babysitter while they went out one night. And while they were out, a terrible storm blew in. It started like an ordinary thunderstorm, at least from what I remember, but then the wind came."

She paused, taking in a deep breath, and Blake kept quiet.

"I honestly don't remember the details," Brooke continued. "A lot of the details I know are things I've learned since. But my parents were driving home in the middle of the storm, and someone crashed into them. From what I heard, my dad died instantly, and my mom died in the ambulance. I was an only child, and my only other relative was my grandmother, who already lived in a nursing home. So I became a ward of the state, basically, and I spent years bouncing back and forth between foster homes before I was finally adopted eleven years ago."

She took another breath before reiterating, "But, like I said, I don't actually remember the night of the accident too well. The only memories that I know for sure are mine, and not images I made up to go with the stories, are memories of the storm. I remember the rain pelting the windows, and the trees bending in really weird ways. And the wind … it was so loud that night." She shivered involuntarily as her voice trailed, the echoing howl of the wind from her memory sending a chill through her heart.

Blake was silent for several seconds before he finally said, "I'm sorry. I never meant to bring something like that up."

Brooke shook her head, finally looking back over at him. "No, it's okay. I know it's kind of messed up, but, I don't really remember my parents. I was only four when they died."

"Still." Blake hedged, as if understanding her point but feeling bad all the same. "Is there something I can do to help take your mind off it?"

Her lips curving up ever so slightly, Brooke replied, "Well, you are kind of good at distractions…" But she didn't want to make him uncomfortable, and whatever might be budding between them she didn't want to screw up. So she quickly offered an alternative to keep the mood light. "Or you could … tell me your own deep dark secret? You know, make us even." Personally, she hoped he'd opt for the kiss. But she supposed learning something new and maybe significant about him would be good, too.

Blake chuckled and wrapped an arm around her shoulders, pulling her into his side. "Those are my choices, huh?" he said teasingly.

****

He was silent for a long moment after, keeping a loose hold on her shoulders. A dangerous impulse had popped up in his head. Something he hadn't considered until he'd seen Brooke sitting, so sad and lonely, on the beach. He disliked seeing her that way. But was he *really* considering telling her his secret? His *family's* secret?

Suddenly, Blake's lips tingled in memory of Brooke's earlier kiss.

Yes, he was considering telling her his secret. Maybe for less than solid reasons, but, his instinct was that he could trust her. And wasn't that really the only requirement? Trust? That trust certainly hadn't backfired on him when he'd told his best friend, Jason. Granted, that entire situation had been different. Jason had nearly drowned during a late-night swim and Blake had had to use his powers to save his friend's life. As a result, Jason was the only one Blake had ever revealed himself to.

Until now.

He wasn't sure how long it took him to work up the nerve to ask a simple, clichéd question. "Can you keep a secret?"

****

Thrown by his question, Brooke angled her head to look up at him. "Yeah, I suppose… What kind of secret are we talking about, exactly?"

He held her gaze as he replied, "An ancient one."

Now thoroughly intrigued, Brooke slowly nodded. "All right … on one condition. I don't want anyone hunting me down for knowing about it."

Blake's lips twitched and he shook his head. "Don't worry. It's not life-threatening."

"That's good." Brooke reached over to run her fingers along the collar of his shirt and tease his skin. "Because I'm ridiculously curious now."

"The best way to explain it," Blake began, pulling away and pushing to his feet, "is for me to show you. So watch closely." He offered her a quick smirk before he took two steps backwards, away from her, and held out one hand towards the ocean. The wave, which had been rolling in at its steady, calm pace suddenly stilled, holding the line several feet lower than usual. Then, abruptly, the water reversed, rushing back into itself.

Brooke was confused as her eyes flicked between her companion and the strangely behaving sea. Was it possible for the ocean to be behaving like that? *It must be,* her brain told her, *because otherwise I have to believe it's possible for* Blake *to be doing that.*

As if sensing her disbelief, Blake curved his hand slowly so that his palm was angled towards her, and then swept his arm in almost casually.

The flow of the tide seemed to return to normal, but as the water came up, a stream separated itself and continued moving forward even as the rest of the water receded. This stream lifted off the ground as it broke free and glided with an unnatural grace through the air until it had curved completely around Brooke's seated form. It swirled around her, separating completely from the ocean and spiraling up.

Brooke was wide-eyed, and barely breathing, as she watched the seawater move around her. It was like magic, and she had no idea how to react. The water curved around her one final time before continuing on, this time flying toward Blake. She watched as he held out one hand, palm up, and the water gathered there, forming a type of puddle and hovering above his hand.

With a flick of his wrist, the water snapped quickly back to the ocean before collapsing, as if the spell that had possessed it had suddenly broken.

"Wh-what … was that?" Brooke asked shakily as she drew in a ragged breath. *That was impossible, that's what that was.*

Blake stayed put, letting his arm fall to his side, and met her gaze solidly. "That was my power. I have the ability, if you will, to control water. It's as natural to me as breathing."

He said it with such a straight face, and such a serious, calm voice, that Brooke found herself inclined to believe him. Except that it was impossible. She just didn't know how *else* to explain what she'd just witnessed. And that was a lot to take in. Did she—could she—really believe what he'd just shown her?

She tried to surreptitiously look around, to see if there were a more logical way to explain what she'd seen. But no one was there. No boats lingered just off shore. The *only* explanation was the one he'd offered. No matter how impossible it should have been.

Blake remained silent as he watched her process what she'd seen. What he'd told her.

After several minutes, Brooke finally spoke. "Is that … why you like rain so much?" It was such a stupid question that she couldn't actually believe she'd just asked. And yet it was the only real question she could wrap her mind around.

His lips twitched again, though he contained the grin this time, and he nodded. "Yes. The closer I am to water, the stronger I am, and the better I feel. Which is why I live in a coastal town, and why I spend as much time outside on rainy days as I can without looking like a freak."

"Can you breathe underwater?" The question was past her lips before she had even consciously wondered it, but she managed not to clamp her hands over her mouth in embarrassment. At this point, she figured, it was as legitimate a question as any other.

Blake allowed the grin to show this time as he said, "Yep. But I can do more than that. If I want to, I can actually *become* water."

Brooke blinked up at him. "I'm sorry," she began slowly. "You can do what?"

"Just watch," Blake replied. He took a deep breath, closed his eyes, and after a moment water began dripping from his fingertips. And then, without warning, Blake disappeared entirely. His clothes collapsed, no longer supported by a body, and it wasn't until they landed that Brooke realized there was a puddle of water where he'd been standing.

The puddle moved as she watched, pulling away from the pile and somehow gliding along the top of the sand. It stopped after moving only a couple of feet, and turned in a strange circle, like a ribbon of water being spun around by an invisible pole, almost as if it were showing off. Then it reversed course, returning to the pile of clothes. When the pile was entirely encompassed, the water shifted, pushing against the fabric. Filling it, giving the clothes an odd three-dimensional effect on the sand. The water seemed to thicken for a moment, and then just as suddenly as he'd disappeared, Blake was back, kneeling in the sand.

Brooke opened her mouth reflexively, intending to say … *something* … but she quickly found that she had no idea what, exactly, she would actually say. So she snapped her jaw shut and watched silently as Blake pushed to his feet.

He released a heavy breath and adjusted the collar of his jacket, before brushing some loose sand off of his jeans and letting his hands fall back to his sides. "Believe me now?" he asked with a lopsided grin.

****

Over the course of the next hour and a half, Brooke learned that Blake was not as unique an individual as she'd first thought. His ability was, quite literally, in his blood. For as far back as his family could trace, the mother of the family always gave birth to five children: quadruplet boys and, later, one girl. The first-born boy was born with the ability to control water; the other three were born with the ability to control air, earth, and fire respectively. It was the sister who would eventually birth the next generation.

At one point, Brooke had asked how their family had come to possess powers like that. It sounded convoluted to her, like trying to puzzle out the idea behind the chicken and the egg. And Blake admitted he didn't have an answer.

"We weren't always the only family with these powers," Blake explained. "Rumor has it that there used to be dozens of families like ours. But over the centuries they've died out, and so far as we know we're the last ones."

"So you don't know your own origin story?" Brooke asked, surprised. "That sounds sort of messed up."

Blake shrugged and leaned back on the beach, resting his palms on the sand behind him to hold himself up. "There are lots of theories that have cropped up over the years," he said. "But all we know for sure is that by the time of our earliest official record, our ancestors already had these powers."

Intrigued, Brooke shifted to better face him. "Tell me some of the theories."

"All right," Blake said, pausing a moment before a slight grin curved his lips again. "Apparently my great-grandmother had decided that our ancestors were actually born from the elements themselves. For whatever reason, each of the four basic elements came together and gave birth to a human who had complete mastery of that element. She said she suspected that Mother Nature was angry at man, and these elementals were supposed to somehow remind the people of their time to respect the world around them.

"And according to her theory, there was one spot of overlapped space where each of the four elements had gathered. It was from that spot that the fifth sibling—the female—was born. And since each of the elements had equal influence over the space that had created her, she was not able to be a representative of any one element. But neither could they allow any one being to control *all* of the elements, so Mother Nature intervened one final time and gave the female a different power. A different purpose. She was to protect and nurture the other four, and to ensure that there would always, from that day forward, be four elementals to fight for the planet."

It was so much like one of the old Greek mythology stories Brooke remembered reading back in high school that she couldn't help but smile. In a strange way, it was exactly what she'd expected. But she was still left with one new question. "Okay, but I'm still confused. I get the 'ensuring a future generation' thing, from what you already said, but how is your little sister supposed to 'protect and nurture'? And what if she just doesn't want kids?"

Blake stared for a beat before shrugging. "Then we're the last generation, I guess. As for your other question, she has a power, too. She can't manipulate any of the elements, but she can heal herself and others."

"Heal?" Brooke repeated in disbelief. She couldn't quite wrap her brain around that one. Though how someone being able to heal someone else seemed more unbelievable than someone being able to turn into water, she wasn't sure. And then another, much more disturbing, thought popped into her head. Even as she chastised herself for watching one too many episodes of

The Walking Dead, she asked, "So, can she … bring people back from the dead?"

Blake valiantly attempted to muffle his laughter as he shook his head. "No, no. Death is impossible to reverse, even for her."

Brooke breathed a sigh of relief. "That kind of works for me."

Blake grinned knowingly, but before he could say anything, his phone began ringing from his jacket pocket. Grin shifting to an apologetic smile, he dipped one hand into the necessary pocket and pulled his phone out. "Hey, bro."

Brooke watched as Blake listened to the man on the other end, her calm patience turning into concerned confusion as his expression changed. In the space of a few seconds, he went from easygoing to angry, sitting upright and almost as quickly springing entirely to his feet in alarm. And he hadn't even said anything yet.

"I'm on my way," he finally replied, before disconnecting and dropping his phone into his pocket.

"Blake?" Brooke asked, standing carefully.

"I have to go, I'm sorry," he said, already shrugging out of his coat. He paused, tugged his car keys free from his jeans, and tossed them to her, adding, "Could you take my stuff to my parents' for me? It's okay if you have to leave my car here."

Brooke blinked at him, entirely thrown. "What's going on?"

He shook his head with a frown. "No time. I'll call you later." And before she could even find the right argument to go with he was dripping again. Only it didn't seem to take as long for his body to liquefy this time, but Brooke couldn't really dwell on that because the puddle he'd become immediately rushed to join the incoming tide. And then she lost sight of him entirely.

"What…?" Shaking her head at herself, Brooke looked down at the keys in her hand. Something bad must have happened for him to react like that, she was sure. And in that case, she couldn't begrudge him his haste. *But I don't know where his parents live.* Still, the Hawkes were apparently fairly well-known around town. Georgia would surely know. Although if she asked Georgia, she'd be stuck figuring out a convincing lie, too. Instinct insisted what Blake had revealed to her that day was supposed to be a secret, and no one with a brain in their head shared a secret like that with Georgia Clarke.

Sighing, Brooke pocketed the keys and gathered up Blake's clothes. Maybe she could unlock his phone and find the address that way. Otherwise she'd be stuck bringing it all home. And all the way up the sandy slope she kept rounding back to one ridiculous thought: she was attracted to Aquaman. She was *really* attracted to Aquaman.

Chapter Six

Angela was walking home from a friend's house, her purse hanging over one shoulder and her earbuds tucked securely into place, attached to the iPod resting in her pocket. The weather was fairly mild, as winter was finally coming to a close, and there was barely a cloud in the sky. It was an almost beautiful Saturday, and it made her hopeful for the rest of the weekend.

Maybe me and Eric can do something more interesting than going to another movie, she mused with a small smile. They always scheduled a date for Sunday afternoons when they weren't saddled with family plans, and if the weather was anything like this tomorrow, she intended to suggest doing something outside. *Like going to the park.* The park was her favorite place in town, even over the beach.

She was about halfway home, having taken her favorite scenic route in order to prolong her time outside, when her iPod made a strange static-like sound. Stopping, she reached into her pocket and pulled the slim device out, as if looking at it would tell her what the sound was. But the music had already resumed, and nothing on the screen indicated any sort of problem. So she shrugged and slipped it back into her pocket.

A particularly strong gust of wind kicked up, blowing her long, dark hair into her face and dragging a sigh from the teenager. She reached up to move her hair from her face, but paused with her fingertips just barely brushing her skin when she heard a strange crackling sound. It wasn't coming from her iPod this time, but from somewhere up above her. *What—?*

The question hadn't even formed in her mind before there was a flash of blinding light off to her right.

The flash had barely faded before she registered the sound of a nearby explosion, which was followed almost immediately by more crackling and a sudden surge of heat.

Angela spun, wide-eyed and confused, and felt her breath catch in her throat. She was on an old paved path that ran alongside a steady stream which eventually curved into the ocean. In the spring and summer, the trees that were scattered alongside the stream were in full bloom and brought a sense of serenity to the area, which was why she loved it so much. In the winter time, of course, the trees were barren, the branches craggy outcroppings of wood. And now, as Angela stared at the quickly building fire only a dozen or so paces away from her, those barren trees were nothing but fire accelerant.

It was at this point that Angela realized what that flash of light had been. *Lightning,* her mind supplied. In her memory, she could see that the flash had started in the sky above her before extending down, out of her peripheral vision. Lightning had struck the ground, and since the ground was dry and covered with burnable twigs, the lightning strike caused an immediate fire. And now Angela was trapped between the growing inferno and the cliff overlooking a rushing stream.

She immediately moved backwards, away from the heat of the flames, and thrust her hand into her pocket to pull out her cell phone. Her fingers automatically found the speed-dial button she needed, and she put the phone to her ear. Fortunately, her brother answered almost right away.

"Dean," she gasped when she heard the line connect. "I'm trapped between a fire and Darien Creek." She was trying to keep her voice steady, to get out all the words he would need to know, but the more she thought about it, the more the reality of her situation settled in. She wasn't sure that even Dean could drive that fast.

****

Fortunately Blake's phone lock was only a swipe-lock, and Brooke had easily located his parents' address. Since she didn't know how to work his GPS, however, she'd taken a couple of wrong turns before finally winding up on the correct street.

And what a street it was.

The homes were set widely apart from each other, and deep driveways coupled with tall shrubbery and tall fences of brick or steel added a heavy level of privacy. These homes weren't houses but mansions. It was no wonder Blake thought nothing of the size of his house! The gate to the first home on the street was open and a large moving van was parked in the drive, its back open. Brooke couldn't stop herself from gawking at what she glimpsed of the property. It looked like the owners were moving, and for a brief moment she wished she could afford a place like that. Would she ever even feel the need to lock her front door again?

You're being ridiculous. Sure, it'd be nice to have enough money to live comfortably—let alone lavishly—but that was the last thing she should have been focusing on. What she needed to do was navigate the magnificent piece of machinery she was sitting in further down the lane until she found the correct number. Returning Blake's belongings, which he had so valiantly entrusted her with, was much more important than lamenting her lack of finances. She was a working college student—wasn't she pretty much required to be broke?

There!

Up ahead, the next driveway—that was her destination. At least according to the mailbox on the side of the gate. The gate itself was open as if inviting her in.

Or perhaps they were expecting her? She had no idea what had startled Blake so much, after all. What if he'd actually come here and just hadn't had the time to drive? *That would make explaining easier.* But somehow she doubted it was that simple.

Brooke eased Blake's Mustang to a stop between the garage and wide front steps, not wanting to block anyone in. Then she gathered his clothes, and phone, in her arms and climbed from the car with a stupid pang of remorse. He had a beautiful car.

Up the steps, shift the pile, and the familiar chime of the doorbell rang beyond the expensive front door. And it wasn't until that moment that Brooke wondered what she was actually going to say. Would Blake get in trouble if they knew she knew? But how else would she explain the clothes? *I could say I found them abandoned by the shore...* She'd come off looking more like a bad stalker if she did that, though.

The door swung open before she could think up a better option, and Brooke found herself looking into the faded blue eyes of a stranger. A woman, maybe in her mid-forties, with dark hair piled up in an elegant bun and a natural smile. Brooke felt immediately at ease in front of her despite having no idea who the woman was.

"Can I help you?" she asked politely. Her eyes flicked past her as she spoke and lingered on Blake's car. The smile on her face dipped into a frown, and Brooke could guess what would have followed.

"I'm sorry to bother you," she offered lamely, "but Blake asked me to bring this stuff over for him... That is, you are Mrs. Hawke, right?" Oh, how awkward would *that* be?

Frown fading a bit, the woman returned her attention to Brooke and nodded. "I am. Call me Lillian. Please, come inside."

Brooke awkwardly stepped into the foyer, trying not to gawk or restlessly juggle the bundle in her arms. She hadn't expected to be invited inside.

"Is Blake all right?" Lillian asked as she guided her guest down the main hall.

"I … think so," Brooke offered. "I don't really know what's going on. He got a phone call and it seemed pretty urgent." She paused, remembering how he'd answered the phone, and added, "From one of his brothers."

Lillian arched one perfectly manicured brow at her as she indicated one of the massive sofas. "And he left his clothes and car keys with you?"

Well, it sounds awkward when you phrase it like that. Swallowing, Brooke carefully set the pile down on the cushion beside her. "Yes. He asked me to bring it to you, but he didn't have time to say why or what was going on." The tricky part was next, and Brooke sincerely hoped she wasn't messing anything up. "He just took off his jacket and, uh, liquefied. Or whatever the word is for that. Then he disappeared in the ocean."

"I feel like I walked in at the wrong time to this conversation," an amused male voice declared before the man Brooke could only assume was Blake's father stepped into view. Extending a hand, he added, "I'm Christopher, Blake's father. And I'm going to assume he trusts you if he willingly told you about his abilities."

Brooke shook his hand as a sort of surrealism overtook her. Lillian's expression had betrayed surprise at Brooke's words, but Christopher seemed calm. Almost happy. "I'm going to assume that, too," she said honestly as her arm fell back into her lap.

Claiming a seat beside his wife, Christopher asked, "So what's going on?"

****

At first, she had been mildly hopeful, because the flames had spread out to the sides more than toward her. However, soon enough that had changed. And now the flames were coming closer and closer.

They were licking at the air in front of her. It was only a matter of moments before she felt the burn when the wind unexpectedly picked back up, blowing fiercely against the flame and holding it back—if only slightly.

Hope lit up in her heart, and Angela turned her head to try to find her rescuer. "Nate!" She could hear the desperation and relief in her own voice, but she didn't care. What mattered, she realized, was that she couldn't see her brother. And that only meant one thing. Angela groaned and clapped a hand over her eyes firmly. "You better blow me out of the way if the fire gets too close!"

The words were barely out of her mouth when another sound reached her ears. This one was wet and roared not unlike waves on the ocean in a storm. The waves in her mind's eye crashed onto the fiery shore, producing a chilling, terrifying sizzle and undoubtedly thick, black smoke. But she could still feel the heat; still hear the crackle of stubborn fire. It wasn't all out.

"Blake!" she called, praying her brother had been riding *on* the wave like an epic movie-star surfer. No way was she going to risk peeking.

The wind died down for a second before kicking up again, and the faint crunch of twigs beneath someone's feet indicated that Nate had pulled himself back together. A hand landed on her shoulder, and Nate's familiar voice said, "Just stay close, Angie. Dean's almost here. I saw him when I was flying over."

"No offense," Angela began, her hand still firmly over her eyes, "but I don't want to stand *that* close when you're naked. It's gross."

"Glad you think so," Nate returned, his humor noticeably more strained than usual. But he dropped his hand from her shoulder obligingly.

"Blake's not naked, too, is he?"

"'Fraid so," Nate replied, his voice strained.

"Stay where you are, Angela," Blake called from several feet away. "The fire's almost out."

Doing her best to melt her fingers permanently over her closed eyelids, Angela said, "Trust me, I'm not moving until no one's naked!"

She barely heard the shift in the crackle of the fire over her exclamation. It sounded as though the fire was receding, but she hadn't heard another rush of water. She hadn't felt an increase in the wind. *Dean.* The only answer was Dean. *Please don't let him be naked, too.*

The sound of crunching, rolling gravel reached her ears shortly before the accompanying sound of heavy breathing. "Angie! You okay?" It was Dean. And that could only mean the fire was finally out.

"No!" Angela replied, turning her face in the direction of his voice. "Two of my brothers are naked and one of them touched my shoulder! I'm scarred for life!"

It was Blake who commented next. "Ange, seriously, are you hurt?"

Angela sighed. "No, I'm not hurt. But someone please tell me Dean's at least wearing pants."

"Fully dressed, I promise," Dean replied, his voice closer now.

The ground beneath their feet lurched just slightly before anyone could comment further, and Angela knew that meant her fourth brother had arrived.

"You're late to the party," Nate called a moment later, confirming her suspicion.

"And you better be dressed," Angela added pointedly.

Ignoring both Nate's and Angela's comments, Logan asked, "Is she hurt?"

"She's not hurt," Angela said. "She's just scarred enough as it is. I don't think I could handle three of you not wearing pants."

There was a pause, and her stomach sank. She might have even thrown up if it had lasted any longer.

"I'm dressed," Logan assured her.

"Speaking of," Nate interrupted, "I don't suppose either of you has any clothes handy?"

"Pants, at least, would be great," Blake added.

"In my trunk," Dean replied, unknowingly saving his sister yet again. This time from having to blindly navigate a hillside covered in tripping hazards.

Angela remained quiet until the crunch of their feet had mostly faded. "So … is it safe for me to look yet?"

"Yeah," Logan promised. "It's safe. We'll give them a minute before we meet up with them."

Angela lowered her hand, blinking her eyes rapidly for a second as they readjusted to the sunlight.

Logan was scowling again when she looked his way. "What happened?"

Her eyes drifted up, toward the sky, reaffirming what she remembered. Like before, there were only a sparse few—white—clouds overhead. As she lowered her eyes back to her brother, she said, "This is going to sound weird, but … I think I was almost struck by lightning."

Logan's eyes widened at her statement. And after several seconds, she knew he had come to the same realization she had.

They'd lost an uncle to a lightning strike, back when their mother and father had only been dating.

Chapter Seven

Concern in her voice, Lillian asked, "Did something happen?"

"Yeah," Dean said as Blake led the way inside. His brother's heavy tone fit their mood perfectly.

"Mom," Angela started with a glance toward Brooke. Her voice trailed, but the implication was fairly obvious.

"Hi, Angela," Brooke said, seeming to sense the younger girl's point. "I'm Brooke. I'm a friend of Blake's."

"Blake sent her here a short while ago," Lillian explained calmly. "We couldn't let her spend money on a cab and she wouldn't let us drive her to the beach, so we've opted to wait together to learn what the emergency was."

With a pointed look at his son, Christopher added, "Seems she was worried."

Blake cringed and looked to Brooke, hoping she could see the apology in his eyes. "I'm sorry about earlier."

Brooke smiled. "It's okay, I'm sure you had a reason. And your parents are really nice."

"Now," Lillian interrupted, "about that reason?"

Nate emerged from the kitchen, two sandwiches plated in his hands, and extended one to Blake before claiming the seat next to Dean.

"You two look a little pale," Christopher said as realization dawned.

"I'm fine," the brothers echoed. Blake wasted no time biting into his sandwich, knowing he needed the rejuvenation.

Lillian cleared her throat pointedly. "We're still waiting for answers. Is someone hurt?"

"No," Dean replied quietly.

Angela pulled in a breath and Blake paused in his eating to glance over at her. She was preparing to explain, and he felt guilty at the news they were about to drop on their parents.

"When I was walking home," Angela began slowly, her blue eyes focused on the carpet at her feet, "I was ... almost hit by lightning." She paused, swallowed, and added, "It started a fire, so I called Dean, and then Logan."

When she paused again, Blake stepped in. "Dean called me from the road. Said he was calling Nate next. Nate managed to get there first, and held back the flames until the rest of us got there." If Dean had had the energy, Blake was sure he'd have been interrupted by now with some kind of outcry. Blake wasn't exactly the brother most known for revealing their family secret on a whim, but it must have been obvious to his brothers—and sister, for that matter—that he'd said something about it to Brooke already. That, or he was willing to get into the details later.

Christopher nodded, and his voice was strangely detached as he looked between Blake and Nate, saying, "But you had to transform to do it."

Blake nodded, his mouth full with the final bite of his sandwich.

"Yeah," Nate said with a swallow.

Before another word could be said, they all heard the familiar rumble of Logan's truck as it pulled into the driveway.

Silently, they waited until the final Hawke had joined them in the living room, claiming the seat beside Nate.

****

Lillian excused herself shortly after Angela had reiterated the story, in detail, for her parents. And Brooke. The family sat in semi-awkward, dark silence as they listened to Lillian move up the stairs. Blake was debating whether or not to offer Brooke a ride home when his mother's muffled voice carried down to them. None of the words were distinguishable, and it became clear she was on the phone.

Curious, Blake looked across the living room to his father. "Who would she be calling?"

Christopher shrugged, his confusion as obvious as theirs. "I have no idea."

"What I don't understand," Angela suddenly said, her eyes still fixated on an invisible spot on the coffee table and her hands fisted in her lap, "is where could the lightning have even come from? It's a clear day."

"I was wondering that, too," Logan admitted even as his brothers nodded silent agreement.

No one had anything more to add, and once again the room fell silent. Lillian's muffled voice became all that could be heard as she continued whatever conversation she was having.

Brook shifted her weight on the loveseat, drawing Blake's attention, and their eyes met. He could read her confusion and concern as easily as he could discern his own. But he didn't have the opportunity to try to get her alone before his mother returned.

Lillian stepped back into the room, her gaze downcast and her lips drawn into a tight, thin line of unhappiness. Her eyes were slightly puffy, and there was a faint tinge of red around the white.

"Lillian?" Christopher asked, curiosity and concern mingling in his voice as she reclaimed her seat beside him.

She took a deep, heavy breath, keeping her eyes closed for a long minute. When she finally looked up again a new layer of tears was visible around her faded blue eyes, though they did not fall. "I just got off the phone with Nicholas," Lillian declared, only the faintest wobble detectable in her voice.

Blake's eyes widened. Nicholas was one of her brothers, and therefore one of their uncles. He, like Dean, controlled the fire element. Unfortunately, due to a horrible car accident which had left him crippled from the waist down, he had very little influence over his natural element. None of the Hawke children had seen their uncle since the boys had been ten, though he did send cards reliably on birthdays and holidays.

"Why did you call Uncle Nicholas?" Angela asked when her mother paused.

"I always thought it was strange," Lillian began softly, in a tone that indicated she was divulging a shameful secret, "that one of my brothers was struck and killed by lightning, and two more of my brothers were caught in a freak snow storm where one of them died, and the other very nearly died, too."

Blake looked away from his mother's saddened gaze, and beside him, his brothers and sister shifted. Angela's gaze was back on the coffee table. No one knew what to say, or where she was going with this, so they held their tongues.

"After the accident, Nicholas had nothing better to do, so he threw himself into our family's history. I always knew he had done the research, but I always assumed nothing had come of it. After today, I thought it was worth asking. I don't want to lose any of my children … the way I lost two of my brothers."

Christopher's hand wrapped around one of Lillian's, which had been curled in her lap, as a tear slipped down her cheek.

Lillian took only a moment to push aside the lingering pain of her lost brothers, dragged in a breath, and said, "Even so, I really wasn't expecting what he said." She paused and wrapped her free hand over the top of the hand her husband still had around hers. "A long time ago, when there were still many other families with powers like ours, there were other kinds of elemental families, too."

"Other kinds…?" Angela repeated, clearly confused. Around her, her brothers shifted again, their expressions turning from concern and frustration to confusion of their own.

Blake noticed a similar expression on Brooke's face when he glanced in her direction.

Lillian nodded and continued. "There were families with the ability to control the weather, in a more direct way than any of us. The stories that Nicholas was able to dig up all said that these other families were supposed to be a sort of balance to our own ancestors. So the power that these other families were best known for was the ability to control, or summon, lightning."

She let that hang for a long moment, knowing it wouldn't take them long to figure out what she meant. Electricity was the main weakness for all of the elementals of their family, and of course lightning was the purest form of electricity. Blake's stomach clenched at the thought.

Blake tried to wrap his mind around what his mother was telling him. "So, what happened to these other families? How come we've never heard about any of this?"

"What Nicholas found also said, at some point, that a feud broke out between our ancestors and the ancestors of these other families. In fact, that rumor suggests a good reason for why so many elemental families died off so quickly. But by the same token, the majority of the other families were also eliminated."

It was Angela who spoke up next, faint disbelief in her voice. "Then … I'm assuming the surviving families on both sides moved apart … and lost track of each other?"

Lillian nodded. "That's the assumption, yes."

Logan's voice was low and tight when he added, "So the lightning that nearly hit Angela wasn't an accident."

"That's … a possibility," Lillian replied, her voice wavering again for an instant.

"We would never even know if we were standing next to the descendants of those lightning-families," Blake said, frustrated.

"But how would they know who we are?" Nate asked. "I mean, why should we believe their records are any more accurate than ours?"

Logan answered his brother's question before their mother could, turning his attention to Nate and saying, "We lost two uncles to freak accidents of weather. Uncle Nicholas was crippled in the same storm that killed Uncle Trevor. *Today* Ange was nearly hit by lightning. What are the chances of that?"

Before Nate, or any of his siblings, could respond to Logan's argument, Lillian spoke up again. "We don't know anything for sure," she said. "We need to be careful, and be sure to stay in touch with each other. And for now, if there's anyone you've told anything to, I have to ask you not to talk to them about this.

She turned her gaze to Brooke, who was watching silently, and said, "I'm sorry, Brooke, but we need to ask you not to talk about this with anyone outside of this room, too. Can we trust you to do that?" Her question was direct, but Brooke nodded without hesitation.

"Absolutely," she said, never breaking Lillian's eye contact.

An odd tickle of pride danced through Blake's stomach.

"Angela," Christopher added after Lillian fell silent again. When his daughter was looking at him, he asked, "I don't suppose you noticed anyone around before the lightning hit? Or did you hear something strange?"

Slowly, Angela shook her head. "There wasn't anyone around, at least that I saw. And I don't think there was anyone behind me. My music wasn't that loud."

Looking back toward his mother, Blake asked, "What other sorts of things can these lightning-families do?"

"According to the stories Nicholas found," Lillian began, "in their prime they could control all types of weather. Creating a snow storm, like the one that put Nicholas in that wheelchair … would have been child's play."

"Well," Dean said, leaning back against the couch, "I'm distinctly uncomfortable now."

Christopher sighed, ignoring his sons as Logan reached over and smacked Dean upside the head, and released Lillian's hands as he stood. "All right, that's enough of this for now. We're incredibly glad you're all safe, and we're proud of you boys for saving your sister. And in light of all this drama, I think we should have an outrageously large dinner. Family only. And Brooke, of course."

****

The diner was strangely busy, and both Georgia and Brooke were being forced to stick to their assigned sections. Therefore, when Emma had come in with a slightly older man Brooke didn't know, it was Brooke—and not Georgia—who had gone to greet them. The man, probably in his late twenties, kept his eyes on his menu as he ordered his drink. His tone was clipped, verging on rude, so Brooke opted not to push conversation. Emma's tone was similarly short, though she managed an apologetic smile.

In the back, as Brooke poured the two glasses of iced tea, she ran into Georgia and asked, "Hey, do you know the man sitting with Emma?"

Georgia paused, her hand hovering with a fresh straw over a glass of soda, and said, "There's a guy with Emma? I didn't know she was with anyone…"

"It didn't really look like a date," Brooke elaborated, sticking her own straws into the glasses. "And if it was, you should really suggest she look elsewhere. He didn't look like much of a catch."

"I'll try to remember to ask her about it later," Georgia decided as she slipped the soda onto her tray. "Let me know if anything interesting happens!" And then the currently-blonde woman sashayed out the door.

Brooke followed suit a minute later, still pondering that nagging feeling in the pit of her stomach. There was just something odd about that man; for that matter, about the whole atmosphere around them. *Not that it's any of my business,* she reminded herself as she approached their booth.

She was coming up from behind the man's position, and she noted curiously that he hadn't bothered to remove his trench coat. Emma, who was facing her, had her eyes closed and was pinching the bridge of her nose, head slightly bowed, as if in frustration.

"What were you thinking?" the man demanded with a rough, aggravated growl in his voice. His words were spoken in an appropriately low tone, but Brooke was near enough that she caught them.

Emma opened her mouth before she opened her eyes, saying, "I saw an oppor—" She cut herself off when she registered the sight of Brooke even as Brooke came to a stop at their table.

This time Emma's companion cut an irritated, evaluating glance in Brooke's direction, but he remained silent. His eyes moved away from her as soon as she'd set his tea in front of him, and he offered no words of gratitude.

"Thanks," Emma supplied as her own tea was placed in front of her. She kept her eyes focused on her drink.

Feeling like she'd intruded, Brooke took a deep breath before she pulled her notebook from her apron and asked if they were ready to order. And as soon as their orders were placed, she scurried away.

The man sitting across from Emma had given Brooke one more look before she'd walked off, and though she wanted to be annoyed or upset by the superiority in his eyes, all she'd felt was discomfort. Her stomach had twisted in an incredibly unpleasant way, and she suddenly wanted to find Paula and tell her she wasn't feeling well. Home sounded like the place to be. But of course she couldn't; she needed her paycheck, after all.

Still, she sincerely hoped that she would never see that man again.

****

Brooke didn't have to work until mid-afternoon on Sunday, and though she'd originally intended to use the time to run necessary errands, she'd agreed to meet up with Blake at the beach instead. She'd hesitated at the idea of the beach initially, as it was open to the public year-round, but conceded when Blake had pointed out that with him there, the beach was probably the safest place to be. It wasn't like it was her secret—or her life— potentially on the line, anyway.

The parking lot was empty aside from Blake's Mustang when she swung back into the space her Honda had last occupied the night before. She climbed from the car, not bothering to lock it, and started for the shoreline as she pocketed her keys.

There was more than one reason she was excited to meet up with Blake this morning. Sure, discussing everything crazy that had happened the day before was important. And she was certainly interested. The problem was that she was *interested* in Blake, too. Very, very much. She already knew he was a good kisser, and as ridiculous as it was, her lips were practically aching to feel his again. And meeting like this, they were going to be all alone on the beach. Just the two of them and the rolling tide. That was a pretty clichéd romantic setting all in itself.

It was all she could do to keep from jogging to the shore when she spotted him, sitting on the edge of the tide with his feet in the water.

As she drew nearer, she slowed, taking in the sight of him with his elbows resting on raised knees and his chin cradled between his linked thumbs and index fingers. It was a thoughtful, reflective position. Sobering. She almost felt bad for some of the thoughts that had been swimming around in her head a moment ago. *Almost.*

"Hey." Brooke settled next to him on the sand. She kept her feet curled up and out to the side at her knees so as to keep her shoes from getting wet.

Blake turned his attention to her, his posture relaxing as a smile lifted his lips. "Hey, thanks for meeting me."

She returned his smile. "So what did you want to talk about? Did something else happen?"

"No. I just thought maybe we should talk one-on-one, you know, after you'd had a chance to sleep on everything." He paused and studied her, looking for something. Whether or not he found it, Brooke had no idea. "How are you handling all that?"

Releasing a breath, Brooke said, "Me? I'm handling it okay. I mean, for me it's more surreal and startling to learn about the existence of people with powers like yours. I'm not being targeted, remember? So it's only scary in the abstract."

Blake arched a brow at her choice of words. "Abstract, huh? And how's that?"

Brooke allowed her smile to feel a little flirtatious as she leaned forward and brushed her fingertips along his cheekbone. "I don't want anything to happen to you is all," she whispered.

Blake swallowed and the tide rolled in a little higher, just barely brushing her knees. Then he'd threaded his fingers into her hair and crushed his lips to hers, his other arm winding around her waist to hold her in place.

It was all she could do to swallow the moan in her throat as she kissed him back. His hair was soft over her fingers when her hands slipped behind his head, and his tongue was hot in her mouth when her lips parted. She'd nearly forgotten how good he tasted.

She could've sworn she purred as his tongue stroked hers, desire burning low and hot in her belly. It was such a contrast to the cold water that continued to tease her knees. Blake's fingers dipped beneath her lightweight sweater, his soft touch teasing her skin and finally pulling free the moan she'd been fighting. He sucked on her tongue, putting more weight into his touch, until his thumb found the right spot to have her arching into him.

He released her lips as her breasts pressed firmly into his chest, trailing his kiss down the side of her throat. She held onto him, moaning again as he shifted to cradle her body more properly against his.

"Blake," she breathed as his tongue danced around the hollow at the base of her throat.

He rumbled and lowered his head, tongue and lips sliding to her collar bone and down to the line of her scoop-neck sweater. And oh, how she wanted him to keep going. To tear off her clothes and kiss the rest of her aching body with the same tender hunger he was bestowing to her collar and neck. How she wanted to feel his heady touch in private places. Brooke doubted she'd ever been so immediately hungry for a man.

Blake made a sort of groaning sound and removed his lips from her skin. "God, you're distracting."

"That's a bad thing?"

He grinned. "Not really. I just feel like there's more that should be said first."

"And you can't talk while you're kissing me." Her words were resigned, because she knew he was right. She just didn't want him to be.

"Exactly."

Looping her arms loosely around his shoulders and making no move to otherwise adjust herself, Brooke said, "So talk. What's on your mind?"

The question was ridiculous, of course. She *knew* what was on his mind in more ways than one. She just suspected she hadn't properly absorbed it all yet. There was still some sort of surreal distance between her sense of reality and the ideas the Hawke family had discussed the day before. *People who can throw lightning. Really?* But then again, the man she was currently embracing could *become* water—she'd seen it herself. So was the rest really so far out there?

Blake released a breath and pulled her in enough to rest his head on her shoulders. "Everything, I guess," he admitted. "I really want my uncle to be crazy, but … that's not his style. He's a realist, even if his 'realism' sounds impossible."

"And you're worried," Brooke guessed gently, her fingers weaving through his hair and massaging his scalp in an attempt to comfort him.

"Yeah."

"Blake, that's natural," she said. "They're your family, and you just found out you might have enemies who can generate your kryptonite at will. That's heavy." As she said it, she realized she was exactly right. She could only imagine how terrifying that would be for him and his brothers. To go from *knowing* they had more power than the people around them—*knowing* they were stronger—to learning they had invisible enemies designed specifically to hurt them. *Although that might be over-simplifying...*

Blake straightened after a moment, taking his time dragging his gaze up to hers. "I know. And I swear I really did want to make sure you were okay, all things considered." He paused and brushed his lips lightly over hers again. "But it's possible I was also hoping for a distraction."

Swallowing a schoolgirl giggle, Brooke raised exaggeratedly dramatic eyebrows at him. "Weren't you just complaining about that?"

"I was confused," Blake insisted, sliding the hand still beneath her sweater a little higher. "I understand now."

"Understand what?" she challenged, fighting her natural response to his touch.

Blake met her challenge with a confident grin and caught her mouth in another hot, demanding kiss. Brooke immediately melted, letting him take her weight as one of her hands dipped beneath his collar and down his back. She couldn't wait to get him out of his shirt—couldn't wait to see the body underneath.

His tongue stroked hers, sliding and curling over and over with a rhythm that made a very different part of her anatomy clench in anticipation. So she adjusted her grip to tug on his shirt, needing to touch more of him. To see and feel and taste his skin. Blake wasted no time heeding her request, pulling back to yank his shirt over his head and toss it to the sand. Brooke followed suit, enjoying the look that heated his blue eyes when his gaze fell to her chest and the lacy bra she'd chosen for the day.

Her hands landed back on his shoulders and slowly slid down to his chest. His chest was smooth and taut. *Perfect swimmer's body.* She couldn't help but wonder if his body was actually a side-effect of his power, but it didn't matter. After his initial sharp intake of breath at her touch, and a moment where his eyes closed as he let her fingers explore, Blake's own hands came up and landed on her bare waist.

Brooke was distracted by his touch, and her exploration stalled. His hands were wandering up as hers were wandering down, and something inside her pulsed eagerly. She wanted to skip the foreplay and get right to the main event as badly as she wanted to linger in this slow, deliciously torturous moment for a while longer. With such confusing, conflicting desires, all she could do was moan low when his knuckles brushed the underside of her covered breast.

One of Blake's hands anchored back over her hip, his lips landed on her throat, and his other hand dipped beneath the cup of her bra to palm her breast. Her next moan was longer, possibly louder, and her arms curled around his torso so that she could hold onto his back.

And that was when Brooke's cell phone rang.

Her first instinct was to ignore the offensive device—she wasn't expecting any calls, after all—but Blake had immediately ceased his caresses and lifted his head. There was no reason not to at least check the Caller ID.

Releasing a frustrated breath, Brooke eased back enough to extract the phone from her jeans pocket and look at the screen. And then she cringed. It was Paula. Flicking a semi-frightened, conflicted glance up to Blake, she answered the phone.

"Hey, Paula."

Blake immediately grimaced.

Chapter Eight

When Brooke answered the phone, Blake knew their stolen moment was done. Especially when the caller turned out to be her boss—and the Queen of Gossip—Paula. If Paula had any clue what she'd interrupted, the whole town was bound to hear about it, which made Blake incredibly glad they were alone.

"Ah, Paula," Brooke hedged, guilt taking root in her expression. "I don't know if I can... Well, I was just, uh, doing laundry. I can't leave my stuff in the laundromat all day." She was silent as Paula spoke again, but Blake could only make out the other woman's voice. After another moment she sighed, the sound heavy with resignation, and Blake reached for his shirt as she said, "No, no, I understand. Okay, I can be there in about half an hour." She accepted what Blake assumed was an apology and disconnected.

"Going in early?" He shook the sand out of her sweater as best he could. Sand wasn't exactly his element.

Pouting adorably, Brooke returned her phone to her pocket. "Yes. Two people called off last-minute. Damn them."

Blake laughed as she took her sweater and tugged it on unceremoniously. "Don't worry," he teased as he stood and extended a hand to her. "I'm not gonna leave town while you're working."

At this, Brooke finally laughed, accepted his outstretched hand, and replied, "You'd better not. I hear your brother is friends with the local police."

"I can't tell if that was meant as a reminder or a threat," Blake said as they began the climb up to the parking lot.

"Maybe it was both?" Brooke returned lightly.

When they made it to their cars—parked one space apart—Blake turned to her and wrapped his arms loosely around her waist. "Don't work too hard," he murmured as he dipped his head for another, sweeter kiss. He held himself in check this time and pulled back, adding, "And I'll see you in class tomorrow."

Brooke graced him with a smile and played with the collar of his shirt. "Yes, you will," she promised.

****

"You were right," Georgia declared before Brooke had even finished securing her apron around her waist. She was standing several feet to the side, leaning against the row of old lockers that the employees used to store their things during their shifts.

Brooke looked over, feeling entirely confused, and cocked an eyebrow. "What do you mean? Right about what?"

"That guy who was with Emma last night." Georgia gave the faintest shake of her head, as if she couldn't believe that Brooke didn't know. "I saw her this morning at the grocery store, so I asked her about it, and she was really … weird."

With her hand poised to pick up her notepad and pen, Brooke paused and asked, "Weird how?"

Georgia lifted her hands, fingers splayed, and moved them back in forth in front of her chest, palms down. "Shifty-weird. Not that I like describing any of my friends as 'shifty', but I don't know how else to say it. She kept looking around while we were talking, like she was afraid someone was spying on her, and she didn't really say much, either."

The image in Brooke's head had her suddenly wondering if maybe Emma didn't need supervision—and it certainly clashed with the image she'd had of Emma prior to this conversation—so she hesitantly asked, "Did she ... look sick, or anything?"

"Sick?" Georgia repeated, her head tilting ever so slightly. "No, of course not. Just ... paranoid, I guess. Oh, but she did clear up one thing. Although it took me *forever* to drag it out of her, I swear!" She shrugged and added, "Whatever."

"What did she clear up, exactly?"

"That weird guy she was with is definitely *not* her boyfriend," Georgia replied as she fell into step beside Brooke.

"That's good." She paused, waiting for Georgia to continue, but when it became obvious she had nothing more to say, Brooke asked, "Did she get any more specific?"

"Nope," Georgia said. "I barely got her to say that much before she said something about a tight schedule and went running for the check-out aisle."

"You're right, that is weird. I hope she's all right."

"Me, too," Georgia replied, her lips scrunched for a moment in thought. She smiled again and picked up a tray. "Anyway, off to work!" Then she flounced into the main room, leaving Brooke standing behind her and shaking her head.

Paula came around the corner before Brooke could gather herself enough to follow after her friend, and she swallowed back her apprehension as she smiled at her supervisor.

"Brooke! Thanks so much for coming in early," Paula said with a genuine smile.

"It was no trouble," Brooke replied. "Is anyone waiting on me?"

"Shelly just sat the Buchannons at table seven," Paula stated easily. But before Brooke could take more than a step away, she added, "Oh, and before you leave tonight, you have to tell me what you were doing earlier with Blake, got it?"

Brooke froze. *How could she possibly—* Realization swept through her, and she barely bit back a groan. Paula had to drive that way to get to the diner; if she'd had to run home or been late, she could've seen their cars in the parking lot. And she would make far too much out of any situation that involved Brooke and Blake interacting no matter what the reason. Turning back to smile again, Brooke said, "It was really nothing. I should go greet Mr. and Mrs. Buchannon."

"I suppose you should," Paula agreed with a knowing smile. She said nothing more, and Brooke took the opportunity to slip away, praying her face wasn't crimson.

When Brooke was within sight of the table, she realized it was not just Mr. and Mrs. Buchannon this time. They had brought their two daughters, Chloe and Clarabelle, as well. Chloe, the recently engaged elder sister, was sitting beside her father and opposite her sibling.

"I'm feeling special," Brooke declared as she stepped up to the table.

The family turned their attention to her and smiled. It was Katherine who spoke first, saying, "Brooke! We haven't seen you in a couple of weeks now, how are you doing?"

Brooke returned their smiles. "Oh, I'm doing fine, Mrs. Buchannon. But I'm horribly curious, what brings all four of you out my way?"

"That would be my fault," Clarabelle declared with a light laugh.

Chloe spoke up before her sister could continue, leaning forward slightly and saying, "It's Clare's twentieth birthday, so of course we had to celebrate."

"Birthday, huh?" Brooke teased easily. "Well, I firmly believe in going all-out on birthdays myself, so I'll see if I can't help a little." Throwing in a wink for good measure, she added, "But you should definitely come back again next year, too."

With a laugh, Clarabelle said, "I'll try to remember that."

"Good," Brooke replied with a nod. "Now then, as the Birthday Girl, you get to order first. So tell me, what would make you happy today?"

****

"We should make a list," Logan declared as the conversation again fell silent. He, and all of his brothers, were gathered at Blake's house Monday evening. They had agreed to meet up to talk more about everything they'd learned after Angela's near-death experience.

"List?" Nate repeated, clearly confused. "You mean like a grocery list of possible suspects?"

Logan narrowed his eyes slightly and shifted on the couch, leaning forward and resting his elbows on his knees. "No, genius. I mean a list of people that we know know our secret. People we've told."

Dean shifted his weight on the couch. "What good's that going to do?"

Swinging his serious gaze around the room, Logan replied, "It's a solid place to start, for one. We could eliminate the people we know are out of town— and have been. And the people who'd have struck years ago if they were guilty."

"What about the people we've lost contact with?" Dean asked slowly as he leaned forward, removing his feet from the coffee table in the process.

All three brothers looked over at him with silent expectation.

Dean sighed and looked away, saying, "It's possible I said something to one or two of my ex-girlfriends…"

Blake sighed and shook his head. "You told Lila, didn't you?" He was referring to the cheerleader Dean had dated for over a year in high school. They had been very solidly together, until one day Lila had shown up at school holding another guy's hand. Dean had lost his temper, words had been exchanged, and it had taken all three of them to keep him from hurting the guy. Dean and Lila hadn't spoken since.

Dean cringed and nodded. "Yeah, I told Lila." He fell silent for a minute, but it was obvious from his tone that he wasn't done. And then he quietly added, "I told Emily, too."

"God, Dean," Nate exclaimed, slumping back against the couch beside Blake. "Did you tell that reporter girl you dated freshman year of college, too?"

"Of course not," Dean defended immediately, glaring at his sibling.

Blake lifted one hand and massaged his forehead for a long minute as he interrupted their budding argument to say, "It doesn't matter now. You've lost touch with both of them, right?"

Dean shifted his attention to Blake and nodded. "Yeah. But last I heard, Emily moved out of town anyway."

Inclining his head, Blake replied, "I heard that, too. So probably we wouldn't have to worry about Emily."

Nate sat up once more. "But shouldn't we consider their families, too? I mean, anyone we told could have talked to their parents, or siblings, or close friends."

Logan nodded. "That's part of my point. The list is a starting point, not a hardcopy of our only suspects."

"Okay," Dean acknowledged, "but we still wouldn't have to worry about Emily. Her family never lived near here, and from what I remember, her closest friends didn't live in town, either."

"That's good," Blake said. "Then you're probably right. And I remember hearing that Lila left town after high school."

"Who'd you hear that from?" Dean asked curiously, unaware that his brother had more information on his ex than he himself did.

Blake shrugged. "Mom heard it from Katherine Buchannon. Remember Lila's mom was close to Katherine before she died?"

Dean made an embarrassed sound and leaned back into the couch, and as his feet returned to the coffee table, he declared, "Nah, I'd forgotten. But that rules out Lila's end, except for any guy she might've talked to."

Logan smirked now and cut a look to his brother. "I hate to break this to you, but she probably didn't go around bragging about you to her *other* boyfriends."

"Shut up," Dean returned, rolling his eyes.

"How 'bout you, Logan?" Nate asked, shifting the focus away from their hot-headed brother.

"I've only told one person," Logan assured them. His eyes were downcast and his voice stable, but tight. They all knew who he was referring to.

After a long moment, Nate said, "I told two. In middle school I told Kirk, and in high school I told Laura." He shrugged. "I haven't talked to Laura in a while, but since her family moved a couple years back to be closer to her, I'd guess she's clean. And I'll vouch for Kirk."

"I think we all trust Kirk," Blake assured him. Kirk was Nate's long-standing best friend, the kind that was as much family as a person could get without being blood-related.

Dean looked over to Blake and declared, "That leaves you, bro. So who've you told besides Jason and Brooke?"

Jason was Blake's own best friend. The two of them had been partners in crime since the eighth grade. It had been their third year of high school when Jason found out about Blake's secret, but the choice to tell Jason had been taken from him. Jason had only grinned after he found out and, voice weak from the water he'd half-drowned in, he'd said, "I'm one lucky son of a bitch, aren't I?"

None of them doubted Jason—not any more than they doubted Kirk.

And Blake just assumed they were all giving Brooke the benefit of the doubt.

"Okay," Dean finally said. "I'll ask the hard questions."

Blake lifted his gaze to Dean but said nothing.

"You obviously trust Brooke," Dean began, sitting forward again. "We don't really have any reason not to, either. But what about her family? Is she from around here? Did she come here to see where her parents or aunts or uncles grew up?"

Remembering what Brooke had told him about her past, Blake shook his head. "She's not from here, and even if her family were I doubt she'd know. She lost her biological family when she was young. She didn't say anything about her adoptive family, really, but I think she'd have mentioned it if they'd suggested the area."

Silence held for a moment as the brothers processed his point. At length, Logan said, "I'm comfortable with that, then."

Nate and Dean nodded, and Dean resettled into his preferred position.

Blake drew the focus from himself and asked, "Does anyone know if Angela's told Eric?" He watched as his siblings exchanged equally uncertain looks before he finally sighed and said, "I take it that's a 'no'."

With a grin, Nate replied, "Hey, you're the oldest—*you* ask her."

"Yeah," Dean jumped in, "you know how much she hates talking about that punk."

Blake gave his brother a pointed look and said, "Gee, that couldn't be because *some* of you always put him down or threaten to massacre him?"

Before Dean could retort to Blake's comment, Logan said, "Well, one of us should talk to her. Whether or not we like him, he's just a teenager. He could've told the wrong person."

"I agree," Blake declared with a nod.

"Great," Dean began, "then you can do it. Probably, if I tried, I'd end up accusing him, and she'd just get all pissy."

Logan reached over and smacked Dean upside the head. "She's our sister," he said. "Don't talk about her like that."

Rubbing the back of his head, Dean said, "Oh, come on, she's *seventeen*. She gets pissy. And I can say it 'cause I'm her older brother. It's expected."

"At the risk of having my head knocked clean off my shoulders," Nate interrupted, "he has a point. She *does* get kind of touchy whenever one of us talks about him."

Blake shook his head. "Do I really need to reiterate myself?"

Dean gave him a pointed look. "Don't tell me you like the kid."

"I don't," Blake assured his brother. "But the more we blatantly dislike him, the harder she's going to cling to him. Or don't you remember the rebellious stage?"

Logan smirked. "He can't remember it, Blake. He's still stuck there."

Nate laughed, and Dean rolled his eyes at them.

Taking a deep breath, Nate pushed down his lingering amusement and said, "Okay, so Blake's gonna talk to Angie about what's-his-name, but we still need to figure out our other options. Does anyone have any other ideas?"

****

Blake was leaning patiently against the driver's side of his Mustang when the high school let out the next day. He'd called ahead and convinced his mother to let him pick Angela up from school, though it hadn't taken much effort once he'd explained his reasons. So now all he had to do was wait for his only sister to come into view. And as he waited, he watched the other teenagers run around, celebrating their temporary freedom. He could still easily recall his high school days, and watching the largely unfamiliar teenagers had him remembering why he was glad those years were behind him.

But none of that mattered, as his eyes locked on to the dark-haired girl he'd been waiting for. She was walking in synch with her now-eighteen-year-old boyfriend and laughing faintly. Neither appeared to have noticed him, parked as he was at the curb off to the side of entrance. When they were close enough that he wouldn't have to bellow, Blake called out, "Angela!"

Several heads turned in startled curiosity, but Blake paid them no attention. When his sister and her boyfriend looked over, he lifted a hand in a lazy wave. He watched silently as they exchanged looks before altering their course and heading over to him.

"Hey, Blake," Angela said hesitantly. "What're you doing here?"

Cocking an eyebrow and keeping his tone light, Blake replied, "What's it look like? I'm giving you a ride."

"It's a nice day," Angela argued, "we were going to walk."

"I was gonna walk her straight home," Eric offered helpfully.

"No need," Blake said, pulling his keys from his pocket. "I'll drive you home, and then take her home."

Angela frowned at her brother. "That's not necessary," she insisted.

Holding her gaze pointedly, Blake said, "Humor me." He clicked the button as he spoke and unlocked his car. When he had the door open, he smiled and said, "Hop in."

Heaving a martyred sigh, Angela looked over to her boyfriend and said, "I'm sorry. Apparently my brother's in a strange mood." Then she turned and ducked into the car.

Eric hesitated, his eyes flicking to Blake, and Blake inclined his head. "Go ahead, I won't bite."

"Uh, thanks." Eric moved around him and ducked into the car.

Once the teenagers were settled in the backseat, backpacks at their feet, Blake re-positioned his seat and angled himself into the car. He had it in motion in no time, and as he eased into the after school traffic, he called over his shoulder, "Your sister hasn't moved, right?"

"No," Eric replied easily.

Blake nodded to himself and started the easy drive to Emma's home. He said nothing, keeping his music low and pretending to ignore the hushed conversation going on behind him. It took him only a few minutes to reach the suburban neighborhood that Emma and Eric Matthews called home.

As he pulled into the slightly slanted driveway, Blake couldn't help but reflect on what he knew of the siblings' history. Emma was a couple of years older than him, and so he'd only seen her in passing during his first two years of high school. From what he'd heard through Angela, Mrs. Matthews had died only a couple of years earlier, and when she had, she'd left her two children alone.

"Here you go," Blake declared as he put the car in park and set the brake. Then he eased out and pulled his seat forward so that Eric could actually exit the car, stepping back to try to keep the situation from being more awkward.

Eric unbuckled and grabbed his backpack in one hand. Turning to Angela, he said, "Uh, I guess I'll see you tomorrow, then."

"Yeah," Angela replied, cutting a pointed look at her brother before returning her attention to Eric and quickly leaning forward to cover his lips with hers. She pulled away a heartbeat later, blushing, and murmured, "See you tomorrow."

Eric swallowed and nodded but said nothing as he scrambled from the car. He deliberately kept his gaze on the ground as he stepped wide of Blake, and it wasn't until he was several feet from the car that he turned back to call, "Thanks for the ride."

Blake nodded silently and remained standing until Eric had disappeared inside the house. Once the front door had shut, he turned to look into his backseat. "You want shotgun?"

Angela crossed her arms. "I'm fine here."

Oh, good, Blake thought with an internal sigh as he reclaimed his seat and pulled the door shut. *Her being angry will make this so much easier.*

Chapter Nine

Awkward silence settled over the car after Blake switched off his radio and eased out of the driveway. When he was back on the main road, he heaved another sigh and finally said, "Angie, I'm sorry. I wasn't trying to be rude, but I need to talk to you about something."

Keeping her eyes pointed out the small back window, Angela replied, "That's what they invented phones for, Blake."

Blake tightened his grip on the steering wheel. "I need to talk to you about what Mom learned from Uncle Nicholas."

In the rearview mirror, Blake watched as Angela's eyes widened marginally and her posture relaxed. After another moment, she turned her gaze forward and let her arms fall to her sides.

"Did you figure something out?" she asked, her frustration almost gone from her voice.

Blake shook his head. "No, we're still pretty much clueless. But the four of us got together yesterday, and Logan suggested we run over a list of everyone we know of who knows about us."

Her frown returned, but her voice was much the same when she asked, "And you want to know if I've blabbed to my boyfriend, right? Like Dean and Nate with their girlfriends? Like *you*?"

Fearing where she was going to take the conversation, Blake replied, "Well, I wasn't going to word it that way, but … yeah."

Pursing her lips for a moment, Angela finally said, "I haven't. I certainly could have, and we've been together long enough none of you would have the right to give me a hard time about it, but I haven't."

97

Genuinely surprised, Blake asked, "Why not?"

Angela shrugged, her gaze returning to the side window. "I don't know, it just … hasn't felt right. Besides, I don't know for sure what he's doing for college yet; if we end up breaking up, or doing the long-distance thing, then it'll be better if I don't."

Curiosity mounting with each word she said, Blake found himself asking, "Are you two having trouble?"

"No!" Angela asserted quickly, turning forward again and meeting his gaze fearlessly through the rearview mirror. She took a breath and calmly explained, "I'm just being cautious. I know that most high school relationships don't work out, so I'm not going to assume it will until I have a little more to go on. But we're *fine*, so don't go celebrating or something."

Blake couldn't help the grin that curved his lips as he said, "I wouldn't dream of it."

They fell into silence until Blake pulled to a stop in front of their parents' garage. He was reaching for the handle on his door when his sister's quiet voice carried to his ears.

"Blake," she said softly, her eyes faded and distant with thought. "You'll let me know when we figure this out, right?"

Frowning at the strange tone in her voice, Blake shifted so that he could turn slightly to face her. "Of course."

Angela dragged her eyes to his. "And … we'll be okay, won't we? All of us?"

"What are you worried about, Angie?" Blake returned, concern welling up inside of him.

She swallowed and her eyes flicked to the house through the windshield before she looked back at him. "Mom … lost two of her brothers, remember? And she barely hears from the others now that Grandma and Grandpa are gone. I … don't want that to be us, that's all."

Blake offered his sister a soft, reassuring smile and reached over to pull one of her smaller hands into his. Giving it a light squeeze, he said, "That won't be us, Angie. I promise."

Releasing a heavy breath, Angela returned his smile and squeezed his hand briefly before pulling away and saying, "So are you letting me out of this car or not?"

****

Brooke was relaxed on her couch later that night, enjoying the couple of hours she had to herself before the guilt would send her to bed. It had been a fairly slow night at the diner, and so Paula had sent her home over an hour before the end of her shift. With a contented sigh, Brooke shifted, tucking her feet closer to her body as she curled up in the corner of her couch beside the window wall.

For once, she reflected as the next set of commercials finally ended and she quickly hit the 'play' button on her remote, *I might actually get to watch my Tuesday-night shows on Tuesday night.* It was a strange concept, considering that she was usually too tired from work or too swamped with homework.

As the show resumed, Brooke registered the faint howl of wind on the other side of her window, but she thought nothing of it. Soon enough she was once more wrapped up in the mystery of the episode.

A sudden flash of light on the other side of her closed blinds pulled Brooke's attention back to reality, and she turned her head reflexively toward the window at the same time as an echoing crash sounded from somewhere outside. *What the—* The thought had barely formed when, without warning, her living room window exploded inward.

Brooke leapt to her feet in shock, stumbling to get away as glass sprayed everywhere. She cried out and threw her arms up over her face, even as she tried to see what was happening. And then pain was radiating through her, so immediately intense that it took her a long moment to realize what had happened.

She had backed nearly into her kitchen table, and the glass had stopped flying. Her blinds were hanging in a mangled mess from one still-fraying cord on the far side. And a rather large, rather thick, still-crackling tree limb was now resting in the hole where her window was supposed to be. It protruded at least two feet into her living room, and the end that had once been attached to the tree (which was the end on the outside of her apartment) was literally smoking.

Lightning ... some part of her mind whispered.

"Oh my ... God ..." Brooke breathed as her eyes swept over the mess that had once been her living room. For a moment, the shock overrode the pain, and she forgot she was hurt. But it was a fleeting moment, and then she dragged in a deep breath and looked down at herself.

Blood droplets littered the dark carpeting from somewhere in the center of her living room to where she was still standing. And blood was still trickling at a fairly steady pace down her arm. Her arm was definitely where she hurt the most, though she realized her feet were stinging as well.

Lifting her arm, Brooke turned it slightly and sucked in a sharp breath when her eyes landed on the gash taking up a sizable portion of her forearm. There was still a piece of glass embedded in her flesh. It looked like the glass had been torn down her arm, and as she looked at it she realized that the pain had flared up while she'd been lifting her arms to protect her face.

The momentum must have dragged it down my arm, she thought, her mind strangely numb. She could still feel the pain, but it was fading, as if it had been a bad nightmare. Even the stinging in her feet—where she assumed she'd stepped on pieces of glass—was going away. *That can't be good,* she told herself as she tore her eyes away from her bleeding arm.

Beyond the tree branch, Brooke could see that it was hailing outside, and the wind was still blowing. Hail was coming in through the whole in her wall and soaking into her carpet. The sky erupted overhead, and she finally realized that there was a thunderstorm raging. Another thunderstorm. Only, this time, she found herself wondering just how natural it was.

I should call someone, she realized after another minute. She was somewhat surprised no one had come out to investigate the noise, but she was also glad for it. She didn't want her neighbors to know her as the girl with the broken-off tree branch in her window.

Shaking her head, Brooke wrapped her right hand around her still-bleeding left arm and turned to walk carefully around her table toward the kitchen counter where her cell phone was charging. As she began walking again, the stinging in her feet resumed with a force, and she bit back another cry of pain. *Oh, I'm so going to need stitches.*

Without thinking, she braced herself against the counter as soon as she reached it—seeking to get some weight off of her injured feet—and ended up smearing blood along the light-gray surface. She hesitated for a moment, finding herself worrying about getting blood on her phone, and then reminded herself this was an emergency. So she picked up the phone and flipped it open in order to dial nine-one-one. But her fingers paused over the first digit, an image of Blake diving into the sea to save his sister flaring in her memory. If this *wasn't* a natural storm, she didn't need 911. She needed Blake.

****

Tiny balls of hail bounced off the hood of Blake's car as he swung in behind Brooke's Civic. He disregarded the quickly dissipating storm as he yanked his keys from the ignition and rushed from his car to her door. All he'd been able to think about on the drive over had been her voice as she'd told him—in broken, disorganized pieces—what had happened. She'd started crying in the middle of her first sentence, but around her tear-soaked voice he could hear the tightness caused by obvious pain.

His concern left no room for the manners his mother tried to teach him, and so he didn't even pause to tap on the door before he let himself in. But he did pause when his eyes landed on her a moment later.

Brooke was sitting on her counter, beside her sink. She had a kitchen towel wrapped around her left forearm, held in place by her other hand. Her cell phone was plugged into the wall on her other side, in easy reach. And between the phone and herself was a large smear of blood. Several spots of blood dotted the otherwise white kitchen linoleum, leading back to the living-room carpet.

"Brooke." Blake gathered himself and moved quickly towards her, sparing only a glance at the devastation in her living room.

She lifted her head and blinked her eyes several times before attempting to offer him a smile. "You drove too fast," she said, her voice devoid of any appropriate scolding tone.

"No, I didn't," Blake argued, failing at his attempt at levity as much as she had. He was standing before her in no time, and with his new angle he could easily see a piece of bloody glass lying in the sink beside her. That piece of glass was undoubtedly the reason the towel on her arm was slowly darkening.

Her tone curious and forcibly light, Brooke asked, "Are you sure I shouldn't have called 911?"

Frowning at her wrapped arm and the fresh droplets of blood on the floor beneath her dangling feet, Blake replied, "Absolutely. You get free medical. I'll call Logan and have him come over to board up your window and get rid of that branch, okay?"

"You don't have to do all that," Brooke said, her right hand tightening over her injured arm. "I have insurance … and my landlord will take care of my window as soon as he gets home."

Blake lifted his frown to aim it at her properly. "I'm not taking no for an answer this time. Now let's get you in the car and we can talk on the road."

Brooke hesitated, her gaze darting toward the ground. "I'd really rather not walk, if it's all the same to you."

Blake silently reached out and pulled her phone from the charger before dropping it into his pocket. Then he shifted and reached around her, ignoring her half-hearted protests, and wrapped an arm around her torso. He slipped his other arm carefully beneath her knees and slid her off the counter, against his chest.

"What are you doing?" Brooke asked, a tiny bit of life beginning to return to her voice.

"Keeping you off your feet," Blake replied easily as he carried her toward the front door. It was shut, indicating that he'd remembered to close it, but he didn't hesitate. As he walked, his eyes flicked back toward the living room, and the melted hail pulled from the carpet and off the debris. It gathered together and then smoothly slid through the air toward them.

The water expanded as it neared them, and Brooke watched in silence as the water poured into the space between her door and the doorframe. Blake slowed his pace just slightly as the water gathered together and popped the latch. Then it curved, pushing out, and the door slowly swung open.

"That was impressive," Brooke declared. Life had returned to her voice, but so had the pain.

Blake moved them outside, letting the water pull the door closed behind them. He wouldn't be able to use the same method to get into the car, but that was okay.

They were in front of his car a moment later, and he carefully set her down on the hood. Holding her gaze for a beat, Blake said, "Don't move." When she nodded, he stepped back and quickly pulled open the door. With barely a flick of his wrist, he pushed the seat forward, and then he moved back to her.

Brooke didn't fight as he once again scooped her into his arms, and she ducked helpfully as he angled her into the backseat.

"You can sit sideways," Blake said as he helped guide her into the seat. "That way you won't have to put any weight on your feet."

Brooke released her arm in order to adjust herself, though as soon as she was out of his arms Blake crawled in to help her. She cringed visibly, the pain undoubtedly worsening with each movement. "I'm sorry," she managed on a gasp after she had finished adjusting herself.

Blake's gaze followed hers. When he realized what she was apologizing for smearing little bits of blood all over the backseat, he shook his head. "Don't worry about it, that'll wash out."

She looked up at him, her eyes wide and tear filled, and said nothing for a long minute. He crawled backwards out of the car, repositioned the passenger seat, shut the door and ran around to his side. When he was sitting, buckled, and beginning to back out of the driveway, she finally said, "Thank you."

His eyes drifted from the back window to hers for a long moment, and his lips twitched in a bitter, apologetic half-smile.

Brooke leaned her head back against the cool glass of the small window and her eyes drifted shut.

Instead of trying to engage Brooke in conversation when she was so obviously fighting to stay awake, Blake tucked his earpiece into place and dialed Logan. Logan answered on the second ring, and Blake wasted no time with small talk.

"I'm taking Brooke to Mom and Dad's. She's hurt. A large branch crashed into her living-room window. Looks like storm damage."

There was a brief pause before Logan replied, "Storm damage, huh? Okay, I'll head out and cover the hole. I won't be able to get a new sheet of glass in this late at night, though. That'll be tomorrow."

"No problem. Thanks." Blake felt a little bad for his clipped tone, but he was in no mood to be polite and chat. He knew Logan would understand.

As soon as that call was done, he hit another button on his speed-dial and waited impatiently. The red light he was stuck at turned green at the same time his mother answered the phone. "Blake?"

"I know it's late," he offered as an apology. "But Brooke's hurt pretty bad. Please tell me Angie's home."

"Of course she is. I'll run upstairs and get her. You're on your way?"

"Be there in five," Blake replied before disconnecting. He'd never been more grateful for his mother's understanding of emergency situations.

He flicked a glance in the rearview mirror to find Brooke with her eyes half-closed and glazed over. The sight made his stomach roll, and he had to make a conscious effort to keep the bile down. *She'll be okay.*

But he didn't slow down until he was swinging into his parents' driveway.

Chapter Ten

Christopher met him at the door, holding it wide and saying nothing as he watched Blake rush up the steps with Brooke in his arms.

Lillian came to stand at the edge of the hallway, one hand resting on the wall. "Blake," she said, concern in her voice.

Blake came to a stop, his hands instinctively tightening. "Please. Questions later."

Lillian released a breath and nodded, her arm lowering. "Your sister's in the living room, waiting for you."

"Thanks." He carried Brooke silently down the hall, knowing full well that his parents were following them. And then the hall gave way to the living room, where Angela was balancing on the edge of the couch anxiously. "Angie," he said when he saw her.

Angela's head immediately snapped up, and she was just as quickly on her feet. "Put her on the couch," she said, moving to the side and gesturing needlessly.

Blake nodded and approached the sofa, carefully lowering himself to his knees before gently easing Brooke onto the cushions. "Just lie still for a few minutes, okay?" he asked softly as he pulled his arms back.

Brooke's head was propped up against the arm of the couch, her injured arm nestled between her body and the back cushion. She nodded slowly at Blake, her gaze flickering between him and his sister.

Angela cleared her throat, and Blake coughed self-consciously even as he pushed to his feet and stepped several feet back. Then his sister moved up and knelt deliberately beside Brooke, smiling gently. "Try to relax, all right? This will take a few minutes."

With another slow nod, Brooke said, "Um, okay."

It wasn't until Angela had unwrapped the blood-soaked towel, tossed it to her brother, and reached over to hold her hands directly above the gash that Blake recognized a look of realization dawning in Brooke's eyes. In all the chaos, she'd likely forgotten what he'd told her about his sister's healing ability.

Angela released a breath, her eyes fell closed, and her hands began glowing. The glow built, slowly at first, wrapping around Angela's hands like a golden aura. As soon as the golden energy was undeniable Brooke's entire forearm—from elbow to fingertips—became surrounded by it.

Blake knew the sensations Brooke would be feeling as he watched her eyes drift shut. As the healing process began, the injured areas would start to tingle, almost like a low-level massage. Then a relaxing warmth would seep into the surrounding muscles, loosening them and freeing the tension. Those feelings would spread from the injury sites to the entire body until the patient fell into a deep, healing sleep. Angela and Lillian both said the sleep was necessary for the restoration of energy. All Blake really knew was that it was always the best sleep he'd ever had.

Either way, Brooke would be out for most of the night.

****

Once Brooke was unconscious, Blake allowed himself to breathe again and simultaneously registered the weight of her bloodied towel in his hands. With nothing better to do, he turned to throw it away. His parents followed him into the kitchen, as he'd known they would, and so he opted to begin the conversation on his own terms. Keeping his voice low in order to help

Angela focus, he said, "I'm sorry. I know it's late and you probably feel I should've taken her to the hospital."

Neither of his parents spoke for a long minute, and after dropping the towel into the garbage, Blake turned to face them. Just as he registered the lack of anger on their faces, his mother broke the silence.

"We're not angry, Blake," Lillian said, voicing the realization he'd only just made. "You wouldn't have brought her here if you didn't think it was necessary."

Blake swallowed, accepting his mother's faith in him and taking a moment to compose what he had left to say. "It gets worse," he warned. "I think our enemies are responsible for this."

Both of his parents went wide-eyed at his declaration. It was Christopher who asked, "What do you mean?"

Eyes drifting to the hall reflexively, Blake explained, "A thunderstorm hit directly over her apartment. It looked like lightning struck the tree in her front yard, and a branch went crashing through the window. The glass is what caused those cuts."

Lillian's eyes fell closed and she curled her hands into fists at her sides.

Without waiting for their response, Blake continued. "I can't imagine she's ticked off the same people who hate us. So I'm assuming that they went after her *because* of me."

It was a long moment before, with obvious reluctance, Christopher said, "I can't think of a more realistic scenario, either."

Taking a deep breath, Lillian asked, "Were the police called?"

"No," Blake said.

They nodded. After a moment of heavy silence, Lillian released a breath. "Well, she's going to need a safe place to stay tonight. I'll go prepare one of the rooms. I'll put fresh sheets on your bed, too, if you want to stay close to her."

"Thanks, Mom," Blake said before his mother turned and slipped down the hall. He'd always wondered why his parents had kept his—and all of his brothers'—bedrooms intact after they'd moved out. Now he was feeling like an idiot for wondering.

Christopher stepped up to his son and dropped a hand on his shoulder. "Come on, Blake. Let's go keep your sister company." He gave Blake's shoulder a squeeze for good measure before releasing him and starting toward the living room.

"Wait," Blake said. His father stilled and looked over his shoulder curiously. "Do we know anything yet?" The question was past his lips before he'd given it any real thought. "Did Mom or Uncle Nicholas figure anything out about who these people are? What their deal is?"

Christopher offered him an apologetic frown and turned back around. "No, nothing," he said. "Nicholas is still trying to look into things, though. There's always a chance he'll find something."

Blake felt his own frown dip his lips. His father didn't sound any more pacified by that line than he himself felt. But without even a clue as to where to start looking, Blake supposed he had no choice but to sit and wait. And hope.

****

Brooke slowly blinked her eyes open, feeling as though she'd slept for days. For a lingering minute, as she lay on her back, staring up at an unfamiliar ceiling, she was completely relaxed. She didn't want to move. In fact, she really wanted to just close her eyes and wait for sleep to reclaim her.

Then her gaze focused in on the ceiling fan poised almost directly overhead. It was obviously high end, and not the kind of thing that would ever belong in her apartment. *But that could only mean...!* Brooke's eyes shot wide open as she realized that she was not somewhere familiar, and she lurched into a sitting position with a startled gasp. She reached for the comforter that had pooled in her lap with the motion, instinctively seeking to cover herself, but when she looked down to grab it, she realized that she was still wearing her shirt from the night before.

"You're awake." Blake's voice was tinged with sleep.

Brooke lifted her eyes from her shirt-covered torso until they landed on him. Blake was sitting in what appeared to be a well-cushioned loveseat, one arm stretched out and his head propped up by a decorative pillow. As she watched, he yawned deeply. For a moment, she felt guilty for possibly having woken him.

"How do you feel?" Blake asked, the sleepiness in his voice already mostly gone.

It was at this point that she remembered everything from the night before.

Her eyes went wide again, and she immediately returned her attention to her arm, expecting to find stitches, or at least bruising. But, aside from the fact that her left sleeve had been turned into the sleeve of a t-shirt, she found nothing.

Brooke lifted her arm, her heart racing as disbelief encompassed her, and she used the fingers of her right hand to poke and prod at her skin. There was no soreness whatsoever. There wasn't a single marking. No stitched-up gash, no scab-covered cut, not even a slim, white scratch mark to indicate she might have hit something. Her arm was flawless.

Blake settled on the side of the mattress, just within reach, as she explored her arm.

"How is this possible?" Brooke asked, her voice as full of disbelief as she imagined her face was. Her arm slowly dropped back to her lap, but her eyes held his searchingly. "It's completely healed, like it never happened at all. And my feet don't hurt, either. Are they healed, too?"

"Yes." Something flickered in his eyes that looked like restrained amusement. "Are you feeling any pain?"

"I—no, I'm not," Brooke replied slowly. "But … I still don't understand … how is this possible?"

Blake allowed one corner of his lips to tip upwards this time, the faintest of teasing glints in his eyes. "I did tell you that my little sister has healing abilities, remember?"

Releasing a breath, Brooke said, "Well, yes, but …" She paused, scrunching her lips in thought as she searched for the best way to articulate the way she'd interpreted his earlier words. After a moment, she finally settled for, "When you said that, I think I pictured, like, healing away scrapes and bruises. Or maybe turning big cuts to fresh scars or something. I don't know." She held her arm up again, exposing the uninjured flesh. "Not this."

Blake shrugged with deliberate nonchalance. "Well, it's not my fault you didn't imagine it the way I meant it."

Brooke reached behind her, snatched the corner of the nearest pillow, and threw her arm forward. The pillow fell against his face exactly as she'd planned. "Maybe you just should have explained it better!"

Blake shifted the pillow easily into his lap, grinning faintly. "No, I'm sure I explained it fine."

Brooke dragged a deep breath in through her nose, but the light humor that was curving her lips faded as she blew the breath back out. "Blake," she said, dropping his stare and locking her fingers together in her lap. "Thank you."

His own halfhearted humor dissipating, Blake quietly said, "Don't thank me. What happened to you was my fault." He looked up from the bunched comforter as he spoke, and she met his gaze with widened eyes when his words sunk in. "I'm sorry, Brooke."

Her surprise fell into frustration, and she frowned. "Blake Hawke," she scolded, "this is not your fault. You didn't call up the storm and drop it on my roof, so you wipe that guilt right out."

It was Blake's turn to stare at her with widened eyes. Apparently, he hadn't expected that response.

"I assume you're thinking I was targeted by those other elementals we learned about," Brooke began after taking a second to compose her argument. "And I'm inclined to agree with that theory. But that doesn't make it your fault."

Blake met her frowning expression easily. "If they are the ones who attacked you, they only came after you because of me."

He was beating himself up inside, Brooke realized. She could see it in his eyes. But she didn't want him to.

Without a thought, Brooke leaned forward, grabbed the collar of his shirt, and kissed him firmly. If he was going to do the stubborn macho-male thing, then she was going to fight dirty. She was not going to have him blaming himself for her injuries when he hadn't even been around to cause them in the first place. So she held her lips over his until she felt him giving in, but when he tried to take over the kiss, she beat him to it and slipped her tongue inside his mouth instead.

Her grip of his collar loosened so that she could slide her arms around his neck, and his hands came up to land on her hips. She rolled her tongue along his, and his arms wound completely around her waist.

Blake rumbled against her, one hand sliding up the back of her shirt, and Brooke moaned into his kiss. The next thing she knew, Blake had her back on the mattress, both hands under her shirt and teasing her skin mercilessly, his weight braced apparently on his knees as he leaned over her. Brooke stroked his tongue one more time before breaking the kiss in order to hold her arms over her head in silent invitation. An invitation he took full advantage of, ceasing his teasing to remove her shirt altogether. He followed it up by removing his own, and Brooke took the opportunity to discard her bra.

Both articles hit the floor only moments before one of Blake's hands closed over one of her breasts.

Brooke arched into the touch and swallowed another moan when his lips descended on her throat. He kissed, licked, and sucked her flesh from the underside of her jaw to her nipple in sweet, torturous fashion. One flick of his thumb had her gasping, her hands landing on his bared shoulders and digging in. Her body was screaming for his. For more of his touch, more of his passion.

Blake's lips detoured below her collar until his kiss settled over her neglected breast. His hand worked magic on one side—squeezing, flicking—while his lips and tongue drove her crazy on the other. When he took her nipple into his mouth, she gasped sharply and buried a hand in his hair, holding him there. He sucked and licked, even grazing his teeth over the hardened peak.

And for every moment of pleasure his ministrations brought her, another part of her pulsated with need.

Finally unable to stand it any longer, Brooke kicked at the covers until only their respective layers of denim were between them. She adjusted her legs, straddling one of his, and bucked her hips enough to graze his covered erection.

That was enough to get Blake's attention. He lifted his head from her chest, hand pausing, and looked up at her.

"Please," she urged, her voice breathless.

Blake's blue eyes darkened with need. He pushed himself up, hands landing on his belt. As much as Brooke hoped to help him out of those crisp blue jeans, it wasn't happening this time. This time, she was in too much of a rush to get her own off. She didn't even wait to let him remove her panties.

"God," Blake groaned when his eyes landed on her again. She was fully undressed and laid out for him, waiting and enjoying her own view as he climbed back over her. He was hard and ready, and if she had thought she could hold out long enough, Brooke was sure she'd have loved to taste him.

But that was just going to have to wait. She needed to feel him first.

Blake's lips crashed back over hers at about the time she'd managed to glimpse a slim package in his nearest hand. A condom. Thank goodness one of them had a semi-functioning brain.

Hands wandered feverishly. Groping, stroking, teasing. Then Blake inserted a finger between her legs, and Brooke gasped against his lips. She must have wanted him more desperately than she'd realized if just the first touch felt so blissfully good. And he wasn't done. He swept that finger in and out, adding a second at the same time as his thumb found her nub, and she gasped again, louder this time.

Blake's lips locked over her nape, sucking hard as he flicked the nub again, and this time she cried out. Her hips bucked, pleading for that final release, but he refused her. His hand withdrew entirely as he released her neck, and he readjusted above her.

Brooke reached up and caught his jaw when he tossed the packaging aside. "Kiss me," she whispered, letting her thumbnail scratch just a little below his lip.

He trapped her wrist in his hand, placed a kiss on her palm, and bent forward, pinning her arm over her head. "Whatever you say." Blake obeyed her request and claimed her lips in a deep kiss.

Their tongues rolled together as his hips surged forward. It took conscious effort for Brooke to keep her lips sealed to his to contain her outcry of pleasure as he filled her. He felt *so* good.

With a groan, Blake broke the kiss. He trailed his tongue up to her ear as his hips began moving gently. He nipped at her earlobe as he sank back into her center. Brooke wrapped her arms around him, her hips lifting to greet his, searching for any way to take him deeper.

"Don't hold back," she whispered against his ear.

Blake only rumbled an acknowledgment of her words before catching her lips in another hot, demanding kiss. But he kicked up the pace, rolling his hips against hers after filling her. In and out. Their bodies danced, grinding together and coming entirely off the bed as Blake's kisses found their way down her throat once again. He trailed them over her pulse point, past her collar, until he'd managed to recapture one breast between his lips.

Brooke held him tight, one hand buried in hair, the other curled over his spine as she approached that blessed precipice. Blake's tongue played with her nipple, and his hips ground into hers, rubbing with just the right pressure. Her vision went white, and it was all she could do keep from shouting as ecstasy erupted like a volcano inside her.

Chapter Eleven

"I know I can't really keep this from coming down on you," Blake whispered, running his fingers through her hair. "But promise me you won't do anything too reckless if you happen to hear something at work."

Brooke's fingers stilled over his chest. "What makes you think I'll hear something at work?"

"I don't know," he offered honestly. "I just figure with your job you probably overhear a lot."

The slender leg wrapped around his tensed, and Brooke lifted herself to look into his eyes. She was still entirely nude—as was he—and the simple beauty of the sight took his breath away.

"You actually do have a point," she admitted, "but don't worry. Double-O-Seven I am not."

He grinned and kissed her gently. "Good, that'll help me sleep better."

She smiled and resettled herself on his shoulder for all of five seconds before drawing in a sharp breath. "My apartment! What happened to my apartment?"

"Logan's taking care of it," Blake assured her. He wasn't surprised when she sat up anyway, concern marring the light in her eyes.

"How is he doing that, exactly? And what time is it?" The last was clearly an afterthought as she broke from his gaze to look toward the covered window. Light was seeping in now, so it was clearly daytime.

"Time for breakfast, I'd say," Blake replied as he sat up. When she returned her attention to him, he added, "Also, Logan works construction. Fixing up housing stuff is literally his business, so he's got it all covered."

"Huh," Brooke mumbled, her gaze slipping from his to wander down his chest for a moment. "I never knew."

"Brooke," Blake interrupted, not feeling particularly like discussing his brother in the moment. "I only had the one condom on me."

Her cheeks flushed, and she swatted at him. "Get dressed, then, and take me to breakfast. I'm hungry."

Blake couldn't help but laugh as he rolled to his feet. "Yes, ma'am."

****

Hands on her hips, Brooke stood in the front yard and frowned at her living-room window. Or, more accurately, at the board covering the hole in her wall where the window was supposed to be. The branch that had crashed into her apartment the night before was gone, and on the outside, the only evidence of the previous night's storm was her window-wall and the now-lopsided tree.

"I hate this," Brooke declared after a long moment as she finally let her half-curled fists drop to her sides. She turned to face Blake, who was standing beside her. "But I can't decide what I hate more. The damage, last night's chaos, or the fact that I apparently could have died and none of my neighbors would have noticed."

Blake sighed, switching his frown back to her boarded-up window. "That's understandable."

"What I don't get is a large branch *crashed through my window*." Gesturing one arm wide, toward the nearest other apartment, she said, "How did Mr. Pendleton not hear that?!"

Blue eyes flicking in the direction of the indicated apartment, Blake paused a moment before the briefest of grins curved his lips. "Because he's half-deaf."

Brooke cocked an eyebrow at him. "Are you serious?"

"Yeah," Blake replied easily, lifting his own hands until he had hooked his thumbs in his pockets. "He's a teacher at the high school. I had him twice. And according to Angie, his hearing's only gotten worse."

"So, what, is he too stubborn to do anything about it?" Brooke asked incredulously.

Blake shrugged. "Probably. Or maybe he figures he's too close to retirement for it to make a difference."

Brooke sighed and shook her head. "That figures. I mean, I've seen him around a little, I knew he was getting up there in age, but it never occurred to me that he never said 'hello' because he never heard *me* say 'hello'."

"Are we talking about Pendleton?" Logan asked as he walked up to them.

Both Blake and Brooke turned to face him, and Blake's grin broadened slightly. "Yeah."

Brooke's looked past Logan, to the business truck that had settled in behind Logan's own. She recognized the name of the local glass company on the side of the electric-blue truck, and her gaze returned to Blake's brother. "Is he here for my window?"

Logan nodded. "Yeah."

"Don't get me wrong, but isn't that a little fast? I mean, doesn't it take longer than that to replace a window?" she asked.

Logan grinned slightly and shook his head. "Not when the owner owes you about a dozen favors. Anyway, don't worry about it. Your new window should be in place in no time."

Brooke smiled. "That reminds me. Thanks so much for helping with all this."

Logan shook his head again before his gaze flicked briefly to his brother. "Don't mention it." Then he moved until he was standing beside Blake, turning to watch the workers at the truck silently.

After a long moment, Brooke suddenly said, "I suppose I should be glad it happened this week, instead of next week."

Logan asked, "I thought next week was the one you had off?"

"Next week might be Spring Break," Brooke acknowledged, holding one hand up, finger pointing toward the sky as she talked. "But that does not mean 'no homework', and it *does* mean 'more work-work'."

"That's true," Blake agreed, realizing her point. "Hell, I'm scheduled for lifeguard duty for most of the week."

Logan sighed, shoving his hands into his pockets as he said, "I almost forgot. Damn drunk college students."

Blake smirked. "Like you never got drunk when you were in college."

"Yeah, but I never annoyed myself."

Before the conversation could continue, one of the workers from the truck stepped up to them, introduced himself, and began explaining to Brooke exactly what they were going to do. Blake stayed quiet as Brooke talked to him and watched as Logan occasionally joined the conversation whenever he found it necessary. Finally, the worker turned back toward his truck, and Brooke moved toward her door. She would need to leave it open, after all, if they were going to be installing a window.

****

"I want to tell Eric," Angela declared as she joined her parents and Blake in the living room after school that afternoon.

Blake, who had come over for further discussion of the situation, leaned back against the couch and raised

121

an eyebrow at his sister's entrance. But he said nothing, because she wasn't really talking to him.

Lillian released a quiet breath and gestured to the mostly vacant couch. "Why don't you sit, sweetheart."

Angela dropped her backpack beside the couch and claimed her favorite spot against the arm. "I'm serious," she said, obviously unwilling to drop the issue. "I want to tell Eric."

Changing his mind about his silence, Blake kept his voice curious as he asked, "Weren't you just telling me that you wanted to wait a while longer? So why the change of heart?"

Looking over at her brother, Angela replied, "You of all people shouldn't have to ask me that. You're *barely* even dating Brooke, and look what happened to her." She switched her attention to her parents again, completely oblivious to the surprise on her brother's face. "Eric and I have been together for over a year now. If you didn't trust him, you'd never let me bring him to family dinners, right? And yeah, I had been thinking about waiting. But now I think keeping him in the dark just puts him in more danger. He *needs* to know!"

"If that's how you feel," Lillian began carefully, pursing her lips for a moment before she added, "then of course you can tell him. I would have felt the same way if I were you."

"Before you talk to him," Christopher interjected, "keep in mind that you'd be giving him a lot of information very quickly. Take it from me, hearing all of this for the first time is somewhat overwhelming. But you'd be telling him more than your mother ever had to tell me. It could be a lot for him to take in."

Angela frowned in frustration, though her tone was far from accusatory when she asked, "So you're saying I shouldn't tell him? Or do you think I should tell him in pieces?"

"I just think you should be careful about how, and when, you tell him," Christopher said. "If he seems frustrated, or short-tempered, maybe that isn't the best time. This isn't just you telling him about your family. You have to tell him that, by being close to you, he might be in life-threatening jeopardy."

Slumping back against the couch, Angela crossed her arms and released a heavy sigh. "I understand what you're saying," she assured them. "But I don't know what to do. Every minute I put it off could be one minute too many!"

For a long minute, her family said nothing. Lillian and Christopher exchanged knowing looks. Blake glanced at his parents before returning his focus to his sister. It was easy for him to put himself in her place.

As Angela's head rolled back so that she could stare blankly up at the ceiling, Blake bit the proverbial bullet and forced out the words that left an odd, unpleasant taste in his mouth. "The way I see it…" He kept his eyes on Angela though he sensed his parents shifting their own gazes to him. "The only person who needs to be sure that this is the right decision is you."

Angela's eyes widened, and she turned to look at him, startled by his words.

He continued before either party could pull together a response. "Eric may not be my favorite person, but I'm your brother—I'm not *supposed* to like your boyfriend. And more importantly, I trust you." He paused to let his words sink in. "Besides, I didn't consult anyone before I told Brooke about us, and we weren't even dating. It hadn't even occurred to me that they might go after her, and as a result she got hurt. I have to live with that." It was odd to talk so openly about his relationship with Brooke, even if the mention had been miniscule. And technically, he and Brooke hadn't had that conversation yet. They'd had too many other things on their minds at breakfast.

Slowly, Angela pushed out a breath and offered her brother an honest smile. She got up, crossed to the other side of the large couch, and then leaned forward to wrap her arms around his shoulders. Holding him close for a long moment, Angela whispered, "Thanks, Blake."

Blake returned the hug easily. "Anytime, little sister."

Angela pulled back and paused to glance at her parents. "I'll be in my room." She turned and scooped up her backpack as she ran toward the stairs.

When Angela was out of sight—and earshot—Lillian and Christopher turned their attention to Blake, who was suddenly feeling awkward. He hadn't meant to overstep, but it suddenly felt like that was exactly what he'd done. "Uh, I'm sorry," he began. "I suppose I shouldn't have said it quite like that."

"No," Lillian said, shaking her head lightly, a small smile curving her lips. "You said the right thing. And I think, since she knows that none of you really like him, it meant more to hear you say that than it would have had we said it."

Blake sighed, his eyes shifting toward the stairs thoughtfully. "Yeah ... and it's not like I said anything I didn't mean."

Christopher shifted in his chair, lacing his fingers loosely across his lap and grinning faintly as he said, "So, Blake, talk to us about Brooke."

Blake's head whipped around until he was once again facing his parents. "What do you mean?"

"She seems like a nice young woman," Lillian declared calmly, a strange smile lighting up her eyes. "She's perfectly sweet."

"I'm … glad you like her," Blake said slowly, knowing his parents were going somewhere else with this. He knew his family well enough to know there was something odd in the expressions on their faces. And he didn't think he was going to like it.

"The question is," Christopher continued casually, "just how much do *you* like her?"

There it is, Blake thought even as his stomach contorted strangely and his throat swelled. His parents had never gone out of their way to grill him about a girl before. *Or at least never both at once.* Clearing his throat self-consciously, Blake replied, "We haven't really had the relationship conversation yet…"

Christopher lifted one eyebrow disbelievingly. "Yet you never told any of your other girlfriends, if memory serves."

They were right, of course.

He knew that his impulsive need to tell Brooke, with so little consideration and even less hesitation, meant something. And he was even beginning to suspect what that something might be, but he was in no way ready to tell his parents that. First he had to admit it to himself.

"Blake," Lillian called, pulling him from his thoughts and dragging his attention to her. Her blue eyes were gentle and understanding—encouraging, even. "Do you love her?"

The question hung in the air as Blake contemplated his answer. The mere fact that he didn't immediately say 'no' had him hesitating. He swallowed heavily as he realized that the truth was, at this precise moment, he didn't have an answer to that question. So he settled for the best answer he could provide. Gaze dropping to the coffee table, he said quietly, "Not yet."

****

Brooke stepped into the dining area in time to see her new favorite person, accompanied by his three brothers, enter the diner. She was en route to deliver drinks to another table, so she was forced to be satisfied with a smile and a nod when their eyes met. As soon as he returned the gesture, Brooke altered course slightly and shifted her focus back to what she'd been doing.

She delivered the drinks to the college girls she didn't know, took their orders, and then moved two tables over to greet the Hawke brothers. "Good evening, boys." She smiled as she came to a stop at their table. They had claimed a center table this time, and since each brother had his own side, she came to a stop at the corner between Blake and Logan.

"Hey," the brothers chorused as they looked over at her. Logan, Dean, and Nate all offered her honest, friendly smiles of varying sizes, but Blake's smile was different. Warmer.

Wishing she had time for small talk, Brooke asked, "What brings you all my way tonight?"

Dean smirked, his gaze switching to Blake for a moment before returning to her as he said, "It seemed like the place to be."

Blake rolled his eyes before looking up at Brooke and asking, "How's the new window?"

Brooke's smile was easy and genuine as she replied, "Fits like a glove." Her attention shifted to Logan. "Thanks again."

Logan shrugged. "No problem."

"Well," Brooke began as she flipped to a new page on her notepad, "I have an order to run back, so how 'bout I pick up your drinks along the way?"

The brothers easily complied, and in no time Brooke had slipped into the kitchen. She was in the process of putting up the order when, from several feet behind her, a sudden round of heavy cursing filled the air. It was followed almost immediately by the unmistakable sound of food hitting the trash.

Concerned, Brooke turned and moved up to the half-wall that separated her from the actual cooking area. Her eyes immediately landed on the diner's head chef, Ed, as he moved toward the large sink and tossed in a dirty knife. He was still muttering curses as he turned back toward his station and therefore her.

"Everything okay, Ed?" Brooke asked gently. For as long as she'd been working there, she had never heard him talk like that. And though she wouldn't claim to know him overly well, she was pretty sure she knew him well enough to tell that this was unusual behavior.

Ed paused mid-step, and his eyes snapped up to hers. He clamped his mouth shut and a flicker of embarrassment shone in his faded brown eyes before he finally sighed and gave a half-shake of his head. "Just having one of those days is all," he said.

As Ed stepped up properly to his station and began working on something, Brooke asked, "Is there anything I can do?"

"Nah," he replied with another head-shake, this time keeping his eyes on his work. "I just got a little distracted in my head and put the wrong ingredients in. But I gotta hurry to get it done now."

"All right, then," Brooke said, always one to take a hint. She stepped back from the divider. "I hope your night gets better."

"Thanks, Brooke," Ed called without lifting his head.

Brooke said nothing more as she stepped from the kitchen. She could tell he was still upset about whatever it was that was bothering him, but there really wasn't anything she could do to help. *We all have those days,* she reflected as she moved to the drink station.

Georgia was suddenly behind her, a grin in her voice as she said, "I notice your favorite customers are back."

Barely resisting the urge to roll her eyes, Brooke said, "Does this mean you're closing tonight?"

"Yep," Georgia replied. "But, hey, better tonight than this time next week."

Brooke let out a small laugh, setting the last glass on her tray, and turned as she said, "I hear you." She paused and raked her eyes over her friend. "I thought you'd gone blonde for the month?"

Georgia lifted one perfectly manicured hand and tangled it in a loose strand of her red hair. "I thought so, too. But I decided I missed the red. It gives a little color to this place, you know?"

"That it does," Brooke agreed as she carefully maneuvered around her.

"Have fun!" Georgia called after her as Brooke moved toward the dining area.

Brooke ignored her and made her way easily back toward Blake's table. When she reached her destination, she noticed the atmosphere was entirely different than it had been when she'd left. A different type of concern settling over her, she asked quietly, "Something wrong?"

Chapter Twelve

Nate was rubbing his forehead as if he had a headache, eyes closed and one fist clenched on the table. Dean had pushed back in his chair, arms crossed, glaring a hole through the table in front of him. Logan had one elbow on the table, mouth a thin line, with both fists clenched. He flicked his gaze up to her when she spoke, acknowledging her words, but made no effort to speak.

Blake sighed in frustration, moving his arms as Brooke set down his drink. "Not exactly."

Dean shot forward in his seat, but he managed to keep his voice low as he hissed, "How can you say that? What's not wrong about this?"

Brooke's attention had shifted to Dean when he'd spoken, but she was feeling incredibly confused. As she continued setting down their drinks, she asked, "Why do I feel like I'm missing something?"

Again it was Blake who answered her question. "Angela's decided to tell her boyfriend about everything. I was there when she made the decision, so I got to tell them."

She straightened as he spoke. "Um, maybe I'm still missing something, but … why is that such a bad thing?"

"We don't even know if he can keep a secret," Nate pointed out.

"More than that," Dean insisted lowly. "It's not like he's gonna stick around forever. He's not right for her, but she won't see it, and lord only knows how he'll treat her after this!"

Meeting his brother's angry gaze, Blake said, "He's never done anything to hurt her, Dean. We have to give him the benefit of the doubt."

Dean leaned back in his chair once again. "I can't believe you're okay with this."

Brooke tried not to smile as Blake heaved a sigh and opted not to respond to his brother's statement. *It's amazing that girl even has a boyfriend,* she reflected as her eyes moved around the table once more. It was obvious to her they disliked Angela's boyfriend for one simple reason: she was their little sister, and more than likely no man would be good enough.

Still, she felt the overwhelming urge to diffuse the situation, so she said, "I wouldn't worry if I were you. I'm sure it'll all work out just fine."

A long stretch of contemplative silence followed her declaration before Blake lifted his gaze back to hers and smiled faintly.

****

It was the last day of school before Spring Break—for Brooke at least—and she smiled to herself as she stepped into the parking lot after class. She had nothing specific to be happy about, but the weather was nice, and she didn't have to work for a few hours still. In that moment, it was enough. She knew if she actually got to thinking about the workload she had ahead of her, she might rethink her good mood, but she had the time to put off those depressing thoughts for a couple of days.

Her car was in sight when someone called out to her. The voice was male, and faintly familiar, but not one she could place off the top of her head. Still, she stopped walking and turned slightly to the side, looking for the man in question. And then she saw him, jogging toward her with an easy grin on his lips.

"Hey, Josh," Brooke said when he was standing before her. Josh was in her last class of the day, and the two of them had been paired together for an assignment that had been due that afternoon. They had shared other classes together sporadically over the past couple of semesters, but rarely talked.

Josh's grin broadened slightly. "Hey. I'm glad I caught up with you." He paused to take a breath and lifted one hand, gesturing vaguely as he spoke. "Me and some friends are gonna grab a couple drinks tomorrow at that bar downtown, and I was wondering if you wanted to come with?"

For a moment, Brooke found herself speechless. *Well ... I didn't see that coming.* "I'm sorry, Josh, but, uh, I'm meeting my boyfriend after work tomorrow. You'll have to go with someone else." Okay, so they didn't actually have plans, and she had no idea if Blake thought of them in boyfriend/girlfriend terms, but it was a good excuse. That was what mattered.

Josh's grin faltered a bit, though it didn't outright disappear. "Well, damn. Maybe we could hook up when you're not working sometime? We could grab burgers or something if you'd rather."

Brooke smiled politely even as she shifted her weight, preparing to take a step backwards. This guy didn't know how to take a hint, apparently. "The truth is, Josh, I'm just not interested." *Sometimes you have to say it like it is.* Still, she hoped it hadn't come off too harsh. She was going to have to see him at least twice a week for almost two more months.

Grin remaining strong this time, Josh shrugged and said, "Well, let me know if you change your mind." He turned to walk away, pausing to lift one hand in a small wave. "See you around."

Brooke held her ground, and her tongue, until he had walked past another row of cars. Then she sighed and shook her head even as she turned to resume her walk. *Some guys...* But she stopped after taking only two steps as her eyes landed on the male figure leaning casually against her Civic.

"Hey," Blake called without removing his hands from his pockets. And dang did he look good like that.

Her lips twitched, and Brooke quickly crossed the final row of cars until she was standing before him. "Hey," she said. "How long have you been standing here?"

He shrugged. "Not too long. I'd have said something, but I didn't want to interrupt."

Brooke groaned. "You saw that?"

His grin was apparent in his voice as he replied, "Yep. Heard it, too. Was I not supposed to?"

Brooke rolled her eyes at him. "Yeah, it was a hugely private conversation. I can't believe you eavesdropped."

Blake chuckled and pushed off of her car. "Now, correct me if I'm wrong, but we hadn't gotten around to making plans for tomorrow night yet, had we?"

Brooke's own lips curved into a mischievous grin as she said, "You're not wrong. But Josh didn't know that. I was hoping it'd be an easier out."

"Gotcha." Blake's eyes danced to match his grin. "Well, don't worry. Your secret's safe with me." He even threw in a wink for good measure.

Laughing, Brooke asked, "What happened to your last class?"

"He let us out early for good behavior," Blake replied with an almost-straight face.

Brooke let out a brief laugh. "How lucky!"

"I thought so."

As Brooke dug out her keys, she asked, "Hey, how did the boyfriend thing go?" She was suddenly incredibly self-conscious using that word directly toward him after what he'd overheard. *What he overheard and didn't correct ... or comment on at all.* She didn't know what to make of that.

His grin faded, and he sighed almost inaudibly. "Don't know yet. I imagine I'll find out this afternoon."

"Ah," Brooke replied. "Sorry, I know it's not my business. I was just curious."

Blake slipped his arm around her shoulders, pulling her into his side. "No apologies necessary. You are my girlfriend, after all."

Brooke's heart tripped in her chest, and her lips lifted in an automatic smile. She nearly forgot she was probably expected to comment. "True," she finally offered, still smiling.

Blake leaned around and pressed his lips briefly over hers before releasing her altogether. As he stepped back enough to let her access her car, he said, "Well, I'll let you go. Catch up with you later?"

"Definitely," Brooke replied without hesitation as she pulled open her door and tossed her bag inside. Pausing with one hand on top of the door, she looked back over at him and said, "At the very least, we should do dinner tomorrow night."

"Sounds like a date," Blake replied, his lips twitching again.

Brooke smiled silently at him before ducking into her car and pulling the door shut.

****

"You're right," Brooke declared Friday night as they settled together on his couch. He had the arm of the sofa at his other side, and his legs were extended, feet under the edge of his coffee table. Brooke was curled up beside him, head on his shoulder, one hand playing with his shirt. She was comfortable. "Dinner in was a good idea."

When she'd arrived, his house was already filling with the mouthwatering scent of something potentially delicious coming from Blake's kitchen, and he'd declared he felt it was a good night to stay in. She hadn't needed a whole lot of convincing. Time alone with Blake was exactly what she wanted.

Blake chuckled and tightened his arm around her waist. "Glad you agree."

"It was hard not to with the beautiful smells coming from your kitchen," Brooke admitted with a laugh. She leaned up and teased his cheek with a kiss. His skin was warm beneath her lips, rousing fond memories of their previous intimacy. "What are we having for dinner, anyway?"

"Ravioli. It's a recipe I had to pilfer from my parents, but it's worth it."

"Well, it certainly *smells* delicious," Brooke declared with a grin. "And I find it incredibly sexy that you cook voluntarily." Then again, she found *him* incredibly sexy.

Blake rumbled and pressed his lips to the crown of her head. "It does smell delicious," he agreed, voice a little thicker than before. "I should go check on it, actually, but I'm pretty sure it's about ready."

"Wow," Brooke teased, refusing to acknowledge the flicker of disappointment at their loss of contact as she allowed him to find his feet. "You can time things properly, too? I don't think I knew men with that talent still existed."

Blake just laughed, tossed her a wink, and headed for the kitchen.

Brooke eased to her feet as well after several seconds, trailing behind him into the kitchen to watch. It was a strange sight to see her man moving around so confidently in the kitchen, clearly knowing what he was doing and being comfortable doing it. Certainly none of her previous boyfriends had been big into cooking. *At least not anything more complicated than hot dogs,* she reflected with a faint grin. This was a change she could get used to.

And then Blake stepped back. Hands on his hips, he uttered the words she most wanted to hear. "Dinner's ready."

Blake refused to allow her to help set the table and to serve. So she watched with a permanent grin on her lips, a hungry rumble in her stomach, and a trickle of warmth between her legs as Blake strode into the dining room. He had a steaming serving bowl in his pot-holder-protected hands. The sight was picture-worthy, and Brooke sincerely lamented having left her phone in her purse on the couch in the living room.

He set the bowl on a deliberately placed table protector, next to a waiting serving spoon, and Brooke couldn't help but lean forward to get a look. Blake chuckled at her before turning to head back into his kitchen, pot holders in one hand. Brooke's gaze locked onto the steaming food and she took a deep breath. The large raviolis were covered in a thick marinara sauce. She could only barely make out the rectangular outlines of the ravioli beneath the sauce, but they were quite a bit larger than the type she bought at the grocery store. The sauce was the perfect shade of red, with visible flecks of green from whatever spices he'd used, as well as discernable chunks of tomato. And whatever those spices were was undoubtedly what had her stomach practically pleading with her to dig in already.

Blake returned with a large bowl of salad in his hands. Two types of dressing were tucked beneath one arm, and two bottles of iced tea were in the crook of the other. He set everything down, not claiming his own seat until after he'd filled both their plates. And then dinner was on.

They kept the conversation light as they ate, and after Brooke finally bit into her perfectly cooled ravioli she said, "You know, if Ed ever quits, you could be a shoo-in for Head Chef at the diner."

Blake laughed and shook his head. "Oh, no. I don't think I could trade part-time at the beach for full-time in a kitchen." Flashing her a grin, he added, "But I'm glad you like it."

"How could I not? This ravioli is *delicious*," she replied with a grin of her own. *Almost as delicious as that smile.*

"The next time I talk to my grandmother, I'll be sure to thank her for sharing."

"I thought you said you got the recipe from your parents?" Brooke asked after she swallowed another bite.

"I did," he said. "But my father got it from my grandmother, who got it from … I think it was my great-grandmother?"

Brooke scooped up a large, sauce-covered bite of her ravioli and held it up as she said, "It's like we're eating a family heirloom." She winked and popped the forkful into her mouth. In all honesty, she hadn't known ravioli and marinara sauce could taste so amazing. Even the sausage inside the ravioli, which was mixed with cheese, had awesome flavor.

Dinner passed easily, and once again Brooke found herself relegated to the sidelines during cleanup. And as she watched, she found herself suddenly envious. Doing the dishes seemed to go a lot faster when you could control the water the way Blake did. He just wiggled his wrist a few times in a circle, and everything was rinsed and scrubbed at once.

As Blake slipped the final dish into the dishwasher, Brooke couldn't help but ask, "You actually use that thing?" It was a stupid question, and she knew it as soon as she had thought it. *Of course he uses a dishwasher. His power is water, not* soapy *water.*

A single flick of his wrists was all it took for Blake's hands to dry, and he shut the dishwasher with a chuckle. "Of course I do."

"Right." Brooke felt like a moron. By then he was facing her, and her self-conscious laughter faded away as she said, "Thank you for dinner. It was really good." She couldn't wait for dessert.

Blake's lips twitched, and he stepped into her personal space, clamping his hands on her hips and pulling her up against him. When their lips were mere centimeters apart, he murmured, "Thank *you* for the company."

An instant later, their lips were pressed together, parted enough for their tongues to dance, and Brooke's fingers were buried in his hair. She felt like she'd been waiting for this kiss all day.

Blake's arms wound fully around her waist, one of his hands tangling in her long, loose hair, and one of Brooke's hands slipped from his hair to dip beneath his shirt collar. Her fingers brushed along his bare skin, and Blake tightened his hold on her as he deepened the kiss. She arched into him with a faint, muffled moan when his thumb trailed over her spine. It certainly hadn't taken him long to memorize that trick. His hand drifted a bit lower, and then his fingers were teasing her skin, just above her jeans.

"Blake," Brooke gasped when their lips parted a moment later. Both of them dragged in deep breaths. Her eyes were still mostly closed, but she blinked them open when his hold loosened and he leaned back. When her gaze focused, she found herself staring into his deep, darkened blue eyes, and she couldn't help but smile at the desire she saw in them.

He untangled his hand from her hair and adjusted his grip so that he could trail his thumb along her cheek gently, holding her gaze all the while. Her own grip on his hair loosened, and her hand slid to his shoulder without thought. He leaned in and pressed his lips over hers again. But this kiss was tender, brief, and he pulled away almost too quickly.

Brooke was still attempting to find her voice, curious about what else she'd seen in his eyes, when he took a single step back. She was forced to loosen her hold, her hands sliding partially down his chest, and he released her almost entirely as he reached up and pulled one of her hands into his.

"About the movie…" Blake began, his voice low and heavy with something that tingled up and down Brooke's spine as it washed over her. It took her a moment to remember they'd even intended to watch a movie that night.

Even she could hear the desire sneaking into her own voice when she replied, "What movie?"

Brooke's body temperature skyrocketed as she allowed him to lead her down the hall, further from the living room. It had only been a handful of days since they'd first made love, it was true, but she was almost more nervous now than she'd been the first time. The first time had been a heat-of-the-moment thing—an *amazing* heat-of-the-moment thing—but this was different. This was deliberate. This wasn't just raging lust and early morning hormones. This was *desire*. The kind that had her silly heart skipping beats in her chest and made her mouth run dry. Which was probably ironic…

Blake's bedroom was significantly larger than hers, of course. Like the rest of his home. He led her several feet into the room before turning suddenly and pulling her flush against him once more. Brooke met him halfway this time, her hands resting on the smooth planes of his chest as their lips met again in a hungry kiss. His hands rested on her hips, holding her against him as she curled her fingers into his chest through the fabric of his shirt.

Then his hands shifted, and he deliberately slipped his fingers beneath the hem of her shirt, slowly massaging her smooth, warm skin. She moaned against his lips at the contact and curled her tongue around his before pulling back from the kiss. He met her eyes again, and she grinned flirtatiously. Brooke pulled her hands from his chest and then grabbed fistfuls of her own shirt. She tugged it easily over her head and let it drop behind her.

Blake mimicked her, tossing his shirt somewhere to the side, and as he did so he dropped her gaze, his eyes moving down and over her torso as if he'd never seen— let alone kissed—it before. Her light-blue lacy bra had been very specifically chosen for this date. What he'd yet to discover was that she'd bought the bra as part of a set with matching panties.

"Do you like what you see?" Brooke teased, trailing her fingers across his chest. She caught his gaze with another flirtatious grin as she traced the contours of his muscles.

He matched her grin with one of his own and lifted one hand to run his finger along the strap of her bra. "The color looks good on you."

Brooke laughed softly. "I should hope so, water boy." Was it ridiculous that she'd purchased this set—as opposed to classic black—because the color was symbolic of her boyfriend's superpower? *Probably.*

Blake let his hand trail down her back, over the now-bared skin. Her laughter melted into a muted moan, and her hand stilled as her eyes fluttered closed. God, she loved his touch.

Chapter Thirteen

His hands curved around her bare waist and her hand pressed over his chest, above his heart, in a moment of lingering silence. Her head was resting over his shoulder. His was tilted slightly into hers. A beat later, they stepped apart, both quickly shedding their jeans, all the while keeping their eyes locked on the other. And she caught the flicker of a grin when he saw her panties.

Brooke couldn't decide if she was disappointed that he didn't go commando or relieved to see that he didn't wear briefs—an observation she'd neglected to make the first time. Not that it mattered. And when he stepped up to her again, she forgot the dilemma entirely. His hands lifted, fingers trailing along her hip bones and over the thin, lacy sides of her panties. Feeling his cool, smooth skin skimming along her own, Brooke pulled her lip between her teeth and raised her hands to frame his face.

Their eyes met again and she smiled. He smiled back.

Their tongues were clashing again a moment later as he lifted her from the floor and carried her the rest of the way to the bed. She had wrapped her arms and legs around him when he'd picked her up, so they fell together onto the large mattress, her head landing—barely—on a pillow. They broke apart, and Blake bowed his head to begin trailing kisses down the side of her neck.

She was too lost in sensation to note the irony of the power he possessed and the heat that blazed through her with every pass of his tongue along her throat, and she couldn't help but moan faintly when he sucked on the sensitive skin over her pulse point. His hands were moving along her exposed skin deliberately, slowly massaging patterns into her stomach and over her sides. Her own hands were wrapped around him, holding onto his shoulders, keeping him as close as she could. He still wasn't close enough.

His head lowered a bit more, and his tongue trailed across her collar bone as he shifted in order to kiss his way back up the other side of her throat. He earned several more muffled moans before she started to squirm beneath him. Her nails dug into his shoulders, and he was close enough for her to hear his heavy swallow.

When he finally allowed her to kiss him again, she readjusted her hold in order to bury her fingers in his hair. She absolutely loved his hair and the soft way it fell over her fingers. He rolled his hips forward when she nibbled a little on his lower lip, and her body arched in response. One of his hands settled again over her hip, and he used his other arm to brace himself before he rolled onto his back, taking her with him. The kiss broke as Brooke realized that she was straddling him now, his hands curving around her back and sliding slowly up her spine. She found she liked this power position.

He held her gaze as he released the clasp on her bra. She smiled and sat up, still straddling him, in order to shrug easily out of the lacy material and toss it aside. The desire in his eyes doubled as he took in the sight of her, and his increased desire was more than enough to spike her own. With a sultry smile, she leaned down and pressed her lips to the skin beneath his jaw. She wanted to make the fun last this time.

His hands, which had been resting over her hips, slid down to her thighs as his head fell back and she trailed her kisses down his neck. She paused a minute to suckle the skin at the hollow of his throat, before continuing down his chest. He moaned as she shimmied her way ever lower, kissing and licking his cooler skin, until she reached his boxers. She stopped then and lifted her gaze back to his. He was watching her, his expression strained and hungry—yearning. Matching the heat in her own body.

Brooke sat up again, her lips curving into a smirk, and she trailed her hands along his abs before sliding them to his sides and grasping his final article of clothing. She didn't even try to hold his gaze as she hurriedly discarded both his boxers and her own panties. Then she reached out again and, letting her eyes return to his, carefully trailed one finger along the length of him. She was finally getting to touch him and was eager to see his reaction.

Blake's head fell back against the pillow. He groaned, fisting the comforter beneath them at his sides. If she could garner that reaction with just one little touch, she couldn't wait to see what he'd do next. She wrapped her whole hand around him, squeezing and pulling slowly. He made a choked sound that was half groan, so she pumped again. Faster. His hips were straining to arch up, but he was trying to resist. She didn't want him to resist, so she squeezed a little tighter and kicked up the tempo again. The sound he made nearly tempted her to touch herself while she played with him.

It was a long few minutes before she released him, her own desire nearly tripled at the sight of him naked and straining beneath her. It was all she could do not to just impale herself on his rigid cock then and there. But instead she crawled back up his body until she was leaning over him, her lips barely an inch from his. He was watching her again, and she smiled seductively, slipping her tongue out to lick her lips.

He reached up with one hand, framing her face and guiding her lips to his for a passionate kiss. His tongue invaded her mouth and she moaned for him, enjoying his responsive rumble beneath her. His other hand landed on her hip, and she shifted herself around before finally sinking onto him. She kept it slow—or as slow as she could manage—and broke the kiss in order to watch his face as she took him inside her.

Blake's hips rolled in to hers automatically, sheathing himself entirely within her. Both of his hands skimmed along her sides, sending little jolts of electric desire throughout her body. Then he found one of her breasts with one hand and curved his other around her spine, tugging her forward again as she began rocking against him. Their lips reconnected as his hips arched up to meet hers, and they fell quickly into a hot, barely controlled rhythm.

He continued to surge into her, matching her rhythm with his own. She couldn't describe the sensations she felt. It was like she was melting into him. And then his hand left her breast, and before she knew it, he had flipped them back over.

He continued to thrust into her even as he abandoned her lips to trail hot, steamy kisses along the length of her throat. Brooke gasped loudly, her arms curving around his torso and her nails digging into his skin. They picked up the pace, and one of Brooke's legs lifted, wrapping around his hip in an effort to take him deeper.

Blake trailed his tongue back up the column of her throat before reclaiming her lips in a hard kiss. He was braced above her now, one forearm on the mattress beside her, and his other hand had wandered to her breast. He molded the pliable flesh masterfully, and their lips parted again as he finally collided with just the right spot. He sheathed himself once more inside of her, and they both cried out.

It was a long moment before her leg slid back to the bed, her arms loosening around him as she tried to regain her breathing.

Blake dragged in another breath and leaned down to press a soft kiss to her cheek even as he eased himself out of her. He half-rolled, half-collapsed beside her. Brooke wasted no time rolling into him.

After several minutes, with Brooke tucked beneath his arm, Blake tiredly murmured, "So … ravioli for dinner tomorrow?"

****

Tuesday was Blake's first shift at the beach. Unsurprisingly, by the time he showed up, the shoreline was littered with college students. He talked for a minute with Judd, the colleague he was replacing, before reaching his station and wrapping his hand around the lower rung of the ladder leading up to his tower. His feet hadn't left the ground yet when a familiar female voice called out to him.

"Blake!" It was Brooke.

Releasing the ladder, Blake turned to face her with a smile. He allowed himself a lingering glance at what she was wearing—cut-off jean shorts and a loose light-blue t-shirt with the straps of her swimsuit exposed and tied around her neck—before he said, "Hey."

Brooke came to a stop just inside his personal space and returned his smile with a teasing grin. "You better not have been trying to run away from me."

Blake chuckled. "I wouldn't dream of it."

"Good," Brooke said. "Did I catch you clocking in?"

"Yeah." He shrugged and added, "It's not a big deal. It's not like we're not allowed to talk to people."

"That's a relief. I'd hate to get you in trouble. But the better question is, what's company policy on girlfriends?"

Blake responded by planting his hands on her hips and stealing a lingering, playful kiss. "That answer your question?"

Brooke grinned and let her fingers trail along his arm. "More or less." She paused before letting her arm fall to her side and somberly asking, "I don't suppose you've made any headway on figuring things out with that … other group?"

Grin vanishing, Blake's eyes flicked toward the ocean. "No, we haven't. As far as I know, there haven't been any incidents since yours."

"That hardly seems fair," Brooke grumbled, crossing her arms over her chest. Neither spoke for a moment until she said, "Hey, I forgot to ask before, did you ever hear how Angela's conversation went?"

"It went pretty well from what I heard. She told him after school last week, and they went to a movie Friday afternoon. Angie didn't say anything about him freaking out, or not returning her messages."

"Well, it is sort of a surreal thing to try to wrap your head around. Maybe he's in denial?"

Blake shrugged. "That I don't know." He jerked his thumb toward the water. "Are you going to swim while you're out here?"

"I was thinking about it," Brooke replied with a teasing smile. She tilted her head up towards the clear sky. "I mean, how often does it almost hit seventy in mid-March?"

Blake chuckled. "Not very often, that's for sure."

Returning her eyes to him and keeping her grin firmly in place, Brooke asked, "Are you going to watch my back if I do?"

Lips curving upwards once more, Blake replied, "That is my job, remember."

Waving her hands in a shooing gesture, Brooke said, "Then you should get back to it. I'm going to go get my feet wet." She threw in a wink for good measure and promptly turned toward the shore.

Blake watched her go for a moment, grin still plastered on his face, before he shook his head and once again reached for the ladder. As he scaled the distance to his designated seat, his mind replayed their conversation. It may not have been her intention, but she'd raised a good point. Despite the fact that his mother could only recall two instances of attacks from her youth, Blake's instincts screamed that they weren't out of the woods yet. They all needed to be on their toes.

****

Brooke did her best not to grin like an idiot as she moved closer to the shoreline. Flirting with her sexy lifeguard boyfriend was fine and all, but strutting around like a love-struck high school freshman was ridiculous. Not that it was her fault. No, as a matter of fact, it was entirely his fault she felt this way.

She'd been wrong when she'd assumed that he'd look out of place in the requisite red trunks of a lifeguard. And while she still preferred seeing him in shades of blue, the red worked just fine. Or perhaps she was just too distracted by his toned chest to pay any real attention to the contrast between his lighter skin tone and the trunks.

And that thought sent her mind straight to the gutter. It wasn't near the first time she'd seen him shirtless, but getting to see him shirtless in *public* added a whole new level of excitement. It was almost like sneaking something your parents said you weren't supposed to have right under their noses.

But this wasn't the time to be daydreaming about that kind of thing, and so Brooke did her best to shake her mind onto a new topic as her toes met with cool sea water. The change in temperature around her feet was distracting, and for a moment she was able to simply gaze out over the gently rolling waves of the ocean and relax.

It was a nearly cloudless day, the morning fog long since dissipated, and birds were fishing not too far out. She could even see the outline of a vessel of some sort in the distance.

I wonder if Blake can feel my toes wiggling... Well, so much for the distraction. But it wasn't like she could turn around and ask, so she was just going to have to ignore the curiosity until later. *Maybe later tonight?*

Heaving a sigh, Brooke took another step forward so that the waves rolled up and over her ankles. She turned enough to watch the groups of people scattered along the beach. There was an intense game of beach volleyball going on to her right, about halfway between the waterline and the parking lot. Numerous couples were scattered here and there, some sitting on beach towels and many splashing around in the shallow water. One couple was even strolling along the water's edge, hand-in-hand. Several groups of three or four were moving around, dancing in the water or walking along the sand. A few yards away, a kid of maybe ten was building a truly impressive sand castle with his father's help.

But there was only one man who seemed to be there by himself. Brooke frowned as she gazed at him, realizing that he was vaguely familiar. He was standing just beyond the reach of the water, staring out thoughtfully toward the horizon. He wore dark slacks, his feet covered by shiny black shoes that did not belong on a beach, and his upper body was clad in a simple light gray t-shirt. His hands were resting in his pockets, and the tips of his brown hair were moving, just a little, with the breeze.

Brooke scrunched her lips as she watched him. She knew she knew him from somewhere, and it was eating at her. Perhaps he was a customer that she hadn't seen in a while? No, she decided. That wasn't it—at least not exactly. *But then where do I know him from?* It was really beginning to bother her, and even that seemed strange. She didn't usually dwell on something that could be brushed off as déjà vu.

But then he turned his head, without moving the rest of his body, and met her gaze solidly. They were standing several yards apart, too far to be heard if they tried talking at a casual level, but there was no doubt that he was staring straight at her. And in his not-quite-glaring brown eyes Brooke found her answer: This was the same man who'd come in to the diner that one time with Emma, nearly two weeks ago. She recognized him as much by his face as by the sudden nausea in her stomach.

Then the man turned completely, releasing her from his stare, and began walking up the beach. He never removed his hands from his pockets, and his walk was calm yet brisk as he made his way to the parking lot. Like a man with a purpose.

Brooke watched, her stomach still churning, as he moved steadily toward a Crown Victoria that was parked apart from the crowd of vehicles. She swallowed heavily, realizing her breathing was slightly uneven, her eyes still riveted on the unknown man. It wasn't until he had ducked into his car and pulled the door shut that the strange spell released her, and Brooke turned promptly back toward the sea.

Dragging in a deep, ragged breath, Brooke gasped, "Who was that?" It was only the second time she'd seen the man. The second time she'd wished she had never been so unlucky. But something about this encounter was worse. Before, she recalled, she had blamed his irritatingly superior attitude. Now, however, she was thinking it was more than that. It wasn't so much his attitude as it was *him*—the man himself was repulsive and terrifying, though she had no solid reason to feel that way.

Maybe I should ask Georgia if she ever figured out anything else about that guy, she decided as she released another heavy breath.

When the water around her ankles shifted slightly, Brooke blinked and looked down, expecting to find a strand of seaweed stuck to her ankle or something. Instead, as she watched, the water rolled and curved, pulling entirely away from the sand and pushing forward in strange patterns. And then, all of a sudden, the patterns solidified. The bare patches of sand had formed words.

EVERYTHING OKAY?

For a moment, Brooke could only stare at the words in front of her. Obviously, Blake had seen at least a piece of her bizarre behavior. It eased away the lingering uneasiness to know that he really was watching. She felt her lips begin to curve into a faint smile, and then it dawned on her that she didn't know how to respond. He'd told her once—because she had actually asked— that he couldn't hear through water. So she doubted speaking would work.

Well, in that case, she decided even as the tide rolled in again and washed away the words as if they'd never been. She turned to face the tower, which was almost directly behind her, and lifted her hand to wave up at him. She didn't know if he could see her expression or not, but she added a smile for emphasis. It was hard to tell from her distance, but she was pretty sure she saw him nod a moment later, so she lowered her arm.

Brooke turned back to the water and sighed. It was true that she no longer felt nauseous or uncomfortable, but she also no longer really felt like swimming. Her good mood had definitely gone down several notches. "So much for this." Telling herself she would try again another day—though it might have to be later in the afternoon—she turned and began trudging back up the beach.

With her head down, Brooke didn't realize that Blake had climbed down from his tower to meet her until he called out to her. Her head snapped up in embarrassed surprise, and she met his gaze even as she adjusted her course to meet him.

"What was going on down there?" Blake asked before she could say anything.

Brooke hesitated a moment, deciding whether or not she wanted to sound utterly ridiculous. "Did you see that guy? The one who was standing over there?" She pointed to the area where he'd been.

Blake's eyes shifted to follow her finger for a moment before returning to her. "The guy in the slacks? Yeah, I saw him walking away. Why?"

"It's stupid," Brooke warned with a sigh. "He came in to the diner with Emma Matthews about a week and a half ago, give or take, and I remember he didn't seem overly friendly. He was never actually rude to me, but something about him just sort of … freaked me out, I guess. Anyway, I hadn't seen him since until a few minutes ago, and he stared at me with this really intense, uncomfortable look in his eyes. And then he just walked away."

"Did he say anything to you?" Blake asked, a frown curving his lips at the edges.

Shaking her head, Brooke replied, "Not this time. And the time before he only spoke enough to order his food. I don't suppose you have any idea who he is?"

It was Blake's turn to shake his head. "No. I think I've seen him once or twice, but I can't place him. You said he was there with Emma?"

"Yeah. Do you know Emma?"

"She's Angela's boyfriend's older sister," Blake explained with a faint nod. "Maybe Angela would know who he is—if this guy's ever around when she's over there."

Brooke pursed her lips, remembering what Georgia had told her. "Who knows. My friend Georgia is pretty close friends with Emma, and Emma wouldn't tell her anything when she asked."

Blake arched a brow. "That seems like an odd thing to keep from your friends."

"The whole thing was strange," Brooke stated, easily recalling that night.

"How do you mean?" Blake asked.

With a half-shrug, Brooke replied, "Well, I walked up to the table at one point in time to catch a bit of their conversation. I don't remember the words now, but whoever that guy is, he seemed pretty upset about something. Even Emma wasn't very friendly that night."

Releasing a frustrated breath, Blake said, "That does sound strange. I'll try to remember to ask Angie about him the next time I talk to her."

Snapping back to her senses, Brooke held up her hands, palms forward. "Oh, no, you don't have to do that. I mean, it's weird, but it's not like he's ever threatened me or anything. Seriously, you've done plenty for me. Don't worry about this."

Blake hesitated, frowning more at her words. After a long moment, he finally said, "All right … but let me know if you see him around again—especially if he does anything strange. And remember, we're dating, so it's not like it's inconvenient for me if you need help."

Her heart fluttered again as her arms returned to her sides, and Brooke smiled. "Deal."

Chapter Fourteen

Georgia all but slammed into the back room, purse clutched tightly in one hand. Her other hand was lifted, patting at her dark red hair in an attempt to smooth it. Her tone was exasperated as she exclaimed, "Holy Mother of God! It's a madhouse out there!"

Brooke offered her friend a sympathetic smile. She had only navigated her way to the back a couple of minutes prior; the memory was still fresh. "It'll be worse tomorrow." she pointed out.

"Don't remind me. Is it too late to call in sick?"

With a bitter chuckle, Brooke replied, "I think so. I'm pretty sure Paula would call the doctor to confirm it."

"Why is Spring Break worse than every other holiday combined?" Georgia asked rhetorically as she shoved her purse into her own old locker.

"I don't know if I'd go that far. But it is pretty bad."

"You're probably right," Georgia admitted. Lifting her apron from the bench in front of her, she asked, "Do you ever wish you'd taken that job at the grocery store?"

"Nope," Brooke replied a heartbeat before the door to the backroom opened once more and Paula stepped inside.

Both women paused, their hands stalled mid-air, and watched as their supervisor pulled the door shut and leaned against it with a heavy sigh. Without even opening her eyes, Paula asked, "Do either of you ladies have any idea what's gotten Ed so worked up today?"

Georgia and Brooke exchanged a brief look before Brooke stupidly asked, "He's upset again today?"

Paula opened her eyes and blinked at her silently.

"What do you mean 'again'?" Georgia asked. "The only time I've ever seen him upset was last year, when the cable company was giving him the run-around."

Brooke looked back and forth between them for a moment before shrugging self-consciously. "Early last week, I think, he was having sort of a bad day. He didn't tell me about it, but he seemed fine the next day."

Paula released a breath and stepped away from the door. "Well, whatever's bothering him today has him in a real fit. Be careful when you go in there. I'm tellin' you, he's got all the other cooks in a tizzy."

"Oh, joy," Georgia grumbled as she resumed adjusting her apron. "Nothing ever goes right when the kitchen's messed up."

"I just hope everything calms down by tomorrow," Paula said. "If that kitchen's not running smoothly on St. Patrick's Day, we'll be in real trouble."

Brooke and Georgia cringed. They were both working long shifts the next day, and Brooke doubted Georgia wanted to think about how much harder it would be if the kitchen staff wasn't on their A-game any more than she did.

"All right, well, enough stalling," Paula said, her tone switching flawlessly to the closest thing she ever came to authoritative. She moved to push the door open again. "You've probably both been seated by now, so you'd better get out there." And then she disappeared from sight.

"Have you ever heard a more motivating speech?" Brooke asked.

With a light laugh, Georgia grabbed her notepad. "Yep. You should've heard the speech my tenth-grade English professor gave us right before our final."

Leading the way through the door, Brooke replied, "Do me a favor, and don't talk about school right now. I can only handle so much at once."

Georgia laughed behind her as the women made their way into the crowded dining area.

****

Most of Spring Break passed in a greasy blur for Brooke. It was already Saturday, and she was working again, but this time only until mid-afternoon. And she would have just enough time to run home and clean up before her boyfriend picked her up. She couldn't wait.

But first she had to get through her shift.

"I can't wait until the college students go back to their dorms," Georgia declared as she met up with Brooke at the drink station.

Brooke laughed as she filled a glass with ice. "I hear you. I'd completely forgotten what a nightmare Spring Break can be."

Georgia reached for a straw, tearing off the wrapper as she said, "That's because it's worse this year. I swear it is." She paused in order to focus on stabbing the straw through the ice without damaging it, and then she asked, "Is enrollment up this year?"

Pulling her glass from beneath the tea dispenser, Brooke replied, "I heard it was down, actually."

"That's impossible."

Brooke offered her an understanding grin. She set the first glass aside and reached for a second as she said, "Maybe we got more of Mimi's crowd this year."

Mimi's Kitchen was the other local non-chain diner in town. Because of this, for nearly as long as the two diners had co-existed, they had been engaged in a friendly rivalry. Brooke was pretty sure Earl's Diner had come first, but then again she'd only ever asked Paula, and Paula was just slightly biased on the subject.

Georgia paused, her second glass just millimeters from the soda tab she'd been aiming for, and turned to offer her friend a laughing smile. "Well, in that case, I think I can suck it up for a few more days."

Brooke set her two perfectly filled glasses on her tray. "That's good, because I imagine they won't disappear until Tuesday."

"Wait," Georgia called as Brooke had turned to re-enter the dining area. "I thought Spring Break ended on Sunday?"

"It does, but that doesn't mean everyone goes back to class when they should." Laughing again at the look of horror on Georgia's face, Brooke looked forward and walked out.

She navigated to the table that had ordered the drinks, setting the two iced teas in front of her customers before pulling out her notepad and taking their orders. Once that was done, she turned to her newest table and the young couple that had been seated while she'd been talking to Georgia. She was nearly at the table before she realized that she recognized them. Angela Hawke and Eric Matthews.

An easy smile in place, Brooke curved one hand over her hip and said, "I'm not expected to chaperone, am I?"

Both teens looked up at her and grinned. Angela's was simple and honest, and Eric's was lopsided and humorous.

"Hey, Brooke," Angela said easily. "This must be our lucky day."

"I'd say so," Brooke teased. "So how've you two been?"

Angela looked over at her boyfriend. "We've been good."

Eric nodded. "Yeah."

Brooke rolled her eyes teasingly. "Well, don't go getting all descriptive on me." She paused and reached out to playfully nudge the eighteen-year-old in the shoulder. "And you had better tell your sister I said 'hi' when you get home."

With a faint laugh, Eric nodded again. "Yes, ma'am."

Angela flashed Eric a smirk before looking up at Brooke with a faux-innocent expression. "So you and Blake are official now, right?"

One of Eric's eyebrows went up at this, and he turned a curious expression to Brooke as well.

"Yes, yes we are."

"Well, don't worry," Angela said, her lips twitching with her effort to contain her laughter. "I promise to be nice to you. You see, I learned from my mother, not from my brothers."

Brooke echoed her laughter a moment later. "That's certainly a relief. I appreciate it." She extracted her notepad and pen from her large apron pocket. "All right, then, let's see what I can get you so I can leave you two alone."

The teenaged couple ordered their drinks and their meals, and when they were done, Brooke turned and headed for the kitchen. She had four meals to put in for, and two more drinks to prepare. As she navigated around Georgia, who was delivering meals to another table, Brooke spotted one of their other regulars and offered him a quick smile and a wave before pushing through the doors that separated the eating space from the working space.

She passed the drink station easily and let herself into the kitchen. Ed was focused on slicing fish, so she opted to keep quiet as she attached the slips of paper to the rotating metal ring. With that done, she let herself out in order to get Angela's and Eric's drinks.

Brooke had finished Angela's tea, and was in the middle of filling Eric's Coke, when the doors to the kitchen slammed open. The drink station was oddly designed, and so anyone coming or going from the kitchen had to be careful, or they could slam right into someone filling a drink. Because of this, as Brooke started and turned in surprise, she was suddenly bumped by someone's side. The motion jarred her, her arm jerked, and the next thing she knew Eric's soda was all over her shirt.

But she couldn't even focus on that, because almost as soon as the pressure of the other person's side had moved beyond her, she recognized the yelling voice that belonged to him. It was Ed.

"—give a damn anymore! If you don't like it, cook it yourself!" Ed bellowed, stomping through the drink station even as he tore the hair net from his head and tossed it angrily to the ground. He pushed through the doors that led to the dining area as he continued yelling. "I've had it with this place!"

Mortified, Brooke stepped away from the mess at her feet to move to the still-swinging door that he had just stormed through. She watched as every head in the diner—customer, server, and hostess—swirled in Ed's direction with wide, startled eyes.

Ed continued his stomping rampage through the diner, nearly colliding with a costumer's chair in his rage. "I hope this whole damn building burns to the ground!" As he walked, he tore his chef's coat off, ripping the buttons and sending them flying like small missiles. He crumpled it haphazardly in one hand and then pitched it at the register, forcing Shelly to stumble backwards to avoid it. "I'm out!" Ed roared even as he shoved through the main entrance. The doors slammed shut behind him, as if echoing his sentiment.

For a long moment, no one dared breathe.

Brooke shifted her gaze to lock eyes with Georgia, who had been in the process of taking someone's order and was still wide-eyed and slack-jawed. As she shifted her gaze, she noticed belatedly that two of Ed's sous chefs had gathered a few feet behind her.

And then Paula came bustling out of the backroom. The sous chefs moved aside quickly, Brooke pressed herself awkwardly to the door frame as she had nowhere else to move, and Paula strode right past them. She paused in the dining area, earning everyone's attention, and after bending to retrieve Ed's discarded hair net, she said, "I'm so sorry about all of the commotion! Please go back to your meals. I promise nothing like that will happen again. If anyone has any questions or complaints, I'll be happy to hear them in just a few minutes."

Everyone watched as Paula quickly moved through the diner, paused to drop the hair net into the nearest garbage, and then pushed through the door.

It was another long moment before anyone shook themselves out of their shocked stupor. And then Brooke looked down at herself, realizing she was still wearing Eric's soda, and groaned faintly. She still had over an hour left in her shift.

Chapter Fifteen

Apparently, Blake had decided to put a slight spin on the traditional dinner-and-a-movie date, because when they climbed back into his car after the movie, he pointed them in the direction of the beach, a direction which was not the shortest route to either of their homes.

Before she could say anything, though, Blake was speaking. "Now, I know the beach isn't all that original, but I want you to trust me. It's worth it."

Intrigued, Brooke looked over at him. "And what are we going to do on the beach at six o'clock at night?" She certainly had a few cliché ideas she wasn't nearly above trying out, but she wanted to hear his first.

Blake's lips curved in a grin, but he never took his eyes from the road. "You'll see."

Brooke laughed, allowing him his mysterious moment, and let her gaze return to the road ahead. They talked a little about the movie, until Brooke interrupted herself when she realized they had just driven past the parking lot. "Um, Blake...?"

He chuckled, clearly unsurprised by her confusion. "You don't think that's the only decent beach around here, do you?"

Not wanting to admit that the thought hadn't even occurred to her, Brooke was silent a moment before she finally said, "Is this the 'trust you' part?"

"I suppose it could be," Blake replied easily as he slowed.

Brooke watched silently as he eased the Mustang off the interstate and onto a gravel road. The road curved, descending gradually, until it came to a stop on a large, flat outcropping made of dirt and gravel. There was room for probably about six average-sized vehicles, but there weren't any others there at the moment. The rough parking area was just a few yards from the sandy shore of the beach.

And it was then that Brooke realized this part of the beach was separated from the main section by a large formation of rock; rock she had looked at before, from the other side, and wondered what was hidden behind it. *I guess now I know*. She almost felt stupid for not figuring it out before. The gravel road was less than five minutes from the public beach.

As Blake pulled the keys from the ignition, Brooke looked over at him and asked, "Are we even allowed to be here?"

Blake raised an eyebrow at her and teased, "Do you think I'd risk getting you arrested? This beach is just as available as the other one. But it's a little rockier, so they consider it more dangerous, and they think if they don't pave the roads or advertise it that people will stay away."

"Right," Brooke said, understanding. She rolled her eyes. "They aren't very bright, are they?"

"I do have my doubts. Now come on." With that, he pushed open his door and climbed out.

Brooke wasted no time following him and paused to take a deep breath of the salty air after she'd shut the door. Sure, it was pretty much the same as the air in town, and she had spent enough time at the beach to be acclimated to the very slight change, but the air somehow felt different in that moment. She rolled her eyes at herself. *Unless he hid his brother behind one of those rocks, the air's exactly the same. It's not going to change just because you're on a date, you idiot.*

The solid *thunk* of the closing trunk drew Brooke's attention, and she looked over as she realized Blake had retrieved something that had been hidden there. He walked around to her side before she could ask anything, and her eyes landed immediately on the quilt draped over his arm and the small ice chest hanging from his hand. Her eyes widened and darted back up to his face.

Blake was grinning again. He held out his free hand. "I hope you don't mind."

Her own lips curving broadly, Brooke accepted his hand and walked beside him. "Not at all."

They reached the smaller beach in no time, and Blake released her hand to set the ice chest down and unfold the quilt. As he shook it out carefully, Brooke allowed herself to look around.

From the waves crashing against mostly hidden rocks a short ways out to sea, she could see what Blake had meant by it being more dangerous, but that didn't take away from the beauty. The sun hadn't fully set yet, though it was well on its way, and the sky was alight with color. The typical coastal fog was only beginning to roll in, adding a strange, mystical feeling to the atmosphere. And when she tilted her head up a bit more, she realized the moon and stars were just beginning to shine.

Deep, gentle chuckling drew her attention back to her companion, and she flushed despite herself. "Sorry," she said as she realized he was already sitting patiently. "It's just … kind of perfect right now."

He smiled. "Yeah, I was hoping it would be. And when the sun's fully set, we'll stay a little longer so you can see the stars."

Brooke returned the smile and moved to settle herself on the quilt beside him. "Just don't get lost in the fog on the way out."

Blake reached back for the ice chest. "I'll put in a little extra effort, just for you," he promised. As he popped open the lid, he added, "I thought I'd go light. I hope that's okay."

"That sounds great," Brooke replied honestly.

With another grin, Blake dove one hand into the box and wrapped his fingers around the first sandwich.

Brooke's gaze travelled, without conscious direction, back to the sky. She wanted to see a bit more of the sunset before it was gone, but what her eyes found themselves focusing on was something she hadn't seen a minute before. As she watched, the few dark clouds multiplied. It looked almost like they were building upon each other—like they were alive. It was the strangest thing she'd ever seen, and quite possibly the most ominous as well.

Her stomach plummeted to her feet, and she swallowed heavily before saying, "Blake … turn around."

Blake paused, two sandwiches clasped carefully in one hand, and lifted his head from his task. He followed her gaze to see that the black clouds were nearly covering the sky now. And the fog was rolling in far too quickly.

Then the first crack of thunder sounded. It was so loud, and so close, that it practically shook the air around them.

Dropping the sandwiches carelessly back into the ice chest, Blake said, "We need to go—now!"

"Oh my God," Brooke breathed as she scrambled to her feet. Apparently, he thought it seemed pretty unnatural, too. Her heart was already pounding against her ribcage, and her arm hurt with the memory of the glass that had torn into it. She *hated* storms. This kind of situation wasn't helping that in the slightest.

"It'll be okay," Blake said, his tone assuring her he remembered her fear. He used his foot to shove the ice chest out of the way as he hurriedly pulled the quilt off the ground, not bothering to fold it.

The sky above them, now darkened by a thick blanket of clouds, flashed brightly. Another crack sounded, but this wasn't exactly the same as thunder. The couple froze for an instant, and as one their heads turned toward the road they'd driven in on. Lightning had struck the ground between them and Blake's car. Thunder crashed again, seeming to echo the fire that suddenly roared to life.

Blake shoved the bunched-up and dangling quilt under his arm before using that same hand to grab the handle on the ice chest. He reached out and took Brooke's nearest hand into his, holding tightly to reassure her. "Let's run."

Brooke gaped at him. "*Toward* the fire?" Her incredulous tone was understandable, if fortunately misplaced.

"Yes," he replied. "My car's on the other side. We'll be fine."

The sky flashed again, and Blake pulled her against him. Brooke forced herself to keep her eyes open, remembering that lightning was poisonous to him. She could only pray it didn't strike too close.

The lightning struck the sand, but apparently not close enough to incapacitate Blake as he remained standing strong. "Trust me," he said.

Still pressed against him, Brooke forced her hands to release his shirt and nodded. "I do." She wished her voice were stronger.

Keeping hold of her hand, Blake began running forward even as another round of thunder rolled overhead. It was so close they could almost feel it now.

Brooke ran beside him, dragging in deep breaths and trying to stay calm. She needed to stay rational and she knew it. But she really wished her boyfriend's mortal enemies had some *other* kind of power. *Really, there are lots of other terrifying things. Like zombies, or magical, man-eating spiders.*

The flames were close now. Or, more accurately, they were closer to the flames. The fire was, for the moment, largely contained on the small field of mostly dead grass between the parking area and the beach. But they would have a serious problem if it went backwards and made it to the car.

"Blake," Brooke said again as they continued running.

"It's okay," Blake said, his voice stable and strangely calm.

And then, even as the sky lit up again and another crack of lightning hit the sand behind them, Brooke registered the sound of crashing waves. The sound was stronger, more urgent and violent than it had been before the storm rolled in. But she doubted the storm had caused the change.

Before she could think more on it, her eyes widened as a veritable tidal wave rose up, towering over and above them.

Blake drew her nearer before releasing her hand and wrapping his arm entirely around her waist. He held her against him tightly as the water crashed down in front of them, landing squarely on the flames. But he didn't seem to trust that the flames were entirely smothered, because a portion of the wave separated, swirling around the couple and pulling them literally off the ground. The term 'flying water' slowly echoed through Brooke's mind as she twisted her hands tighter in the back of his shirt. Her feet were suddenly half-submerged in water and very much *not* on the ground. Thunder rolled overhead, but she focused on the continuous crash of the waves around her. And she allowed herself to be somewhat amazed as they seemed to glide forward on the wave, curving around the burnt earth safely. It seemed impossible, even fantastical. She might have described it as 'awesome' were they not fleeing for their lives.

The water lowered them almost as quickly as it had lifted them, and Brooke realized that hard-packed dirt and gravel were once again beneath her feet. They were standing beside Blake's car, on the other side of the now-smoldering fire.

"It's still unlocked," Blake told her as he released her entirely. "Get in. I'll be right behind you."

Brooke barely took the time to nod before she darted around the car and yanked open the passenger door. As she quickly clambered inside, noticing that Blake was throwing their would-be picnic dinner into the trunk, lightning lit up the sky once more. Everything was white for a long moment, and Brooke felt her heart lurch.

Surely, after that strike, the air around them was charged with electricity by now. At least enough to do some damage.

"Blake!" Brooke cried, turning to jump back out of the car. She might be afraid of storms, but she wasn't so afraid that she would cower while he risked his life for her.

The driver's side door was yanked open before she could get her second foot back on the ground.

"I'm fine, but we need to go." Blake nearly leapt into the driver's seat. "That last strike was way too close."

Brooke turned, her eyes examining him to see how much he might have been exaggerating.

He looked a little more pale than usual, his eyes were bloodshot, and his breathing was something less than stable. She'd never seen him like this before, and she didn't want to ever again.

"Should I drive?"

Blake paused a moment after he pulled his door closed solidly and looked over at her. With a slight shake of his head, he replied, "No. But you should buckle up."

Brooke obediently yanked her door shut and snapped her seatbelt into place. By the time she was done, Blake had put the car into motion and was moving up the gravel road.

The storm still raged above them, reminding them of the continued threat as the sky lit up again and lightning tore across their line of sight. It crashed onto the road several yards away, and Blake increased his speed.

Neither spoke as he did his best to put the unnatural storm behind them.

The storm was somewhere behind them, out of sight, when Blake pulled up to Brooke's apartment and cut the engine. They hadn't said a word since they'd hit the interstate; for the most part, Brooke's eyes had been glued to the side mirror. But she was watching as Blake tugged the key from the ignition with shaky hands.

He was still too pale, and a fine line of sweat had broken out along his brow. He was taking too-deep breaths, and he clenched his fist around his keys right about when Brooke realized his hand had been shaking.

"Blake..." Brooke began, not entirely sure how to say what she wanted. Her panic was behind her now, and she felt incredibly guilty. She might have been afraid of bad storms, but lightning was literally *lethal* to him. And still she'd let him take charge of the situation. But even more than the embarrassment and guilt, she was worried.

Blake swallowed and said quietly, "I'm sorry. I didn't even think about the danger. Are you all right?"

Brooke frowned at him when he finally met her gaze. He looked exhausted. "I'm fine," she replied pointedly. "It's you I'm worried about."

Shaking his head stubbornly, Blake said, "I'll be fine, don't worry."

Knowing full well he was deliberately trying to down-play how he was feeling, Brooke scowled at him and reached over, snatching his keys from his loosened grip.

"What are you—" Blake started to ask, his eyes widening and his fingers twitching in an effort to reclaim his keys.

Brooke cut him off as she slipped his keys into her pocket. "Making sure you stay put. But feel free to switch seats." Holding his confused gaze a moment longer, Brooke turned and angled out of the car. She deliberately did not look back as she jogged up to her front door and extracted her own keys from her pocket.

****

Blake watched as Brooke disappeared inside her apartment, feeling almost as confused as he was drained. He released a heavy sigh and slumped back against his seat. He wanted to be angry with himself for putting Brooke in danger like that, but at the moment, he couldn't work up the energy. By the time he'd made it into the car, the air around them had been ripe with electrical discharge, and that last lightning bolt had been only barely far enough away to keep him on his feet.

But now, as the adrenaline wore off, he was paying the price for his thoughtlessness. *I could've gotten us both killed.* With a brief surge of bitter humor, he decided this was probably not what Dean had meant when he'd advised Blake to make sure it was a date neither of them would ever forget.

Fortunately, for whatever reason, the storm hadn't followed them past the interstate. And a part of Blake knew he should wonder about that, but he didn't have the energy. So he filed it away for future reference and refocused his attention on his surroundings.

It wasn't until Brooke was once again in sight—locking up her apartment, with a duffel bag on the ground at her feet—that Blake remembered she had told him to move. Dragging in a deep breath, Blake pushed open the driver's side door and stepped out. He was glad, if not a little surprised, that he didn't seem to need to lean on his door for support.

"Can you walk?" Brooke was already standing in front of him, with the duffel bag now slung over a shoulder. There was genuine concern in her eyes that touched him and made him feel even more like an idiot at the same time.

Still, he did his best to smile. "Yeah. What's with the duffel bag?"

"I'll tell you on the way." Brooke gestured for him to move to the other side.

Blake sighed and did as she instructed. He noticed, as he walked at a slower-than-usual pace, that Brooke took the time to shove her duffel into his backseat. Then she straightened and watched him until he had opened the passenger door.

They both ducked inside, and as Brooke pulled the door shut, she dug his keys out of her pocket.

"Where are we going?" He suspected he already knew the answer as he watched her stick the key in the ignition.

"I'm taking you home," Brooke declared, starting the car. "Whether you exhausted yourself using your powers, or because of all that lightning, I don't know. But you need to rest and regain your strength."

Blake allowed himself to lean back in his seat as Brooke backed out of the driveway. Eyes falling shut, he said, "It was the electricity. That little bit of power I used would never drain me like this."

"Little bit of power?" Brooke repeated incredulously. "You summoned, like, a ten-foot tidal wave back there, and then crashed the whole thing onto that fire!"

"It was a little more than eight feet," Blake clarified, his lips twitching even though his tone lacked the humor he'd wanted. "And that wasn't enough to slow me down." He wondered what she thought about that—if it was impressive, frightening, or something else altogether—but he didn't have the strength to even study her reaction.

Blake allowed the silence that followed to rest between them, though he noted with a small amount of reassurance that this silence didn't feel at all awkward. She might be worried about him, he realized, but she didn't seem to be upset or frightened. As far as he was concerned, in that moment, that was all that mattered. Well, that and the fact that they were both still breathing.

The next thing he knew, Brooke was gently nudging his right shoulder. Blake wanted to curse himself when he realized he'd fallen asleep for the last couple minutes of the drive. Blinking his eyes open, he mumbled, "Sorry." It came out as more of a slur than a word.

Brooke smiled faintly. "It's okay. Come on, let me help you get inside."

Blake did what he could to walk on his own, but for the first few steps, he had no choice than to lean on her. Fortunately, he was able to stand properly by the time they'd stepped out of the garage.

"What can I do to help? Do you just need sleep? Should I make you something to eat?"

Blake shook his head. "Food and sleep will help, but what I really need is rehydration."

Brooke stared at him for a beat, processing his words, before an idea obviously occurred to her. "Do you have a bathtub? Or a hot tub, or something that you can soak in?"

"Yeah," Blake replied. "Both, actually." And he was impressed at how quickly she'd grasped his situation. He paused as another thought struck. Sure, he definitely needed a good soak, but that didn't have to mean the date was over. *You nearly got electrocuted and burnt to death,* he reminded himself. *That date's pretty much over.*

"Which would be better for you?" Brooke asked, interrupting his self-berating.

Blake re-focused. "They'd be about the same."

Brooke nodded, and when her gaze re-focused and she looked at him, she smiled and asked, "Why don't we hit the hot tub, then? I could use a little relaxation, too."

"Brooke." Blake looked away from her smiling face as the guilt returned in force. His eyes narrowed and he found himself almost glaring at the floor of his hallway. "I'm sorry. I never meant for that to happen, and I … I'm glad you didn't get hurt."

Brooke reached out and used her fingertips to drag his face toward hers once more, staying silent until their eyes met. "What happened wasn't your fault. *Of course* you didn't mean for us to be attacked. And because it seems I need to remind you, I already knew about your enemies when I agreed to this date."

Blake swallowed heavily, letting her words settle in his heart. She was right. He knew she'd already known. At length, he said, "Did you bring a swimsuit?"

Chapter Sixteen

Blake let his eyes fall shut for a long minute as he sank until he was nearly ear-deep in water, his head tilted back to rest against the rim of the hot tub.

This was exactly what he needed. A good soak in good company, no lightning or electrical fires or even daily responsibilities hanging over his head. An hour or ten of this and he'd be right as rain—a saying he personally believed had been coined by some long-lost water elemental.

When Blake felt he could hold a conversation without slurring or running too short on breath, he pulled himself into a regular sitting position and looked over at Brooke. His lips twitched again when he saw she had relaxed so much that she was almost floating. "Don't fall asleep. I'm pretty sure I'm the only one who can breathe underwater."

"You must be feeling better," Brooke quipped as she lifted her head and resettled herself in her seat. "Otherwise, I'm sure the delivery of that would have been all wrong."

Blake chuckled despite the truth of her words. "I am feeling better."

"I can tell," Brooke replied, her humor fading as she raked her eyes over his face.

"So, tell me," Blake began, hoping to keep his tone casual as he shifted and lifted one arm to rest on the edge of the tub, his fingers still dipped in the warm water. "What's with the duffel bag?"

Brooke's face flushed adorably, and she looked away. "Well," she said, stalling. "I was worried about you." She finally met his gaze again. "I didn't really think you should be alone, but I thought you'd be more comfortable at home, so I decided I'd just stay here. With you."

Blake grinned. "You were going to stay the night to keep an eye on me?"

She nodded silently.

His grin slipped away as his tone became quietly serious. "Yet you said I shouldn't be saying thank you."

"If you think about it, it was kind of rude of me to invite myself like that. I probably *should* have just called your family and had one of them pick you up at my apartment." She paused, took a deep breath, and went on. "And you shouldn't thank me. You saved my life, not the other way around. You even risked yours to do it. And for the record, I'm *really* sorry about that."

Blake frowned at the underlying guilt he heard in her words. He lifted the arm that was still mostly submerged, and the water in the tub swirled around her.

Brooke's eyes widened when she realized that the water was slowly pulling her away from the side she'd been leaning against. Gently, the water carried her over to Blake, depositing her at his side before fading back into stillness. By the time the swirling had settled down, Blake's arm had returned to the water and curved around her, holding her up against his side.

"I don't want you to apologize for anything that happened tonight," Blake said firmly, though his tone was quiet and gentle. "I might not have caused this ridiculous feud, but it was still my fault your life was in danger tonight. It was the least I could do."

She wanted to argue with him. He could see it in her eyes. She didn't want him to claim sole ownership of the guilt. But instead Brooke let herself relax against him, her head landing on his shoulder.

After a moment, Brooke said, "I would never want you—or anyone, for that matter—dying to protect me. So if you want to help me, okay, but don't you dare die for me, got it?"

Blake's lips curved up again ever so slightly, and his arm tightened around her. "Got it." He leaned down to brush his lips against her hair. He leaned down a bit more then and pressed his lips solidly to the crown of her head.

Brooke sighed. One of her hands came up, her fingertips dancing along his exposed chest. "What time is it?"

With his free hand, he reached over and lifted his watch, which he'd set down on the edge of the hot tub. He frowned at the read-out for a moment, wishing he could believe that it was broken. *If time flies when you're having fun, then it must move backwards when you're running for your life.* Aloud, he said, "It's just after seven."

"Seriously?" Brooke asked, lifting her head to look at him. Her hand stilled over his chest as their eyes met. "That has to be impossible."

Blake shook his head, setting his watch back down. "Apparently not." He held her gaze for a long moment, and his skin tingled beneath her hand. He knew he was biased, but she had never looked more beautiful to him than in that moment. Her hair was piled in a messy bun high on her head, so she could keep it dry, and she was wearing the same maroon bikini that she'd worn at the beach on Friday.

Her hand slid up his chest, slowly curving around the nape of his neck.

She leaned up as he leaned down. Their eyes closed, and their lips met. Brooke's fingernails scraped the base of his neck before her hand plunged into his thick hair, and her other arm lifted, sliding up along his body until she had the proper angle to wrap it around his shoulders. His arm tightened around her waist as his tongue slipped past her lips.

They shifted, and Blake wrapped an arm around her back to pull her flush against him. The material of her bikini left most of her skin exposed, and his hands found vast expanses of her smooth, tempting flesh. With every slide of her tongue against his, Blake found himself feeling less and less tired.

"Blake!" a muffled male voice shouted.

The couple tore apart, startled, and turned wide eyes to the sliding glass door that led to his back porch. They looked back at each other, her hands on his shoulders and his hands on her hips, and she was obviously wondering the same thing. Who had called him?

The door was thrown open with surprising force, and before either could recover, Dean had stepped through. His eyes settled on them, and for a moment, all three were silent and still. Then Dean released a heavy breath, his posture relaxed, and he shook his head, muttering, "I oughta kill you, dammit!"

Too confused to be embarrassed by the situation, the couple pulled apart and Blake shifted to rest one arm on the edge of the hot tub as he raised an eyebrow. "What's going on?"

Dean narrowed his eyes in a frustrated glare and threw his arms wide as he exclaimed, "What do you mean 'what's going on'? We've been looking for you everywhere, you idiot!"

"Why?" Blake asked, fearing that he and Brooke had not been the only victims of the night. "Is someone hurt?"

Dragging in a deep breath, Dean clenched his fists and closed his eyes tightly. "You tell me," he finally demanded. When he opened his eyes again he held his brother's gaze solidly. "The three of us went down to the beach looking for you, 'cause we figured you'd have gone there on your date, but of course you weren't there. And you weren't answering your cell."

Blake shook his head, realization slowly dawning. "I'm sorry. I left my cell in my room and I didn't think to call. We're fine."

Dean lifted a hand and pinched the bridge of his nose exasperatedly. "Dad heard a weather report on the radio that said some freak lightning storm had hit the beach. We all knew you would probably end up there, so of course he called to warn you, but you didn't answer. So he called Logan, who called me and Nate."

The guilt returning, though for an entirely different reason, Blake cringed. "Damn, I'm sorry. I didn't think you'd have heard. We were at the beach when the storm hit. By the time you heard about it, we must have already been back here."

Some of the frustration left Dean's face and his arm dropped to his side. Gaze flicking between them, he asked, "You're sure you're okay? Why're you soaking?"

"There were a few too many lightning strikes," Blake admitted. "But once we got past the beach we were fine. The storm, or whoever was controlling it, didn't try to chase us."

Dean nodded, accepting his answer. "Good. Although I'm still inclined to beat the crap out of you. You should have called someone."

Blake looked away guiltily. "I will next time." His eyes widened, and he looked back to his brother, asking, "Where're Logan and Nate?" If they were still at the beach, they could be hurt. Or worse.

"Nate opted to stay at the beach, just in case," Dean replied as he dug his hand into his coat pocket. "Logan and I split up. He went to check her apartment in case you'd gone there." He pulled his phone out, flipped it open, and hit a couple of buttons before putting it to his ear. Blake's stomach clenched. He hoped Dean was calling Nate first. And he hoped Nate would answer.

Brooke looked back at Blake and whispered, "Maybe I really should have called someone for you."

"Don't feel bad. I didn't even call after you brought it up." He was such a moron. He *should* have called.

They fell silent as Dean began talking into the phone, their attention returning to him.

"It's me," Dean said. A moment later, he added, "Yeah, they're both here, and they're okay. But you should call Nate and get him the hell away from the beach, in case whoever's behind all this crap is still hanging around." After another pause, he told Logan (who Blake assumed he was talking to) that Blake had promised to give them the details the next day, and then he hung up.

Slipping his phone back into his pocket, Dean said, "I'd yell at you some more, but Mom and Angie will probably do that for me tomorrow."

Blake cringed and inclined his head. "I am sorry, Dean." And Dean was right. He was going to get a royal chewing-out, and he had it coming.

Dean sighed. "I know." The air was heavy with guilt and easing frustration for a long moment, and then Dean's lips twitched as his eyes flicked between them again. "Well, since you're both all right, I'll just let myself out. Carry on." His grin was undeniable as he turned without another word and stepped back into the house, pulling the sliding door shut behind him.

"Try to ignore him," Blake grumbled, his voice choked in embarrassment, as he stared at a spot on his porch near where Dean had been standing. He was searching for something to say to push past the embarrassment when a familiar lurching in his stomach reminded him of something else. Lifting his eyes back to Brooke, though she was still staring at the edge of the hot tub, he asked, "Hey, are you hungry? We never had dinner."

Brooke's eyes widened and lifted to his. A moment later, a smile curved her lips and she nodded. "Actually, yes. I'm starving."

With a nod, Blake moved and pushed to his feet. He still wasn't at full strength, but a good meal would go a long way towards changing that.

****

"Are you sure you don't mind?" Brooke asked again as Blake eased into the Earl's Diner parking lot Sunday morning.

Blake chuckled even as he pulled to the curb at the front entrance. "I'm sure, I promise. This way I know I get to see you again today, remember?"

Brooke allowed herself to smile as she slid the seatbelt off and then leaned over to press a kiss to his cheek. "All right, then I'll see you in a while. Thanks for the lift."

"It was my pleasure," Blake replied with a lopsided grin.

Flashing a final smile at him, Brooke grabbed her purse and stepped out of the car. She paused to wave before turning and letting herself into the diner.

After dinner the night before, Brooke had insisted on staying anyway, saying she wanted to be absolutely sure that he was okay. Blake hadn't put up much of an argument, and they had ended up on the couch, watching another movie. But Blake had fallen asleep about halfway through, telling Brooke all she'd needed to know about how much energy he still didn't have. She'd woken him up and convinced him to go to bed a little early, promising she'd wake him if she needed anything. And then she'd settled down right beside him, realizing that she was tired, too.

In the morning, Brooke had been grateful that she'd somehow thought to throw her uniform into her duffel bag when she'd been packing, but she wondered what she'd really been thinking. Her uniform would do her no good if she couldn't get to work. Fortunately, Blake had woken fully recovered and offered to drive her.

And now she was walking into work feeling downright giddy, and at the same time almost like a teenager slipping into the house after curfew. She hadn't seen her adopted family since the weekend after Christmas, even though they emailed or talked on the phone fairly consistently, but in the course of time she'd been living in Darien, a lot of the diner staff had come to feel like family. Paula and Georgia especially had taken her under their wing—and they were more than likely to question her about her chauffeur.

After exchanging a brief hello with the new hostess, Brooke quickly shuffled her way to the back room. It wasn't until she was halfway through the dining area that she remembered what else had happened the day before. *What are we going to do without Ed?* He'd been cooking there for nearly a decade. It would be strange to have a new Head Chef, but the diner wouldn't survive without one.

She pushed into the back room, unsurprised to see Georgia already securing her apron. And she couldn't help but smile, just a little, when she realized that that meant the older woman hadn't seen who had dropped her off. "Morning," Brooke called, moving to her own locker.

Georgia lifted her head and returned the smile. "Morning." Her smile turned mischievous. "How was your date?"

Brooke tried not to cringe, grateful her back was turned. She'd forgotten somehow that she'd told Georgia about the upcoming date. "It was pretty good." She was sure Blake would give her a funny look if he'd been able to hear that response. Yes, someone had tried to kill them. But their enemy—whoever it was—had failed. And how could she not be happy to be alive?

"'Pretty good'?" Georgia repeated slowly, focusing her full attention on her friend. "So it could've been better? Or are you trying to downplay it so I don't ask too many questions?"

That'd be the one, Brooke thought fleetingly before she turned to lift an eyebrow at the other woman. Deciding to be as honest as she could—or at least as honest as she needed to be—she said, "Sure it could've gone a *little* better. Blake ended up not feeling all that great, so we turned in a little earlier than we'd wanted." *There, that was complete truth.*

Georgia's grin faltered. "Oh. Well, that's depressing."

Brooke opened her mouth to agree, since it was something else she could be honest about, but before a sound could come out, the door opened again and Paula stepped in. The look on the older woman's face was enough for Brooke to suck in a breath. *She saw.*

"So, Brooke," Paula began with a knowing smile. "Is something wrong with your car?"

Brooke swallowed and shook her head slowly. "No, my car's fine."

Georgia's confusion was evident in her voice as she asked, "Why would anything be wrong with her car?"

Before Brooke could say anything, Paula replied, "Well, that was my natural assumption when I saw Blake dropping her off this morning."

Turning wide eyes to Brooke, Georgia said, "I thought you said he wasn't feeling well?"

"He wasn't," Brooke assured her, cringing internally. The rumors were bound to be flying by the end of the hour. "It's just that ... we were out when he started feeling off, and I personally hate being alone when I feel bad, so I offered to keep him company. We stopped by my place, I picked up a change of clothes, and then I actually drove him home."

Both women were silent for a moment, apparently deciding whether or not they believed her words. Fortunately, it seemed there was enough truth in the words to convince them. She just didn't have the energy for gossip.

Paula accepted her answer with a nod and a grin. "I assume he's feeling better this morning?"

"Yes," Brooke replied easily. "All he needed was a good night's sleep."

"Good," Paula said.

Seeing an opportunity to change the subject, Brooke waited only a moment before asking a question of her own. "Um, Paula ... what happened with Ed?"

Georgia froze again, her eyes moving between them but the rest of her remaining completely still. Her interest was obvious.

Paula sighed, planting her hands on her hips. "Damned if I know," she replied. "I chased him down, but all he did was yell and rant about how much he hates this place, so I lost my temper and told him never to come back."

Slowly, Georgia asked, "Do we have anyone to take his place?"

It was Brooke's turn to remain silent as she watched her supervisor.

"No," Paula declared somberly with a shake of her head. "For now, me and Earl are gonna help out, but we need to start looking. None of the other kids in the kitchen are comfortable stepping in—and that's just the ones that are qualified."

Brooke and Georgia exchanged a look in silence. Nothing good could come of having no chef.

Paula released another sigh and dropped her arms. "Don't you two worry about any of that nonsense, though. Me and Earl are gonna sit down tonight and figure out if we might know someone interested. We'll have a new chef before you know it. Now get out there and keep our customers happy in the meantime!" With a laughing wink, Paula turned and whisked from the room.

After a long moment, Georgia said, "Well, I for one am not going to worry. Everything happens for a reason, right? See you out there!" And then she followed after Paula and slipped from the room.

Brooke sighed and quickly finished securing her apron. She hoped Georgia and Paula were right, but even if they were, they were bound to be running a bit slower than usual. And days were always longer when they were running slower.

****

"I feel like we're being stalked," Dean grumbled as he paced by the large, elaborate fireplace in his parents' living room once more.

Blake sighed and leaned back into the couch. "Tell me about it."

Angela scrunched her face thoughtfully and said, "It seems to me whoever's doing all of this must be a large family, then. I mean, they'd need to have enough people to actually follow all of us around at any given time, right?"

"But if they are stalking us," Nate interjected, leaning forward from his own seat on the couch, on the other side of Angela from Blake. "Then how come we haven't spotted anyone? I mean, even if they switched it up every day, by now you'd think they'd have had to recycle a few times, and we should've noticed someone following us. Or, what, are they invisible?"

"I don't think they're invisible," Christopher replied with a shake of his head.

"There must be something we're missing," Logan declared gravely, arms crossed over his chest as he leaned into the couch.

"All right," Christopher agreed. "Let's back up. Blake, how many people knew about your date beforehand?"

Blake hesitated. "That's hard to say. I didn't tell anyone who isn't in this room, but Brooke has friends at the diner, she could have mentioned it to Georgia and Georgia could've told … anyone."

"Or someone could have just overheard her mention it," Angela said. "Eric and I were at the diner yesterday, when Ed quit. And I asked her about your date. There were other tables nearby, someone could have been listening."

Nate sighed heavily and ran a hand through his hair. "So we're back to 'it could be anyone'."

Chapter Seventeen

"Fantastic," Dean growled. As he paced past the fireplace again, the small, crackling flame flickered and flared for a moment.

"From now on," Lillian declared, speaking for the first time in several minutes, "no matter what time it is or what you think we might be doing, whenever one of us is attacked in any way, we need to call at least one other person in this family. This is as much to check in and let the rest of us know what's going on as it is to make sure everyone is accounted for."

"Your mother's right," Christopher agreed somberly. "We're still not playing it safe enough."

One by one, the children nodded their agreement. Their father's words were obviously true—there was no point in trying to argue.

"And absolutely *no* skipping family dinners," Lillian added pointedly. "In fact, Blake, why don't you bring Brooke over this weekend?"

Blake tried not to feel particularly flustered by the idea of bringing his girlfriend home for dinner so early in their relationship, and he failed spectacularly. "I'll invite her."

Dean smirked, seemingly forgetting his anger for the moment. "How'd the rest of your date go?"

"Oh no!" Angela interrupted quickly, launching to her feet. "If the family meeting's over, I'm going upstairs. I don't need to hear this!"

Even as Angela darted to the stairs, and Nate chuckled, Blake shook his head and said, "Not the way you're thinking, obviously. But it went fine, given the circumstances."

"So when are you seeing her again?" Nate asked, joining in on Dean's fun.

"This afternoon, when I pick her up from work," Blake replied, his voice slightly firmer than he'd expected.

"Okay, boys," Christopher interrupted with a laugh. "Leave your brother alone. You don't want him turning the tables on you someday, do you?"

"Ah, come on," Nate returned with a mock-whine. "How often do we get to pick on Blake?"

Blake pushed to his feet. "Not nearly as often as I get to pick on you." Switching his focus to his parents, he added, "I'm going to go. But I'll ask Brooke if she wants to come to dinner Saturday."

"Be careful," Lillian called as he started down the hall.

Blake kept his sigh to himself until he was safely seated in his car. As it slipped free, he leaned back and let his head fall against the headrest. It really didn't make any sense. They really *should* have noticed if someone was following them. *But, what, did they just happen to be walking down that gravel road last night? Or by the creek when Angela was walking home? And that wouldn't explain the incident at Brooke's apartment at all.* In his mind, there was no way this was all coincidence.

Muscles tense, Blake reached up and started the car. As he gripped the steering wheel, his mind still going over what little they knew, he cursed under his breath. They needed to figure this out, and put an end to it, before one of them really got hurt. And before anyone else got dragged into it unnecessarily. In the meantime, he could only hope he'd be able to keep Brooke out of danger.

****

"So, is it true?" Clarabelle Buchannon asked in an uncharacteristically conspiratorial tone after Brooke had taken her order. She leaned forward just slightly, letting her elbows rest on the table.

Brooke lifted a curious eyebrow. "You'll have to be more specific, Clare."

"About Ed," Clarabelle elaborated quietly. "I heard that yesterday, he just stormed out of here and no one knows why. And then, about an hour ago, I heard someone saw a U-Haul in his driveway."

Brooke's eyes widened. "The part about yesterday is definitely true," she replied. "I was here when it happened, and it was incredibly awkward. But I haven't heard anything else."

Clarabelle sat back, her fingers absently drumming along the table. "That's so strange. I hope something's not wrong with him."

"Yeah," Brooke agreed. She might not have approved of his outrageous exit, but she certainly didn't wish the man any ill. And then an idea struck her, inspired by the lingering twist in her gut, and Brooke shifted ever so slightly and lowered her voice. "Hey, Clare, can I ask you an odd question?"

It was Clarabelle's turn to arch a slim eyebrow, but she nodded anyway. "Of course."

Gesturing as subtly as possible to the corner booth a little behind her, Brooke asked, "See that man over there? Do you happen to know who he is?"

Clarabelle's eyes flicked past Brooke for a long moment, and her lips curved into a frown before she looked back and slowly shook her head. "No, I don't know anything about him. But I've seen him around town, just here and there, for probably about a month." She paused, lowering her voice even more, and looked away with an almost guilty expression. "Truthfully, he gives me the creeps."

Brooke was glad to hear it wasn't just her, but at the same time she was concerned. Clarabelle was the town sweetheart; she loved *everybody*. And even she was freaked out by the man currently sitting in the back booth. The same man that had given Brooke such a funny look at the beach only a handful of days ago.

Looking back up, Clarabelle asked, "Why?"

"I've seen him around a little, too, and I feel the same way. I guess I'm just curious is all."

With a natural smile, Clarabelle said, "Well, if I hear anything, I'll let you know."

Brooke nodded. "We have a deal, Ms. Buchannon. I'll be back with your drink in a minute." Brooke turned, still keeping her back to the man's booth, and made her way to the drink station.

Georgia followed her in almost immediately. "Did you notice? That weird guy who was with Emma before is back," she said in a hushed voice.

Brooke did her best to suppress an almost sarcastic smile. "Yeah, I noticed. Don't take this the wrong way, but I'm glad he's at your table and not mine."

Now standing directly beside her at the station, Georgia said, "That's the weirdest part. Shelly said he specifically asked *not* to be seated with you."

Her hand halfway to the straws, Brooke paused. She turned her head toward her friend in a reflexive effort to hear her better. "What? Why would he do that? He only sat with me the one time, and I'm sure I was perfectly fine."

Georgia shrugged. "Apparently, he didn't say anything else. But it is kind of weird. Have you run into him since?"

The day at the beach immediately flashed through her mind, and Brooke had to repress a shiver. "That depends on your definition," she replied carefully. "We saw each other at the beach early last week, before St. Patrick's Day. But we didn't talk or anything."

"I take back what I just said," Georgia declared as the ice clinked into her glass. "It's *really* weird."

"Tell me about it," Brooke said on a sigh. She set Clarabelle's drink on the tray and stepped back. "Good luck," she added before she turned and walked back into the dining area.

Brooke did her best to keep her back to the mysterious man in the corner booth while he was there. He stayed for a while, though no one ever joined him. He was there for nearly thirty minutes longer than Clarabelle. And when he finally made his way to the exit, he brushed past Brooke, bumping into her as she was jotting down an order.

Reflexively—and without realizing who had bumped into her—Brooke took a small step forward, trying to move out of the person's way, and said, "I'm sorry, excuse me." Her head turned as she spoke, and the man paused for a beat after he was past her.

When their eyes met, something strange flashed through his dark, haunting gaze. And then he turned his head forward and continued on, not saying a word. He barely paused to set down exact change at the register before sweeping out the door.

The look in his eyes haunted Brooke for the entire rest of her shift, and by the time Blake arrived to pick her up she felt like she was in need of much more than a scalding shower.

"Hey," Blake greeted as she ducked easily into the car. "How was work?"

"I feel like my answer to that is not what it should be," Brooke admitted as she buckled herself in and he pulled away from the curb.

"What do you mean? Did something happen?"

"Technically, no. I had good tables, no one made any type of a scene, and Paula swears we'll survive losing Ed. So, when you look at it that way, it was a good day at work."

Frowning now, Blake said, "But something did happen that bothered you."

Her eyes followed the buildings and trees that passed as he drove toward her apartment. "Do you remember that guy I told you about? The one from the beach?"

"Yeah."

"He came in again today. Apparently, he asked specifically not to be seated with me. Plus he stayed way too long for a guy eating lunch alone. But what bothered me most was when he left. He bumped into me—which, looking back, had to have been deliberate—and when he looked at me…" She paused, shivering faintly, before she said, "There was something in his eyes. Something dark, and definitely not nice."

Blake's grip tightened on his steering wheel as she talked. Brooke could only assume he was thinking the same thing she'd been thinking for the past few hours— that this stranger was somehow related to what was happening. Whether he was directly responsible or working with the responsible party, they had no way to know. Though, Brooke supposed, she had to consider the possibility that the man was simply an anti-social jerk.

They were nearly to her apartment by the time Brooke pulled herself out of her musings to ask, "How'd the meeting with your family go? Nobody else got attacked last night, right?"

"Right," Blake assured her. "We didn't really make any progress, though. Dean's convinced we're all being stalked, Logan doesn't think it's that simple, and I don't really know what to believe."

"It's crazy is what it is," Brooke declared on a sigh.

Blake made a noise of agreement as he pulled into her driveway, parking once again behind her car. "Your duffel's in the back."

Brooke hesitated even as her eyes traveled to the backseat, confirming his words. She didn't particularly want to be alone at the moment, knowing she'd just dwell even more on everything that had—and hadn't—happened. But she also didn't want to come off as clingy, or annoying. At length, she asked quietly, "Are you busy?"

He didn't look remotely surprised by her question. Probably because she had no poker face. "No. Do you want some company?"

"I've always prided myself on being independent. Ever since I was a kid, bouncing around from foster family to foster family, I knew I could only really rely on myself. But there are still times when I know I really wouldn't be my own best company, you know?"

Blake offered her a small, reassuring smile and tugged the keys from the ignition. "I think everyone has days like that. But I hope someday you'll realize that it's okay to rely on other people sometimes."

Brooke reached around to tug her bag into her lap. "I'm learning that, too." And though she meant it, in her heart Brooke knew she was talking specifically about Blake. It was almost frightening how strongly she trusted him already. Instead of saying that, though, she merely added, "Thank you."

They climbed together from the car, and Brooke led the way to the door. It wasn't until he was closing it behind them and she was opening her mouth to tell him to make himself comfortable that she realized she needed a shower. She, of course, had already *known* she smelled like a diner, but she hadn't given it a single thought. *And how rude would that be?* Or she could invite him to join her… But no, she just wanted to wash the smell of greasy food out of her hair. She didn't feel clean or desirable.

"I'm sorry," Brooke said, earning a silent, raised eyebrow from Blake. "I probably smell like stale grease or something. I'm going to go change real quick."

Blake chuckled and shook his head. "I don't think you smell. But if it'll make you more comfortable, I think I can entertain myself if you want to take a quick shower or something."

Brooke smiled at him. "I'll be fast, I promise." When he nodded again she turned and dashed down her short hall, to the bedroom, where she could grab a decent change of clothes. She detoured in the hall to pull a towel from the closet and then disappeared inside her bathroom. She was going to take the fastest shower on record, but if it would get the smell out of her skin and hair, then it would be worth it.

****

As Brooke disappeared into her bedroom, Blake shook his head and migrated to her couch. He paused, standing before it, and found himself studying the far end. It was that end that would have been cut up by the imploding glass, and he hadn't heard anything about her getting a replacement. Curiously, he moved to the window side and knelt down to get a better look.

When he ran his fingers lightly along the arm, he found a couple of spots that felt stitched together. Then he saw another patch job on the seat cushion, near the arm. It was smaller than the two he'd found with his fingers, but it was still obviously a repair from something slashing through the material. He doubted very much she'd taken a knife to her couch at any point.

His fingers moved to run along the small repair on the cushion, and he frowned. He could easily picture Brooke curled up on the couch, relaxed and winding down from a long day. He already knew she'd been caught completely off-guard by the storm. And it would have been so easy for her to have been caught by a large shard of glass while she'd still been sitting. *She could've been hurt a lot worse.*

It was a fact he'd already known, and something that had kept him up late on more than one night. But he hadn't really been inside her apartment since then—at least not for any length of time. He hadn't had the opportunity to visualize it from the inside. And as he did so now, he felt his temper boiling all over again. His earlier frustration returned in force, and Blake pulled his hands from her couch.

With clenched fists, Blake stood and moved to the other end before forcing himself to sit and wait. Twice she'd been attacked; twice she could well have been killed. Twice he almost hadn't been fast enough. He refused to allow for a third.

We need to figure this out and find the monsters responsible. These were the same people—probably— that had already killed two of his uncles, and crippled a third. It was so easy for him to forget that, as the accidents had all happened long before he'd been born. He'd never known two of his uncles, and he didn't know the man Nicholas could have been. If they weren't careful, something similar could happen again, this time to them. Only now the people close to them were being dragged into it, too.

For the briefest of moments, he considered breaking up with Brooke. His heart clenched painfully at the very idea, but the pain wasn't why he dismissed the notion almost as quickly. Breaking up with her wouldn't keep her safe. Their enemy already knew that he cared about her; she would still be a target. *In fact,* he realized, *she might actually be safer this way. At least I'm around, and she'll call if she needs me.*

His eyes traveled to the clock hanging on the wall above her television, though he stared at it for nearly a minute before registering what it said. He'd known, of course, what time she'd gotten off work. But it had only just occurred to him how close the dinner hour was. *We never did do anything really noteworthy for dinner last night,* he thought as his mind finally switched topics. Dinner the night before had really only been thrown together as a necessity, not because either of them were particularly inspired.

"Sorry to make you wait," Brooke declared as she re-entered the living room. Her hair and skin were still damp, she was wearing clean clothes, and he instantly loved the way she pulled off the 'fresh from the shower' look.

"I wasn't waiting too long," he promised. "I never even got bored."

She laughed softly and walked around him to settle on the other end of her couch, but she sat sideways so that she could see him. "That's good," she said as she tucked her foot behind her opposite knee.

Her sitting in the exact seat that had been damaged by her exploding window was not at all helping him keep the image of her covered in blood out of his head. But he tried not to let it show as he adjusted himself to properly face her. "So," he began lightly. "What are your plans for the rest of the evening?"

"I don't have any. I'm sure I'm supposed to pretend like I'm super busy, but the truth is, I'm all caught up on my homework and I have nothing to do between now and school tomorrow."

Blake's lips twitched. "That's interesting. I'm pretty much in the same boat." He paused, more for effect than anything else, and then he asked, "Think you'd be up for dinner? I figure we could try it more traditionally and keep our fingers crossed."

With another soft laugh, Brooke said, "That's awfully brave of you. What did you have in mind?"

"Well, for one thing, I was thinking we could try ditching our stalker. There's a place about ten minutes past the college that I've always wanted to try, if you're up for a little drive?"

"I can handle a little drive," Brooke assured him, a teasing glint in her eyes. "But it better not turn into a medium drive."

Blake laughed and pushed to his feet. He held out a hand to her. "Duly noted. Come on, by the time we get there it'll be a good dinner time."

Brooke reached out and placed her hand in his, allowing him to help her to her feet. "I suppose it will," she agreed. Before she could say anything more, Blake tugged her into his chest.

He dipped his head and captured her lips with his even as he released her hand and curved both of his arms around her. She immediately responded to his kiss, her hands clenching fistfuls of his shirt as their lips parted and their tongues met.

Blake trailed one hand along her spine slowly before he forced himself to pull away from her lips. His hands slid to her hips, and he smirked flirtatiously. "Ready to go?" he asked, his voice low and thick.

Brooke offered him a slow, seductive smile. "Yes," she replied, her voice still slightly breathless.

He stepped back from her. "Good."

Brooke rolled her eyes even as she laughed at him, and together they moved toward the entryway. Along the way, Brooke snatched her purse off of the dining table, and they paused just beyond her door so she could lock it back up.

They were still settling in the car when Blake decided he should probably let his family know he'd be out of town for a couple of hours. He pulled his phone from a pocket and began typing, having opted to just send a single group text to his siblings. He explained that he was taking Brooke to dinner out of town, telling them not to worry, and sent the message.

Though both of his parents had cell phones, neither were particularly text-oriented. Watching his mother try to text was akin to watching a dog trying to follow a cat up a tree—they tried the same thing over and over again, and the more they failed, the more determined they became. More frustrated, too. His father wasn't much better.

As he dropped the phone back into his pocket, he remembered his earlier promise to his mother. "I have a question for you, by the way."

Brooke raised an eyebrow. "Oh?"

"You've been invited to our family dinner this Saturday. Do you think you'd be interested?" It was certainly early in a relationship to be bringing his girlfriend home for dinner, he knew, but she'd already met his entire family. And the more he had thought about it, the more he hoped she'd come.

Her eyes widened in surprise, and it took her a minute to compose her answer. "Yeah, of course."

He smiled at her response and inclined his head. "I'll let them know, then."

Brooke nodded as Blake put the car in motion. It was true she had already met his family, on multiple occasions now. But to have her over for an official family function, even if it was just a dinner, was unexpectedly heady. When his parents had first suggested it, he'd thought the idea awkward, but now it seemed significant. Now he felt the beginnings of very different nerves.

By the time Brooke spoke up again, having seemed lost in thought, Blake had navigated them to the interstate. "So, where are we going?"

"A steakhouse."

Brooke waited a beat, but when he didn't say more, she turned an exaggerated frown to him. "Is that all you're going to tell me?"

"Yep," Blake replied calmly. "I've heard their food's good, but I've never been there. So we'll find out together."

Arching a pointed brow, Brooke asked, "You remember I used to live in that area, right? I might have been there."

"I doubt it," Blake said confidently. She'd told him she'd been living in Darien for two years, give or take, and the steakhouse they were headed towards was barely a year old. So the odds were in his favor, in his opinion.

Brooke was silent for another minute, watching the traffic slide by, before realization dawned and she asked, "Are we going to that new place?"

Blake laughed, the sound escaping from him without warning, and he flashed a quick smile in her direction before returning his gaze to the road. "Yes, we are."

"I knew I'd figure it out," Brooke declared proudly as she shifted and stretched out her legs as best she could. "But you were right, too. I haven't been there."

"That's something, I suppose," Blake agreed, still laughing faintly.

They fell silent again for a couple of minutes, Blake focusing on the road and Brooke relaxing into her seat, until she grumbled, "I just wish I knew who he was."

Blake's attention shifted to her for a moment. "You thinking about that mystery guy again?"

Brooke sighed heavily. "Yeah. He's just so … haunting, I guess. And every time I see him I wish I would never see him again, but apparently I'm not that lucky."

Blake scowled out his windshield. "Do me a favor. If you ever see him when I'm out with you, point him out to me, okay?"

"Sure." Her brows crinkled in thought and she asked, "Do you think he has something to do with everything?"

"It would sort of fit, yeah. But I have no proof."

"Did you talk to Angela about him?" Brooke asked curiously.

The question threw him for a minute, until he remembered the story Brooke had told him before. "No," he admitted. "But I'm definitely going to now. Even if all she can give me is a name, it's still more than we have right now."

"That's true," Brooke agreed. "But what good would a name really do?"

"If we could get a full name, we might be able to track him down somehow."

"Maybe," Brooke allowed, her fingers absently picking at the hem of her shirt. "But you probably don't want to start poking around before we know enough; you could get hurt."

Blake's grip tightened over his steering wheel, but he kept his voice calm as he replied, "We're already getting hurt. This has to end."

Silently, Brooke reached over and let her hand land on his thigh. She gave his thigh a squeeze, and then moved her hand around a little in a rubbing motion before she pulled it back to her lap.

He took one hand from the wheel and reached out, catching her hand and holding it in his. His thumb ran over her knuckles lightly before he laced their fingers together. He made no move to pull away.

Chapter Eighteen

Their impromptu date went off without a hitch, and before Brooke realized it, several days had gone by and she was once again working the late shift on Wednesday. She'd seen Blake in class, and they had talked on the phone a couple of times, but otherwise they hadn't gotten any time together. And she knew she was ridiculous for being bothered by that, since she had technically seen—or at least spoken with—him every single day, but she had spent a majority of the weekend in his presence and had quickly discovered she liked it that way.

I'm a moron, she decided as she secured another dinner order. *A complete, love-struck moron.* It was official, though she couldn't quite believe it herself. She had realized the truth of her situation after Blake had dropped her off Sunday night. She, Brooke Munroe, had fallen in love. And miracle of miracles, he was a decent, respectable, reliable, family-man. *Wait until Mom hears about this. If I don't tell her in person, she won't believe me.*

The only problem was, she had no idea how he felt about her.

That's not exactly true, she corrected herself as she maneuvered her way back into the dining area, to greet her newest table. *He definitely cares.* She only wished she knew how much, and how long she would undoubtedly have to wait before he returned her feelings. She absolutely refused to consider the possibility that he might never feel that way.

But before she could dwell on it further, her new table was in sight, and she found herself pausing just to make sure that she wasn't hallucinating. She blinked several times in rapid succession, but he was still there. Still sitting opposite his sister, who was talking quietly and hadn't seen her yet. Releasing a deep breath, Brooke didn't try to stop the smile that instantly curved her lips. She wasn't at all surprised by the faint fluttering of butterflies in her stomach.

"Well, this is a surprise," she declared as she stepped up to their table.

Blake and Angela looked up at her and smiled. "A good one, I hope," Blake teased with a lopsided grin.

"Always," Brooke assured him, laughing faintly.

Angela rolled her eyes dramatically. "For the record, it was my idea. I think he thought it'd be awkward to take his little sister to his girlfriend's work."

Brooke laughed a bit more, raising an eyebrow at Blake. "Is that so?"

It was Blake's turn to chuckle as he mock-glared at his sister. "Only partially. She suggested it before I could."

"Right," Angela declared sarcastically as she leaned back against the booth.

Reluctantly extracting her notepad, Brooke said, "Well, I can talk more when I bring your drinks, but for now I actually have another table to check on... So, what can I start you with?"

Blake allowed his sister to order first, before ordering his own beverage and smiling once more at his girlfriend before she walked off.

Angela was laughing at him when he returned his attention to her, and he frowned pointedly. "That's not very nice, you know."

"I'm perfectly allowed to laugh at my brother." She paused before leaning forward again, resting her arms on the table, and lowering her voice in order to ask, "Do you love her yet?"

Blake nearly choked on his own breath at her question, and as he recovered himself, he raised an eyebrow at her and said, "I'm surprised you're willing to talk about that."

Angela gave him a pointed look. "Girls love to talk about love; even you should know that. It's the physical stuff that sisters don't want to know about. And you're avoiding the question."

Having this conversation with his seventeen-year-old sister was not exactly ideal. Especially since he'd only recently admitted the answer to himself. Returning her pointed look with one of his own, Blake said, "That's not what I wanted to talk to you about, Angie."

Never one to back down, Angela said calmly, "Well, it's what I want to talk about. Conversations have to work both ways, you know."

"Not here," Blake insisted firmly. He knew he was going to get stuck answering her question, but he wasn't going to do so when the woman they were talking about could walk up to them at any given moment.

Angela sighed exaggeratedly. "All right, fine, you can tell me later." She shifted and reached over to pluck a couple of sugar packets from the porcelain container. "So what *did* you want to talk about?"

Pausing a moment to glance around, making sure no one had settled in the booth behind him, Blake leaned forward and proceeded to tell her about Brooke's mystery man. When he was done describing both the man and his suspicions of him, Blake carefully asked, "Is there a chance you've ever seen, or heard of, someone like him?"

Angela frowned and slowly shook her head. "I've definitely never seen anyone who fits that description. But that just means he's not stalking *me*."

Blake sighed and clarified his question. "That's good, but I actually meant specifically when you're at

Eric's. Remember, I said the first time Brooke saw him, he was here with Emma."

Angela's eyes narrowed in defensive anger, but a heartbeat later, the look passed and she took in a breath. She took her time answering the question, her voice thoughtful as she finally said, "No. I don't know anything about him."

Blake nodded and relaxed into the booth. He had sort of hoped to get a name, or a clue as to the man's identity, but all the same he was glad the guy seemed to be staying away from his sister. "This probably goes without saying, but … if that ever changes, you'll let me know, right?"

"Of course. But I really don't think the thing with Emma had anything to do with this. Eric was pretty shocked when I told him everything."

"I was more hoping his association with Emma would give us a clue about him."

Brooke stepped back up to the table a moment later, tray over her shoulder and balancing two drinks. "I come bearing gifts," she joked as she readjusted her load in order to set down their glasses.

As she set down Angela's tea, Angela once again lifted one of her pilfered sugar packets and exclaimed, "Thank you!" She wasted no time in tearing the little packages open and dumping in the contents.

Blake chuckled as Brooke set his soda down. "Thanks," he said, shifting his gaze to her and offering her a smile.

Brooke tucked the tray against her side, grinning with amusement. "You're both very welcome. So, did I miss anything interesting?"

Removing her lips from the straw, Angela said, "Your boyfriend told me about your stalker. And fortunately, I have never seen the guy in my life."

"Lucky girl," Brooke said with a faint laugh.

"So we're back where we started," Blake declared, frustration evident in his tone.

Brooke's eyes drifted to follow the host of the night as he sat an elderly couple two tables over. "As much as I don't want to cut this conversation short, it looks like I've got more customers."

****

Blake came to a stop in his parents' living room late the following morning, unsurprised to see his mother perched carefully on the edge of the coffee table and one of his brothers sleeping on the couch before her. Lillian's hands were curved over Nate's right forearm, hands and arm encompassed in a soft, golden glow. He took a deep breath and let his gaze move to his father, who was sitting in the armchair, fists clenched in his lap and frowning. His gaze shifted next to the loveseat, where Logan sat. Logan was scowling darkly, and his arms were crossed over his chest.

At length, Blake moved toward the loveseat. "What happened?"

Lillian's voice was tight, but not quite strained, as she replied, "He was on his motorcycle when he rode into some sort of hail storm. He's lucky his injuries aren't worse."

For a long moment, the silence returned. The accident that had crippled their Uncle Nicholas—and killed their Uncle Trevor—had been eerily similar. They'd been driving, and driven straight into a freak snow storm that had frozen the road. The car had spun out of control before either man could have reacted. And Blake, as well as his brother and their father, knew that Lillian was comparing her son's wreck to the accident that had taken her brother from her.

Releasing a heavy breath, Christopher unclenched his fists and looked over at Blake, who had since settled into the seat beside his brother. "Did you get a hold of Dean?"

Blake's attention shifted to his father, and he nodded. "Yeah. He's fine, but he's busy. There's a fire downtown. He asked me to call if anything else came up."

Christopher nodded, and once again they fell silent.

As Blake returned his attention to his healing brother, his own lips tipped down in a frown. There was no doubt in his mind this was more than a case of 'wrong place, wrong time'. It was shortly after eleven in the morning on a Thursday. Angela was in school, which meant she wasn't available to heal her brother. And though Lillian had healing powers as well, her powers were slowly fading with the natural progression of time. Injuries that would take Angela ten minutes to heal, leaving her in need of only a few minutes rest, would take Lillian nearly half an hour, and leave her notably tired.

And then there's that fire, Blake reflected as he continued to watch the healing. Everyone in town knew Dean was one of their volunteer firefighters. And of course accidents happened. But the timing was something Blake found himself not inclined to ignore. *We've been separated,* he realized. If that fire was, in fact, not an ordinary accident, then Dean could still be in danger. And if he got hurt, their mother would be hard-pressed to heal him properly.

Blake gave a slight shake of his head, squeezing his eyes shut. *I'm being paranoid,* he told himself. For all they knew they had only one enemy. They hadn't seen any evidence that pointed to a second person's involvement. Never, that he knew of, had there been a coordinated attack. *It's just a coincidence,* he told himself. But that was problem. Blake didn't believe in major coincidences, like the downtown fire and the freak hail storm.

Looking sideways at his silent brother, Blake kept his voice low and asked, "What happened to his bike?"

Without taking his eyes from the pair by the couch, Logan replied, "It's in the back of my truck. I'll take it in later."

Blake nodded, accepting the answer. He imagined it had been Nate's insistence that had made Logan bother with the motorcycle.

"Blake," Christopher began again. "Could you pick up your sister from school today?"

"Of course."

Lillian's voice was somewhat strained when she spoke again. "Do you have work?" Though she didn't specify, the question was obviously directed at Blake.

"I already called in and switched shifts."

Christopher stood without a word and strode heavily out of the living room, headed toward the kitchen. His posture was rigid, matching his clenched fists and jaw.

Blake returned his attention to his mother, whose eyes were narrowed in concentration. Hesitantly, he offered, "I could go get Angie now…"

"No," Lillian insisted firmly. "I'm about done."

Logan quietly said, "Nate's arm was pretty well shattered. But the rest of him was just scraped and bruised."

"That's good, at least," Blake admitted.

After another minute, Logan pushed to his feet, pausing to nod at Blake before he continued forward, toward the stairs. Blake took the silent hint and followed his brother up the steps. Nate would be asleep for a couple more hours at least, and their mother would probably need a nap herself when she was done. The least they could do was make sure Nate's old room was ready.

They were folding down the comforter when Logan spoke. "There's something else."

Blake paused, the edge of the comforter still in his hand, and looked up at his brother. "What do you mean?"

"Nate wasn't exactly on the interstate," Logan explained. "And when I was on my way to get him, I was passed by this old BMW. It was the only car on the road, and going the opposite direction."

"Did you get a look at the driver?" Blake asked, recovering enough to finish adjusting the comforter.

"Only a glimpse," Logan admitted. "But he was older. And he gave me a nasty look when he passed me."

For an instant, Blake was disappointed. He'd honestly expected to hear a description fitting the man that had been semi-stalking Brooke. But then the rest of Logan's words settled in his head, reminding him of another encounter he himself had had. It had been over a month since that night, but all of a sudden the memory was crystal clear. He remembered going to the diner for dinner, wanting to see Brooke, and having an awkward run-in with an older man. The man had glared at him for no reason before shoving past. *And he was with another man, closer to my age,* Blake realized. And then it dawned on him.

He had seen their enemies—the man who'd probably attacked Nate, as well as the one who seemed to be stalking Brooke.

"Blake?" Logan asked, sensing his brother's distraction and raising an eyebrow.

Blake pulled himself back to the present with a shake of his head. "There're two," he declared firmly. "That man you saw today, I just remembered, I've seen him before, too. Before the attack on Angela. And he was with another man, who I'm pretty sure is the same guy that Brooke's seen around a few times."

Logan's other eyebrow rose as well, both arching toward his hairline. "Are you sure?"

"Yeah," Blake said with a slow nod. "I mean, I have no proof, but I'm positive. It's the only thing that really makes any sense."

"Hell, it's more than we had twenty minutes ago. I wish I'd thought to look at his plates."

"Don't beat yourself up about it." Blake stepped back from the bed and crossed his arms thoughtfully. "I'm going to call Dean before I head back down. Even if he doesn't get the message right away, at least he'll know what we do."

Logan nodded. "Good idea." Then he turned and walked around the bed, slipping from Nate's room.

****

Brooke tucked her notepad into a front pocket and stepped into the main room. The diner was moderately busy for mid-morning on a Friday, but even so, Brooke was intercepted before she could reach her first table.

"Brooke!" Shelly, the hostess, called from another table she was sitting. She gestured to the phone on the counter, which was ringing. "Could you get that, please?"

With a silent nod, Brooke turned and moved quickly to the phone. "Earl's Diner, this is Brooke, how can I help you?"

The voice on the other end hesitated a beat, and the signal was slightly scratchy, but the woman's voice was still easily discernable as she spoke. "Yes, hello, is Earl available? Or Paula?" The slightest of accents flavored the woman's voice, though Brooke couldn't identify it specifically.

Brooke's eyes flicked around, though she knew she wouldn't see either of them. She knew for a fact that Earl was in the kitchen that day, but where Paula was, she had no idea. "I'm sorry," she replied. "They're busy at the moment. Can I take a message for you?"

"Oh, I see." Disappointment laced the unknown woman's voice. "Well, could you tell them Missy called? I talked to Paula a few days ago about that new chef position."

By now, Shelly had returned to the front and was standing beside Brooke with a curious expression. Brooke's eyebrows shot up, and she said quickly, "Actually, if you can hold on a second, I might be able to get Paula for you."

"Yes, please," the woman replied immediately, the tone of disappointment gone.

Putting her hand over the mouthpiece, Brooke whispered, "Take this, I'm going to find Paula. She's calling about the job."

Shelly nodded and switched places with Brooke.

As soon as Brooke was free of the phone, she moved swiftly toward the back again in search of Paula. The older woman hadn't been in the back room earlier, but it was possible she was there now. Or in the kitchen with her husband. A quick survey assured Brooke that she wasn't in the drink station, so Brooke pushed open the door to the back room. When she found it empty, she turned and crossed to the kitchen door.

She found Paula standing at the half-wall, talking with Earl. Ordinarily, she was opposed to interrupting a conversation between the two people who signed her paychecks, but she knew they would understand. Still, she cleared her throat first to gain their attention. When the couple had turned their eyes toward her, Brooke hurriedly said, "I'm sorry, Paula, but a woman named Missy is on the phone for you?"

"Oh, thank goodness!" Paula exclaimed, immediately starting forward. She smiled in silent gratitude to Brooke even as she brushed past her and out of the room.

Brooke just stood there for a moment and watched the door swing shut. *I guess this Missy woman is someone they were hoping to hear from...*

Deep, gravelly chuckling from behind her drew her attention, and Brooke turned to properly face her boss. Earl Sanders was the official owner of Earl's Diner—he'd had the restaurant nearly two years longer than he had been married. He was a good, if not overly straightforward, man; a good man who had been incredibly upset about his previous chef's inappropriate departure.

With a lopsided grin, Earl said, "Missy's an old friend of Paula's. They've kept in touch, an' it turns out Missy's little girl took a couple years of culinary school. She also happens to be lookin' for a job, so we thought we'd reach out an' see if we couldn't help each other."

Brooke nodded slowly. "Gotcha." With a genuine smile, she added, "Well, I for one hope she comes through."

Earl held up his hands, which were covered in spice-rub, and said, "Me, too."

Chapter Nineteen

"It turns out Missy's daughter, Madison, is working a temporary job right now," Brooke was explaining as Blake turned onto his parent's street Saturday afternoon. "It should be done in a couple of weeks, and she doesn't like it so she's definitely not staying longer, and then she's going to be moving up here after that's over."

"She's moving all the way up here for a 'probably'?" Blake asked with a raised eyebrow. He slowed the car as he approached the driveway.

"Earl and Paula have promised her a job," Brooke said. "The only part that's not for sure is whether it'll be as Ed's replacement or as a sous chef. They finally talked one of the guys into stepping up if she doesn't work out."

Blake nodded, pulling in behind Logan's truck. "That makes more sense. Well, I hope she works out. I know you've all been a little more frazzled since Ed ditched."

Releasing a frustrated sigh, Brooke replied, "That's one way to put it."

They fell silent for a moment as Blake turned off the car and tugged the keys easily out of the ignition. He released his seat belt and looked over as Brooke did the same. "You ready?"

"I was hoping this would be easy, since I've already technically met the parents," she declared. Her eyes flicked to the house visible beyond the windshield, and she added, "But it's still a little daunting."

"Don't worry about it," Blake replied, reaching over and wrapping a hand around one of hers. Their eyes met. "They already know and like you, remember? It *will* be easy."

Brooke leaned forward and planted a quick kiss on his lips before pulling back and saying, "I'm certainly hoping so."

Without another word, the couple stepped from the car, and Brooke self-consciously smoothed out her new light blue, loose-collared t-shirt. When she'd raided her closet for something other than regular denim to wear with it, she'd discovered a pair of ivory pants that she had thought lost the year before. Now she was fairly confident that she looked fine, but she was still worried about making a good impression. This was actually her first time interacting with the Hawkes as a family, all at once, in a non-emergency.

Blake's chuckling drew her attention, and she realized he was standing before her. "You look great," he promised, his eyes only briefly skimming over her before returning to hers. "Come on."

She took his proffered hand and allowed him to lead her up to the house.

As they stepped into the foyer and Blake paused to ease the door shut, Brooke realized that she could hear talking coming from down the hall. Multiple voices—which didn't surprise her, considering the truck they'd parked behind.

"Sorry we're a little late," Blake declared as he and Brooke stepped into the large living room.

Christopher and Lillian were spread out in two of the three armchairs, and Eric and Angela were settled in the loveseat. Nate and Logan had claimed two spots on the oversized couch. The family looked over when Blake spoke, and multiple smiles were aimed their way.

Angela's smile of greeting morphed into a grin. "The only one who's late is *Dean*. Again."

"Brooke." Lillian rose to her feet and moved toward them, a smile on her face. "I'm so glad you could come."

Brooke returned the smile and let herself be pulled into the loose embrace. "Thank you for inviting me."

"Of course we'd invite you." Nate shifted closer to Logan in order to make more room on the couch for the couple. "We get tired of teasing Angie all the time."

Logan reached up silently and smacked his brother upside the head.

Guilt washed over Brooke as she followed Blake to the couch, realizing she had completely forgotten that Nate had been injured just a couple of days prior. She couldn't believe the attack had slipped her mind after how shaken up Blake had seemed. Still, she knew she had no real reason to be feeling guilty, so she smiled and said, "Hey, guys."

As they settled on the couch, Blake looked over at Nate seriously. "How're you doing?"

Nate's face scrunched unhappily. "My bike's in the shop, and probably will be for a *while*. I'm grumpy."

Blake lifted an eyebrow. And from what Brooke remembered of his story, she understood why. Apparently, Nate's bike had been pretty well totaled. "Why not just buy a new one?"

"I liked that one!" Nate's tone indicated that he had clearly already had this conversation a time or two.

Before another word could be said, Dean's voice called from the hallway. "You can start the party now!"

"You're too late!" Angela called back quickly. "We started without you!"

Dean ambled into the living room a moment later, one hand in his pocket. "Then you'll just have to start over again." He smirked and crossed the living room to drop a hand on his sister's head teasingly. "You wouldn't want us to start without *you* one day, would you?"

Angela dragged his hand off of her hair with one hand, reaching up to try to smooth it back down with the other. "That would never happen. I know how to read my watch."

"Ha!" Dean exclaimed even as Nate burst into laughter. Blake and Logan chuckled quietly, and Dean sighed dramatically, turning and moving to the couch to claim a seat between Nate and Blake. After he'd settled, he leaned forward to look around Blake and grinned at Brooke. "Hope you're ready for this," he said with a wink.

"Bring it on."

They talked only a little about their still-unknown enemies, mostly to make sure that Dean had gotten Blake's message about the second man. The group then spent the majority of the rest of the time talking about other things and arguing over which game they should play after dinner.

When dinner was just about ready, Brooke found herself making her way through a side hall in search of a bathroom. She'd gotten directions from Blake, but she was afraid she might have forgotten a detail. She sure felt lost.

"… more careful, mostly." The whispered words drifted to Brooke from a partially open door to her right. After a moment, she realized the speaker was Eric. Though why he would be hiding out in some random room, and who he was talking to, she had no idea.

Maybe that's the bathroom? Brooke wondered. She hesitated a moment before stepping up and tapping her knuckles lightly along the doorframe. Since the door was slightly open, she wasn't worried about catching him in an awkward position, but she didn't want to startle him by opening the door.

"Obv—" Eric began, cutting himself off when he registered the light sound of Brooke's knock.

The door was pulled open, and even as Eric gave her a curious, slightly embarrassed look, Brooke realized that the room behind him was, in fact, not the bathroom. It looked like a home office. "Sorry!" Brooke stage-whispered with an awkward smile.

Eric's lips curved up at the corners, and he held up one finger as he said into the phone, "Sorry, I have to go, I think dinner's ready. Talk to you later." He pulled the phone away from his ear, then, and slid it shut. To Brooke, he said, "Um, sorry... I know it's kind of weird that I was on the phone in Mr. Hawke's office, but it gets really good reception." He paused and gestured to the large window wall behind him. "I think it's the window."

Brooke nodded and stepped back so that he could leave the room. "No, it's fine... I was actually sort of hoping you could point me toward the bathroom. I think I took a wrong turn after the family-photo wall."

Eric grinned and pointed down the hall. "You didn't," he said. "It's that door there, on the left."

Of course, it's barely ten feet away, Brooke admonished herself. *How embarrassing.* "Thanks," she said. "Dinner's about ready, by the way."

"Cool," he replied, slipping his hands in his pockets and turning back the way she'd just come, toward the rest of the family.

****

"So, was it very bad?" Blake asked as he eased to a stop behind Brooke's Civic in her driveway later that night. They had stayed for several hours after dinner, so it was nearly eleven o'clock by the time they arrived at her apartment.

Brooke laughed and shook her head. "No, you were right, it was fine."

"Good," Blake replied with a chuckle of his own. He turned the car off before shifting in his seat to face her better. "What's your schedule tomorrow?"

"I work at four," she said after a moment's thought. "But I was planning to finish a paper that's due before I went in." She paused, one eyebrow curving up. "Why?"

"I haven't had any time alone with you in days."

Brooke smiled and released her seat belt. "I suppose you can come in if you'd like, Mr. Hawke." She popped open her door with a wink and climbed out.

"Do you want some coffee or something?" Brooke offered as she flipped the lock behind them after they had slipped inside the apartment. "I'm thinking about making some for myself, so it'd be fine."

"I'll take a cup if you're making it anyway," Blake stated, watching her as she moved past her table and into the kitchen. His eyes never left her. The way she looked in those ivory pants, and the way her shirt rode up just enough to tease him when she stretched to reach— and later return—the coffee. He had to restrain himself from going up behind her and sliding his hands beneath her shirt.

"Can I ask you another question?" Brooke suddenly said, pulling Blake from his distracting thoughts. Somewhat.

Blake rested his hip against her table even as she turned to face him. "Of course."

Brooke took a deep breath and Blake recognized the signs of embarrassment in her eyes. "I had this crazy thought," she began, "and I've actually been wondering it for a while, but … when I'm, like, swimming in the ocean or something … can you feel me?"

Blake did his best to fight the grin that immediately wanted to curve his lips, but he didn't quite succeed. "I can," he said. "But only if I'm trying to. So, most of the time, no, I can't. But that's because I'm not trying."

Brooke pursed her lips before turning and moving to her sink. She lifted the lever enough to create a small but steady stream. "So then you can feel my hand if I do this…?" She stuck her hand beneath the water, wiggling her fingers a little even as she turned back to grin at him.

Blake matched her grin and nodded. "I can," he replied. His eyes crinkled with laughter as the water dripping from her hand curved up and swirled over her forearm slowly. "And I can feel you when I do that, too."

Her attention had returned to her arm when the water began curving along it, defying gravity as it circled her skin up to the elbow.

"Of course," Blake began, moving to stand in front of her and reaching out to trail his fingers along her dry arm. "I get a better image if you're fully submerged, like if you're swimming."

Brooke allowed a secret smile to slowly curve her lips and she pulled her arm from the water, which immediately fell back to the sink, as she said, "That could be considered sort of perverted, you know."

Blake reached past her and lowered the lever, shutting off the water flow and giving him a good excuse to trail the fingers of his other hand along her arm. "That's why I don't usually do it. Although, with you, I might start making an exception."

He leaned in and she let her eyes flutter closed as their lips met. His arms curved around her loosely, and her hands came to rest on his chest.

Brooke pulled away after a long moment, mischief lighting her eyes. "Seeing as how I just made coffee, why don't we watch a movie?"

Blake smiled and fought down the heat rushing through his veins. His hands settled lightly over her waist. "I'm game for that. Lead the way, beautiful."

It took her no time at all to find a decent movie and set it up. Then she lowered herself directly beside Blake, shifting so that she could curl into him and use his shoulder as her pillow. His arm came around her automatically, his hand resting over her abdomen as a smile lifted his lips. He could easily get used to this.

With the exception of when they got up to get the coffee, Brooke spent the movie curled up against him, and he was ridiculously comfortable.

He was almost disturbed at how easy it was to do nothing with her and enjoy it. While he'd never been the type who always needed to be doing *something*, he had also never really been the type to enjoy just sitting around for long periods of time. And yet he could sit in one position for nearly two hours, with Brooke curled into his side, and feel as if everything was right with the world. It was a nice feeling. The kind he wanted to hold on to for as long as he was able.

So when Brooke fell asleep shortly before the end of the movie, Blake happily took advantage of the opportunity to stay a little longer. After all, he couldn't in good conscience leave her alone in an unlocked apartment.

****

"Come on, Brooke, pick up," Blake pleaded under his breath as he sped toward her apartment. His hands gripped the steering wheel so tightly that his knuckles were white. He was close enough now that he could see the thick plume of smoke as it reached for the sky. In his ear, the line kept ringing.

It had been nearly a week since she'd come to their monthly family dinner—just over a week since Nate had driven into the hail storm. Blake and Brooke had spent what time they could together, though between their conflicting work schedules and end-of-the-semester school projects, there hadn't been as much time as either would have liked. He wasn't expecting to see her again until Sunday.

But that was before the fire.

Brooke's outgoing message was playing in his ear for the second time, and Blake cursed as he ended the call, not bothering to leave another message. It wasn't like her to ignore her phone when she wasn't working, but he knew she hadn't been scheduled for that night. *Maybe she picked up a shift last-minute.* At the moment, he had no way of knowing. All he could do was hope.

Blake pulled to a stop along the curb barely a block from her complex. He cut the engine and climbed from his car even as the police officer he'd parked behind turned and started toward him. He recognized the man immediately, and after a beat, he looked past him toward the fire. He had really been hoping Dean had been exaggerating.

"Blake," the officer called, coming to stand in front of him. "I'm afraid you have to stand back."

Forcing his jaw to unlock, and hoping his tone was civil, Blake replied, "Yeah, I know. How bad is it?"

The officer turned toward the blaze.

The fire wasn't quite under control yet, despite the numerous firetrucks and firefighters clogging the road just ahead. Flames still licked sporadically out a couple of windows, and thick, black smoke polluted the air above them. From where the two men were standing, it was obvious which apartment had been at the center of the blaze, and fortunately, it seemed to be the only apartment completely decimated.

But it was Brooke's apartment. The sight of the structure charred, destroyed, and still burning made Blake's stomach churn violently. He wanted to find and beat the person responsible about as badly as he wanted to throw up.

The police officer cleared his throat and looked back at Blake. "You can see for yourself the apartment's a total loss." He paused, and the look in his eyes told Blake that he had an idea of why Blake was there. "Dean went through it himself, and he said no one was there."

The first flicker of relief ignited in Blake's heart, and he released a heavy breath.

The officer waited long enough to see that his words had sunk in before continuing. "We've evacuated the front half of the complex. It doesn't look like Ms. Munroe was anywhere around when the fire started."

Blake's gaze trailed away from the apartment, settling on the blown-out heap that had most likely once been Brooke's car. It was obvious that the fire had spread from the apartment, covering the short distance between her front wall and her car.

"We matched the license plate to her car," the officer said, seeing where Blake's attention had gone. "Wherever she is, she clearly didn't drive there. Have you tried calling her?"

"Yeah," Blake replied slowly. "She's not answering."

Chapter Twenty

The officer frowned, but Blake's attention had once again been pulled away. Dean had spotted them and was making his way over, frustration curving his lips in a fierce scowl.

When he reached them, Dean dropped a hand on the officer's shoulder. "You mind if I take over?"

The officer nodded and quietly walked away, toward a group of observing civilians across the street.

"She wasn't home?" Blake asked immediately, his voice tight and strained. He wasn't sure he could believe it until his brother confirmed it.

Dean nodded shortly. "The apartment was empty. It's a disaster inside, though. There isn't anything the fire didn't get."

Blake swallowed heavily and let his gaze return to the building. "Better the apartment, and the car, than her."

"I don't disagree," Dean said somberly. "Have you gotten a hold of her?"

"No. I left her a message, and I called twice, but nothing."

Dean's scowl deepened. "Is she working?"

"She wasn't scheduled to," Blake said. "I think I'm going to head over there and double check, though. It's not like her to ignore my calls." He paused, knowing he had to ask the question, and equally as certain he already knew the answer. "How did this happen?"

Dean's voice was low and angry, his own eyes now focused on the lingering flames and billowing smoke. "Some sort of electrical fire," he said. "Started in the living room. Near as I can tell, something hot and live hit the electrical socket. The rest is history."

"Something like lightning?" Blake asked unnecessarily. Even Dean wouldn't be able to know with absolute certainty, but lightning was more likely than someone sticking a stun-gun into the outlet.

"Exactly," Dean replied.

Blake dragged in a breath and nodded again. Looking back to his brother, he said, "Thanks for calling me. I'm going to try to find Brooke, but…"

Dean forced a bitter smile. "If she comes home, I'll have her call you. And, uh, speaking of calling … you mind calling the family? I haven't exactly had the chance."

"Sure," Blake agreed. "Thanks."

Dean turned and began walking back toward the apartment as Blake returned to his car. Blake wasted no time cranking the engine over, barely remembering to tug his seat belt into place as he made his first call. He talked to his father, giving him the short version, before calling Logan—and then Nate—and repeating the story. Logan offered to drive around and help look for Brooke, an offer Blake wasn't stubborn enough to turn down.

He decided to call Brooke again, just to be safe. It rang four times before going to voicemail. He opted not to leave another message.

He'd barely disconnected the call when he pulled into the diner's parking lot. Since her car had been home, he was fairly certain she wasn't there. But maybe Georgia was, and maybe Georgia would know where to find her. It was that possibility that had him swinging into the first available spot, not bothering to correct his parking job before he got out of the car.

It was an effort to keep his building panic off his face as he entered the diner, but he didn't want to cause a scene. Taking a deep breath, he stepped up to the front counter, but he wasn't able to offer Shelly any kind of a smile. "Do you know if Brooke's here?"

Shelly's smile faltered. She hesitated, glancing at a paper he couldn't see. "Um, she's not listed. But I can grab Paula if you want…?"

"Please," he said. Later, he might feel guilty about confusing or worrying Brooke's coworkers, most of whom he'd known for years. But right now he simply didn't care.

Shelly nodded and turned, quickly moving further into the diner. She wasn't gone long, and Paula was leading the way when she returned. Paula's expression bespoke curious confusion, but no concern. Clearly word had not reached Earl's that one of their employees was now homeless.

"Blake?" Paula asked, coming to a stop in front of him. "Shelly tells me you're looking for Brooke?"

"Yeah," Blake replied with a short nod. "I know she wasn't scheduled to be working tonight, but she's not at home and she's not answering her cell. Do you know where she might be?"

Paula slowly shook her head, her curiosity beginning to give way to worry. "I don't, sweetie. I wasn't expecting to see her before tomorrow afternoon."

"Is Georgia on tonight?" Blake asked, falling back to plan B.

"No," Paula replied. Something lit up her eyes, and she added, "But I just remembered, it's Georgia's birthday. She took the whole day off—she does every year—so you might find Brooke at her place."

Hope bubbled inside him, and Blake released a breath. "Okay," he said. "Could I get an address? Or a phone number?"

Paula hesitated even as Shelly reached for a piece of paper and a pen. "What's the emergency?"

It was Blake's turn to hesitate, though he knew it was pointless. He was honestly amazed she didn't already know. "Her apartment … caught fire," he said carefully. "I know she wasn't home when it happened, but I haven't been able to reach her."

Shelly had frozen, hand poised over the paper, and Paula's eyes were wide with shock. "My goodness," Paula murmured. "Well, when you find that girl, you tell her not to worry about working the rest of the weekend. She's got other things to worry about right now."

"Here you go," Shelly said, holding out the paper. "Georgia's address and cell phone number. I hope you find Brooke."

Blake took the paper and nodded again. "Me, too. Thanks." He left without another word, ignoring the stares of the two women behind him.

He had the address memorized by the time he'd buckled himself back into his car, and in no time he was on the road once more. *Please let her be there*. He still didn't know why she wasn't answering her phone, but he was willing to forgive that entirely as long as she was all right. If she wasn't, he didn't know what he'd do.

****

"And the word is," Emma began, pausing dramatically as her eyes lifted from the card in her hand and she smiled. "Delicious! Mouth-watering, scrumptious, or luscious." She leaned forward and set the card in the center of the circle so that everyone could see it.

"If anyone has the 'Georgia' card," Georgia began with a laugh, "you can play it now and automatically win." Laughter greeted her declaration as each of the other players examined their options. Georgia ran her new press-on nails over the cards in her hand before carefully pulling one free and setting it, face down, beside Emma's.

One by one, Brooke and the other participants placed their own cards on or around Georgia's. When the last card was in place, Emma reached out and gathered the face-down cards. Emma was still going through the offerings when someone knocked loudly on the front door.

The group paused, startled, before exchanging curious looks.

"You didn't order strippers, did you?" Emma asked with a grin as she looked over at Georgia.

Georgia rolled her eyes and pushed to her feet, saying, "I wouldn't do something like that!" With a wink, she added, "At least not when my boyfriend was home!"

The girls laughed as Georgia's live-in boyfriend stood as well and put a hand on her shoulder. "I'll get it, babe. Keep playing."

As he turned to slip from the room, Georgia's older sister hollered, "Bring me another beer on your way back!"

Georgia reclaimed her seat and waved her hands in a simmer-down gesture. "Okay, okay, let's get back to business here. Have I won yet?"

Emma returned her attention to the cards, paused, and said, "Well, the answer to that all depends ... if you're the one who threw Luke Skywalker at me, then no, you did not win." As she spoke, she tossed the aforementioned card from her hand.

"Oh, come on!" the girl to Emma's immediate left exclaimed as the card landed on the discard pile. "He was cute!"

Laughter interrupted whatever else she might have said, and it was several seconds before Emma could speak over them again. "Who wants to see the next loser?" Emma called with a smirk. The girls quieted, and she opened her mouth again, reaching for another card, but again she was interrupted.

"Uh, Brooke?" Georgia's boyfriend said, standing in the entry to the den. They looked at him, and he jerked his thumb over his shoulder. "Your boyfriend's here for you. He says it's important."

The laughter faded, and Georgia looked over at her friend. Brooke shrugged as she stood, hoping her instant worry didn't show on her face. She couldn't think of many *good* reasons why he would have tracked her down, especially without calling. *Or did I miss a call?* She patted her pocket for her cell phone as she stepped from the room. It was only then that she realized her phone wasn't in her pocket at all.

She decided finding her phone wasn't her priority and continued down the hall, rounding the corner that led to Georgia's living room and entry. As she passed the small kitchen, she realized where her phone was—in her purse, which was still resting on the counter. *I probably did miss a call,* she reflected with a guilty wince. But there was no time to dwell on it, because Blake was already in sight.

Worry shrouded his face, fading his eyes and tightening his jaw. That worry edged away visibly when he saw her, and her guilt intensified. Something had happened, and he'd been worried, but she had stupidly forgotten to remove her phone from her purse and therefore hadn't heard it ring over the music and laughter.

"Blake," she began when she reached him. She'd meant to say more, but as soon as she was within arm's reach, he pulled her into a tight embrace, and her breath caught in her throat. He'd been *really* worried.

He said nothing for a long moment, holding her close and breathing deeply. With every second that passed, Brooke cursed herself for worrying him so much. She could feel the tension in his body—tension that wasn't leaving very quickly.

"Blake," Brooke said again, whispering this time and not trying to break his hold. "I'm sorry. I think I left my phone in my purse. What happened?" She was on the verge of tears and she didn't even really know why. And that was her fault.

Slowly, Blake released her. He met her gaze and swallowed heavily. She wasn't going to like his answer. "It's okay," he began, hedging. "I'm just glad you're all right. But … I have bad news."

Brooke drew in a slow breath, knowing it must be pretty bad if he was stalling so blatantly. Her brain was still functioning enough for her to hold up a hand before he could say more, and she quietly said, "Let's step outside first."

Silently they moved back to the front porch of Georgia's apartment, and Brooke pulled the door closed behind her. She turned back to face him then, but said nothing.

"There … was a fire," Blake said carefully. "It started in your apartment. By the time the firefighters got there, there wasn't much they could do. Your car was still there, so they looked for you, and when you didn't answer your phone I checked in at the diner, and Paula led me here."

Brooke was breathless again, but for an entirely new reason. *My … apartment?* She'd been happy in that small, out-of-the-way apartment. She'd been planning on living there until she had a reason to need a bigger place. It was comfortable. And now it was gone. All she had was her car, and whatever was in the trunk—she hoped. "What about … my car?"

Blake slowly shook his head. "It got caught in the fire." He paused. "Why was it not with you?"

"Emma offered to give me a ride," Brooke explained numbly. Her breath stalled somewhere in her throat. She should have at least driven herself. If she had—

That settled it, then. She had nothing left. The clothes on her back, the money in her purse, her cell phone—which would need to be charged soon, and she no longer had a charger—and nothing else. She'd been without a family for several years, and without a reliable roof for most of those years, too. But she'd never been truly homeless. She couldn't exactly afford to live out of a hotel for however long it would take to find a new apartment. She really didn't want to have to drop out of school and move back in with her adopted family.

She had no idea what she was going to do.

"I'm sorry," Blake said softly.

Brooke blinked, re-focused her attention on the present, and shifted to let herself slump against the outer wall of the entryway. "Everything," she mumbled disbelievingly. She shook her head, looking back at him. "There must be something that survived, right?"

"Dean didn't seem to think so," Blake admitted.

Brooke groaned and lifted a hand to her forehead, her eyes squeezing shut. "I can't believe this … I don't know what I should do!" Those tears were back behind her eyes, and for a moment she focused entirely on fighting them back. *Crying won't help anyway.* It was her old childhood mantra. It'd been a long time since she'd needed it, but she needed it now. She needed the strength she'd found when she'd realized she had no one to rely on.

A strong, steady hand landed on her shoulder, and the burning faded as her eyes snapped open. She found herself staring into Blake's intense, guilty, concerned blue eyes, and a bit of the weight that had settled over her heart slid off. She may have lost her possessions, and her home, but she wasn't alone this time. And that was something.

"I'll help you through this," Blake said firmly. It wasn't a tone to be argued with, or an offer he would easily allow her to refuse.

Without warning, a single tear escaped and slid down her cheek. Brooke swallowed past the painful lump in her throat as she nodded. She couldn't speak. She was afraid she'd break down if she attempted to make a sound. But Blake seemed to understand. He moved closer, pulling her to him once again.

She tucked her head beneath his chin, her arms wrapping around his torso, and allowed herself a minute to let the tears fall. If she could let out just a few, just enough to take the edge off, she'd be fine. She sniffled into his shirt as his arms tightened around her, his hands rubbing soothing circles over her back. By focusing on him, on his embrace, Brooke was able to lock away the rest of her tears. His thumbs rubbed over her spine, and her skin tingled. She focused on that until she was sure she wouldn't shatter.

Her emotions once more reined in—at least for the minute—Brooke gently eased out of his embrace. She wiped quickly at her face and offered him a small, shaky smile. "Thank you. Will you ... wait a minute? I should say goodbye to Georgia. It's her birthday, after all."

Blake inclined his head. "Of course. I'll wait right here."

****

Blake had taken her, at her request, to her apartment after she'd left Georgia's a short while later. It had taken Brooke nearly a full minute to make herself step from the car after he'd pulled to a stop at the curb, but she had managed it. And though the fire was out by then, it was far from safe for Brooke to go sifting through the debris, so they hadn't stayed long. She had spoken with Dean, the fire chief, a couple of police officers, and her landlord, but then she had turned and let Blake lead her back to his car.

He drove back to his house in silence, trying to give her an opportunity to come to terms with what had happened. For the duration of the drive, Brooke stared out the passenger window. She was jerked out of her thoughts when the car came to a stop.

Her eyes slid forward, looking through the windshield, and her gaze settled on the garage wall in front of them.

Blake paused when she didn't move. He looked over at her and hesitantly reached out, wrapping his hand around her nearest one. "Hey," he said gently.

Brooke blinked and looked over at him. "Hmm?"

"Come on." He gestured toward his house. "You can stay with me, I don't mind."

She smiled, albeit faintly, and nodded. "Thanks," she said.

Together they climbed from the car, and Brooke followed Blake into the house silently.

They were nearly to the sofas in the living room when Brooke said, "I'm sorry. It's all just a lot to take in."

Blake offered her an understanding smile. "You don't have to apologize. Hell, it's my fault this is happening to you in the first place." And the guilt he felt about that was only surpassed by the anger still boiling in his gut. These men, whoever they were, were going to answer for their actions.

Brooke frowned at him. "No it's not."

He took his usual seat in the corner and shook his head. "Sure it is. They're *my* enemies."

Lips scrunched disapprovingly, Brooke moved and sat beside him. "Maybe, but I knew about them as soon as you did. So your excuse for feeling guilty is voided."

Despite himself, and despite the situation, Blake chuckled and curved his arm around her shoulders, pulling her closer. "Fine, fine, you might have a point."

Brooke leaned her head over his collar and let her eyes close. "Blake … thank you for letting me stay here tonight."

Blake frowned at her hair, which was all he could see of her. "Where will you stay tomorrow?" he asked quietly. *Georgia's, maybe?* He wasn't sure; he doubted she had even given it thought.

It was a long minute before Brooke mumbled, "I don't know. I don't have any idea…"

His heart ached at her words, and his arm tightened around her. There wasn't much he could do in this situation, especially not before they figured out who was after them, but he could offer a little help. If she was willing to hear it.

He leaned down and pressed his lips to the crown of her head before whispering, "You can stay with me. I've got plenty of room, and the rent's free."

Brooke pushed herself up enough to look into his eyes. "I can't do that!" she insisted. "I couldn't impose like that—and I have no idea how long it'll take to find a new apartment!"

Blake held her gaze firmly, wanting her to see that he was serious. He reached up with his free hand and let his fingertips trail over the side of her face lightly, saying nothing as his thumb traced her lower lip. When his hand stilled, cupping her cheek gently, he said, "I don't care how long it takes, and it's not an imposition. I'm *offering*. You won't have to pay for a hotel, and if I can help it, you won't have to pay for a taxi, either."

Silence stretched between them as he watched her process his offer. Her eyes went wide, and she swallowed heavily, but he saw the moment of realization when it struck. She clearly saw his logic, whether or not she would heed it. He could only hope she would.

Finally, her lips tipped up at the corners with a small, genuine smile. "Okay," she said. "I see your point. Thank you."

Blake returned her smile and tugged her forward enough to press his lips to hers. The kiss was tender and lingering, and when he pulled back, he murmured, "You're welcome."

Brooke sighed, her eyes dimming as her mind undoubtedly wandering back to the day's events, and she re-settled herself against him. Her eyes closed again, and she inhaled deeply.

Blake tightened his arm around her shoulders, holding her close. She likely wasn't ready to hear it yet, but he hoped she'd realize soon that everything would be okay. He'd make sure of it.

Chapter Twenty-One

Brooke spent nearly two hours talking with her landlord the following morning, only to be told that there wasn't much he could do. He released her from her lease, stating he didn't have any other units to transfer her to, and wished her luck. With a frustrated sigh, Brooke led the way back to Blake's waiting Mustang in silence.

"Can you take me by the mall?" Brooke asked as they pulled onto the main road.

"Sure," Blake said. "Which store are we hitting up?"

"I need a new uniform," she replied. After a beat, she added, "Well, technically, I need new everything..."

Blake glared out his windshield. "Try to think of it as re-booting your wardrobe," he offered after a short pause.

Brooke's lips twitched, more in appreciation of the thought behind his words than of the humor itself. "Was there something wrong with my wardrobe?" she asked, opting to go with his tone. She could certainly use a little good humor.

"Well, I mean, it was, what, a couple of days old?" Blake asked, only the faintest of laughter tingeing his voice.

"God forbid," Brooke agreed with matching laughter. It was swallowed up a minute later, however, when yet another realization dawned on her and she groaned aloud.

"What is it?"

Eyes closed and head back, Brooke replied, "My computer. I need a new freaking computer!"

Computers were certainly an expense she didn't need. But they were also highly necessary, especially considering that most college courses had required online elements.

"You can use the one in my office until you get your own," Blake offered.

"You don't mind?" Brooke asked hesitantly. "You're already doing so much…"

"I don't mind. I use my laptop mostly, anyway." And she got the distinct sense he was willing to argue her into submission, too.

"All right," Brooke accepted, releasing another heavy sigh. There really was no point in the argument. "Thanks," she added as Blake turned in to the parking lot.

Blake just smiled and shook his head as he searched for a parking spot. It was mid-morning on a Saturday, so the choices weren't as nice. But he found a satisfactory spot in the third aisle, and less than a minute later, the two of them were walking toward the clothing store.

Holding open one of the large glass doors, Blake said, "You know, I think you could put off the uniform hunt for an hour or two. Remember, Paula said you don't have to go in today."

"I know," Brooke admitted as she made her way toward the women's clothing section. "But I can't really afford to miss too much work, so if I can go in tomorrow, I will. Today, though, I realize that I should focus on other things … like re-booting my wardrobe."

Blake's lips twitched, and he shoved his hands into his pockets. "We can at least agree on that last part."

****

Blake opted to skip his last class on Monday in favor of making an overdue phone call. Up to now, he'd been leaving the bulk of the investigation into their enemy to his family. But surely he could do more. Surely there was something he could contribute besides a random chance encounter at a diner. And the only way to know for sure was to talk to the one person who most understood what was going on.

Uncle Nicholas.

"Howdy," Nicholas answered after the second ring. His learned Texas accent was thicker than Blake remembered, but not by much.

"Uncle Nicholas, this is Blake. I'm sorry to call without notice, are you able to talk?" He hadn't spoken to his uncle in a while—most of their news and messages came through his mother. But they were still on good terms.

"Blake! Of course I can talk," Nicholas said. "How's my oldest nephew? Not too dry, I hope!" He laughed at his own joke and Blake pinched the bridge of his nose with his free hand. He'd forgotten this part. Nicholas found it hard to focus. For as much information as he knew, it'd taken him most of his life to learn it because he was fairly easily distracted.

"Actually," Blake said, leaning back and tapping his fingers on the steering wheel of his car. He'd opted to have this conversation from the car in order to insure its privacy. A college campus was no place for this sort of topic. "I was hoping to talk about the other elementals you and Mom have been discussing."

Nicholas's laughter subsided quickly. "Oh, of course. But I've already told your mother everything I know."

"Everything?" Blake pushed. "There has to be more information somewhere. Do they have predictable family lines like we do? Even just knowing how many people to look for would help." *Anything* would help, really. The information they had was too vague, too basic.

"I'm sorry, Blake," Nicholas said. Papers shuffled in the background, and Blake pictured his uncle balancing a manila folder on his lap. "I don't think they have heritages like us. But they used to be pretty prolific, I think." Nicholas made a stalling sound, more shuffling filled the line, and then he added, "Lightning is their main power. The rest is, ah, it's not clear. A side effect, maybe. No, looks more like it's just harder to do." This time the shuffling stilled. "Have you seen this power up close, Blake?"

The botched beach date flashed through Blake's mind, and he nodded. "Yeah. On a date. And now these guys burned down my girlfriend's house."

Nicholas released a bitter laugh. "Dating at a time like this? Boy, I can't decide if I'm proud of you or ashamed. What do your parents think?"

Blake ground his teeth. "Mom and Dad like her," he said. "Uncle Nicholas, please, focus. These people are trying to kill us."

A rush of air crinkled over the phone line. "You want my advice, Blake? The smartest thing to do is run. Run until the lightning stops falling."

****

Over the next couple of days, Brooke did what she could to pull her life back together. She contacted her family, spent too much money on things she should have already had, and explained the situation to her professors when she went back to class on Monday. But despite all the things she got done over the weekend, by Tuesday she was still far from whole. Because of her greatly decreased bank account, however, she volunteered to take an extra shift on both Tuesday and Friday.

She was in the back room late Tuesday afternoon, using her ten-minute break to rest her feet, when Georgia slipped into the room. Brooke lifted her head from the locker it was resting against and offered a smile to her friend.

Georgia's returning smile was sympathetic, if not slightly guilty, and she moved toward her. As she set her purse down and reached for her own locker, Georgia said, "Brooke, I'm so sorry. Are you doing okay?"

Brooke sighed. "I suppose I could be doing worse."

"You're still staying with Blake, right?" Georgia asked after a moment.

"Yes," Brooke replied. "He's been really helpful. And patient."

Georgia grinned lightly and turned so she could sit beside her. She lowered her voice and said, "Now, as your best friend, it's my responsibility to make sure you're remembering all of the essentials. How's your supply?"

Brooke was sure her confusion showed on her face. "What are you talking about?"

Giving Brooke a pointed look, Georgia said, "You're sleeping in the same bed, aren't you?"

For an instant, Brooke was still confused. "Wha—? Oh, don't worry about that."

Georgia frowned. "It's not like they survived the fire. Do you need some money to buy some more? I'll run you by the drug store after work if you want."

Brooke squeezed her eyes shut, trying not to be mortified, and held up one hand defensively. "No, no, I already bought more. And even if I hadn't, I can't take your money for something like *that*!"

"You could if you needed it," Georgia replied, grinning now. "I mean, I wouldn't want to have to hold back."

"Shouldn't you be getting ready?" Brooke asked pointedly.

Georgia waved her off even as she pushed back to her feet. "Yeah, yeah." They were silent for a minute as Georgia pulled out her apron and began dressing for her shift. At length, she asked, "Do you need a ride after work? We're closing together, so I totally don't mind."

A genuine smile eased onto Brooke's face and she shook her head as she pushed to her feet. "No, thank you. Blake's picking me up." She paused and turned, jerking her thumb toward the door. "I'll see you out there, okay?"

Georgia nodded, still adjusting her apron, and Brooke turned and quietly stepped from the room. She appreciated everyone's concern, but all the same, she was tired of only talking about the fire and everything she'd lost whenever she saw someone. All she wanted was to forget—if only for a minute—about her own problems.

Shelly nearly ran into her as she bustled into the drink station, and she stumbled back to avoid Brooke, saying, "Oh! I'm so sorry, I know you have another minute left, but we got a little busier … and you have a family at four."

Brooke nodded, smiling. "That's fine. I was on my way back out there anyway." The two parted ways at the door, and Brooke took a deep breath as she approached the family of three. She didn't recognize them, which told her only that they probably weren't local.

They were dressed well, though not overly so, and the mother and father sat opposite each other, with their son settled between his father and the wall. The son, who was probably seventeen or eighteen, was the perfect combination of his parents. He had his mother's thick blond hair and blue eyes, but he had his father's strong, masculine features.

She smiled politely as the parents set their menus down. "Hi," Brooke began easily. "My name's Brooke, and I'll be taking care of you tonight. Is it your first time here?"

The mother returned her polite smile and nodded. "Yes," she said. "We're going to be moving to the area in a couple of months, so we're in town for a few days to do a little house-shopping."

Of course you are, Brooke thought fleetingly. Aloud, she said, "That's always fun. We've got lots of nice places to live around here, so I'm sure you'll find what you're looking for."

"We're not too worried," the father stated with an easy, confident smile.

Allowing herself a moment to indulge in a conversation that wasn't about her own life, Brooke asked curiously, "What brings you to Darien, though?"

The father's smile turned into a teasing grin, and he dropped a large hand on his son's head as he proudly declared, "Vaughn here's going to be going to college nearby starting next semester, and we've always wanted to live near the beach, so it seemed like the right time."

Vaughn grumbled something Brooke couldn't decipher and dragged his father's hand off his head without looking up.

"Graduating high school soon, then?" Brooke asked, directing the question to the boy deliberately.

The boy in question shifted his eyes from the table to hers and nodded. "Yeah," he said.

Continuing to purposefully ignore his anti-social attitude, Brooke said, "Well, congratulations, Vaughn. Now then, what can I get for you tonight?"

****

"I bought you something," Blake declared casually as he pulled out of the parking lot a few hours later.

Brooke looked over at him. "Oh?"

Grinning, Blake gestured toward the backseat. "It's in the bag."

More curious now than she had been initially, Brooke shifted and looked behind them. Her eyes easily found the small, unmarked plastic bag on his backseat, and she stretched her arm until her fingers had grasped it. It was lightweight, and she pulled it onto her lap. "What is it?" she asked as she found the opening and eased her hand inside.

"You'll see."

Brooke's hand had already made contact with the hard plastic casing of the object, and she pulled it out of the bag quickly. As soon as she saw the object packaged within, she couldn't help but laugh. It was a new phone charger. "You didn't like me using yours, huh?"

"Not true," he defended, still grinning. "I just thought it might be easier if we each had one."

Returning her gift to the bag, Brooke said, "Thank you. I knew there was something I was forgetting to replace."

"Don't mention it."

Settling the bag in her lap, Brooke leaned back against the headrest and told him a little about her day as he drove. She had fortunately few stories to tell, and by the time she was done Blake had pulled to a stop in his garage.

As they walked into the house, Blake only slightly ahead of her, Brooke asked, "You know what I want to do?"

Blake arched a brow at her words and glanced back at her over his shoulder as he walked. "Enlighten me," he said, a slight curve to his lips.

Brooke angled past him, setting the bag with her new phone charger on the kitchen counter. "I want to go for a nice soak in your hot tub. Feel free to join me if you're interested." She continued on down the hall and waved over her shoulder. Her casualness was feigned, of course; she very much wanted him to join her. But she was also pretty sure he would. So she grinned silently as Blake followed her down the hall.

Brooke paused in the large master bath after she had secured her bikini, taking a moment to admire herself. She'd never considered herself vain, but she wasn't afraid to admit when she knew she looked good. Nor was she unwilling to admit, at least to herself, that there was only one reason she'd purchased this particular bikini.

The suit itself was royal blue, with little ivory seashell-like clasps. The top tied around her back and behind her neck, and slim, borderline inappropriately small triangles of fabric covered her breasts. The triangles of fabric were connected in the front by the first of the two seashell clasps. The bottom piece was just enough to cover her, though her hips were only encircled by a single string of fabric, which tied over her left hip by looping through the other clasp.

With a self-satisfied smile, Brooke stepped out of the bathroom. She didn't bother to grab a towel on her way to the hot tub; it was a moot point, anyway.

She was unsurprised to see Blake already settled in the hot tub, arms stretched out over the sides and head back, looking relaxed. Even if she hadn't known his secret, there could be no denying that he was truly relaxed in the water.

"Got room for me?" she teased even as she stepped into the perfectly heated water.

Blake lifted his head, offering her a private smile as he said, "Always." His eyes left hers in order to take in her appearance, and he swallowed heavily.

"You like?" Brooke asked with a small laugh, stepping to the floor of the hot tub and slowly twirling around. When she was facing him again, he dragged his eyes back up to hers, and she recognized the desire swirling around in the depths of his gaze.

"You could say that," Blake replied, his voice low and thick. He pulled one arm from the rim of the hot tub. "Come here."

Even as his arm extended, reaching for her, Brooke felt the swirl of water suddenly, gently, pushing at her legs. She allowed the water to tumble her forward, into her boyfriend, and laughingly smacked at his shoulder. "Cheater!"

Blake's arms came around her, hauling her properly up to him, and he grumbled, "I'm more about results, really." He caught her ensuing laughter in a hard kiss as his mouth slanted over hers.

Brooke moaned against his lips as he devoured her, and her hands clenched over his shoulders, searching for purchase. One of his hands slid up her back, over the ties of her swimsuit, until he had tangled it in her hair. His other arm wound entirely around her waist, holding her tightly against him as his tongue swept over hers.

He was holding her tightly, her breasts pushed up against his chest and her nails digging into his shoulder, when she shifted against him and tore a muffled groan from his throat. Her leg dragged across his lap, and then she was straddling him. She allowed one of her hands to slide, nails still scraping his skin, up and into his hair.

As Blake sucked her tongue into his mouth, he slid his hand from the small of her back to her barely covered backside and squeezed deliberately. The action, synchronized with his tongue moving against hers, caused Brooke to roll her hips forward and into his straining arousal. They both groaned at the contact, neither quite breaking from the kiss.

Brooke took a deep breath through her nose and pulled her lips from his in order to trail hot kisses along his jaw. His hold on her remained strong as she kissed and licked her to way to his ear slowly. She angled her head to nibble on his earlobe. He groaned faintly, his own hips lifting off the bench and rolling into hers.

"I have a confession," Brooke murmured, her lips brushing the shell of his ear. He hummed an inquiry without actually saying anything, and she paused to let her tongue run along his ear. "I've always wanted to have sex in a hot tub."

Blake swallowed as her tongue resumed its torture on his ear. "I think I can help you with that."

"Yeah?" Brooke asked teasingly, her hot breath fanning over his moistened ear and down his throat.

"Yeah," Blake replied. He released her hair and trailed his hand over her throat until he found the tie on her new swimsuit, and in one swift tug, the tie came loose. Without skipping a beat, his hand trailed lower, finding the second tie and pulling it free as well.

Brooke leaned back, removing her lips from the skin beneath his ear, and used one hand to pull the bikini top off. She released it carelessly, letting it float away on the water. She watched him, a seductive smile on her face, as her hand returned to his shoulder and she lightly traced her nails over his skin. Her hand went down, nails skimming his collar, until she was able to trace her fingers over his nipple.

Blake sucked in a breath even as his own hand pulled around her until he had cupped one of her breasts in his palm. Her hand stilled immediately, and he squeezed gently, watching as her head fell back, eyes closed, and she arched into his touch. Her hips rolled into his again as he rubbed his thumb along her hardened nipple. She gasped his name, and he repeated the motion, his other hand releasing her bottom in order to trail up her side.

He paused, taking a minute to caress her other breast simultaneously. His own groans tore from his throat as she continued to roll her hips into his, both of her hands now clinging to his shoulders as she let him pleasure her. He released her breasts then and slid his hands up to curve over her shoulders and behind her throat, tugging her forward.

Their lips met again hungrily, and one of Blake's hands immediately slid back down, dipping again beneath the surface of the warm water. In no time, he found the seashell clasp over her hip and tugged it free. With her straddling his hips, it was no effort at all for him to tug the material away from her body and release it to float alongside her top.

Her tongue plunged into his mouth as his fingers began trailing along her upper thigh. His other hand slid down her spine a little, holding her close, and they both groaned again when his wandering hand found her center and he slipped a finger inside her. Her hands released his shoulders in order to frame his face, and she dominated the kiss as he pumped his finger in and out of her over and over again.

She pulled away a minute later, sucking in ragged breaths and gasping his name as she continued to roll her hips forward. Her hands slid back, tangling his hair.

****

Blake leaned forward and locked his lips over her throat, sucking and licking the sensitive skin for a moment before he pulled his hand away from her center entirely. He heard her groan with frustration at the lost contact and smirked against her skin. His hands shifted, and his arms wrapped around her before he lifted his own hips off the bench beneath him. The water swirled at his mental command, acting as spare hands, and easily tugged his trunks from his hips.

When he was free of the discarded fabric, he re-settled against the bench and lifted his head enough to see her face.

Their eyes met. One of her hands disentangled itself from his hair in order to frame his face as she breathlessly gasped, "Now would be good."

He grinned, whole-heartedly agreeing with her sentiment, and huskily replied, "Your wish is my command."

Their hips rolled together, and he was immediately sheathed within her. Blake's head fell back, and a groan tore from his throat as his arms tightened around her. Brooke's eyes fell shut, and her head collapsed against his shoulder as he surged within her, a gasp escaping her lips.

After a moment, Blake's arms loosened and his hand slid down to her bare hips. His grip tightened again and his hips rose, his arousal thrusting back into her. Brooke lifted her head from his shoulder and let her nails drag down his chest as she rolled her hips against his at an almost desperate pace.

Blake couldn't take his eyes off her. Her nails scraped up and down his chest, sides, and arms, and the faint stinging only heightened the sensations coursing through him. The water was swirling and sloshing against their bodies, lapping at the undersides of Brooke's breasts teasingly, and Blake allowed himself to expand his senses.

Suddenly, he could feel her everywhere, and he could feel every curve of her body simultaneously as she moved against him. Like he was caressing each smooth, delectable surface with his hands. The pleasure was indescribable. All he wanted was to bury himself inside her and stay there.

Brooke gasped as Blake increased the pace, pulling her flush against him again and crashing his lips to hers. She fell into the kiss willingly, eagerly, clinging to him as she met his new rhythm thrust for thrust.

Their tongues were still dancing together when Brooke's orgasm hit. Her inner walls tightened and squeezed around him just moments before she tore her lips from his, choking on a gasp that sounded a lot like his name. And her release was the final push he needed to find his own.

Neither moved for a long minute, their bodies still joined and Brooke mostly collapsed against his chest and shoulder as they breathed.

Slowly, carefully, Blake eased out of her. The motion pulled Brooke from her haze, and she shifted, half-climbing, half-sliding off him until she was resting at his side.

Feeling ridiculously comfortable, Blake's arm encircled her loosely. He let his head fall back as he asked, "So, how was your fantasy?"

Chapter Twenty-Two

Brooke laughed, the sound soft and tired at first, but it built into full, honest laughter. "Let's just say we really need to do that more often."

Blake chuckled, his fingers absently skimming along her smooth arm. "Definitely."

Brooke took a deep breath, but it was another long, comfortable minute before she said, "You know what, though? I'm starving, and we haven't had dinner."

"That's a good point." Blake lifted his head from the rim of the hot tub. "It would be bad to go to bed without having dinner, especially when we both have class tomorrow."

Cringing, Brooke reached up and put a hand to his chest, halting his movement. "Let's not talk about things like school and work tonight, okay? I'm not feeling that responsible."

Blake's lips curved into an easy grin. "Whatever you say, beautiful." He shifted and pressed a kiss to the crown of her head. "I've got a couple boxed dishes that only take about twenty minutes in the oven."

"That sounds perfect," Brooke declared as she sat up properly. She smiled at him before looking around for her discarded suit, which had gathered along the opposite wall of the hot tub. Her bikini was tangled with his trunks, trapped between the currents of two jets.

Blake followed her gaze and laughed faintly as the current of the jets altered course until they were propelling the discarded fabric forward. As he plucked his shorts from the pile, he said, "Special delivery."

Brooke laughed and moved away from him in order to pull her swimsuit back on.

"For the record," Blake added, his trunks already in place and one hand braced on the edge of the hot tub, "that swimsuit was a brilliant purchase."

As she tied the top around her neck, Brooke grinned and said, "You have such a dirty mind."

"Says the one who lured me to the hot tub specifically so that she could fulfill her naughty fantasy." As he spoke, he climbed from the water, his body absorbing the moisture that clung to his skin as he pulled away.

Brooke had finished tying her bikini into place by the time he'd stepped out of the hot tub, and as she climbed out after him, she gave him a teasing smirk. "You say that like you think that was my *only* fantasy."

Blake stopped moving, finding himself watching her as she passed him. He hadn't actually given a thought as to how many inappropriate fantasies she might have, but now he couldn't help but wonder. And the thought had him thinking they'd left the hot tub a little too soon.

Brooke paused, halfway through the sliding glass door, and looked over at him. "Aren't you coming?"

Releasing a breath, Blake smiled. "Of course." *This woman might be the death of me,* he decided as he followed her into the house, belatedly pulling the water off her dripping body. *On the other hand, is there a better way to go?* He shook his head, laughing silently at himself.

****

Brooke detoured into the bedroom—which she was now sharing with Blake—and called, "I'll be out in a minute. There's no way I'm eating dinner in a bikini."

She didn't comment on Blake's resulting chuckle as she moved to her new nightgown, which was draped over the foot of the bed. She might not be willing to eat dinner in a swimsuit, but she had no qualms about eating dinner in her pajamas. So she grabbed the nightgown, moved to grab a pair of clean panties, and continued on to the bathroom.

The nightgown and panties were folded and waiting on the side of the counter, and Brooke's arms were up, reaching for the tie behind her neck, when her eyes landed on a faint red spot on her skin. She paused, realizing immediately what it was, and her hand lowered until her fingertips were brushing the mark. It would undoubtedly be gone by the time she was warm enough to take off her coat the following morning, but she still couldn't stop the grin.

He gave me a hickey. She felt like a teenager for feeling even slightly excited about that fact, but there was no denying she was. Until she convinced him to give her a ring, a hickey was just about the most blatant advertisement of his possession that she was going to get.

She paused again, her hand stilling over the red mark and her eyes going wide. *Until he gives me a ring,* she repeated slowly. *Oh God.* She swallowed heavily. Somehow, there was a big difference between knowing she was in love with the man and knowing she wanted to marry him. But she did, she realized. She wanted it more than she'd wanted just about anything, ever.

****

"I've made a decision," Georgia declared the next night as she met up with Brooke in the drink station.

Brooke, paying only the necessary amount of attention to what she was doing, pulled her focus forward. "A decision about what?" The last time Georgia had made such a declaration, she'd ended up dragging Brooke to a bar and getting more than a little drunk. On the other hand, that was also the night Georgia had met her current boyfriend.

Georgia stuck a glass filled with ice under the soda machine. "We need to do something fun. Just us girls, you know? Get away for a few hours, forget all our problems, talk about our love lives, that sort of thing."

"That sounds like a high school sleepover," Brooke said as she set one filled glass on her tray and then reached for the second.

"Ah, but it'll be better," Georgia insisted as she began filling her own glass. "The next time we have the same day off I'll rent us a boat, and we'll go floating off shore. I love just floating around."

Curious, Brooke asked, "Why not skip the boat rental and just use the main beach?"

Georgia clucked her tongue at Brooke, reaching for a new glass as she said, "Because you can go farther out in a boat, of course!"

Of course, Brooke thought with a mental eye-roll as she secured her second glass on her tray and stepped out of Georgia's way. "I have Tuesday off," she said.

Smiling, Georgia pulled her second glass from beneath the stream. "Great! Then we'll do it Tuesday! We'll pack a lunch and meet in the morning, and make a day of it! Back before the rental place closes, of course."

"Who all are you inviting?" Brooke asked.

Georgia pursed her lips. "Well, I'll probably invite Emma, but I doubt anyone else would want to come anyway. And this is a strictly-girls thing, so no boyfriends, got it?"

With a laugh, Brooke turned toward the dining area and assured her friend, "Relax, he works Tuesday anyway."

As Georgia turned to follow Brooke, she asked, "Will you want me to pick you up? Or do you think you'll have a car by then?"

Brooke swallowed a sigh of frustration. "I'll meet you at the beach. Blake and I are going to the dealership this weekend, but I doubt I'll be able to afford a new car just yet, so I'll ride with him to the beach on Tuesday."

"That'll work, too," Georgia allowed. With barely a pause, as the doors swung shut behind her, Georgia asked, "Hey, when's the new girl supposed to get here again, do you remember?"

Brooke paused for a beat as she tried to re-orient her brain. "Uh, Monday, I think. Why?"

Georgia came up beside her so that she could whisper, "I always get nervous with Earl in the kitchen. Anyway, talk later!" And then she sashayed off to her patiently waiting table.

Brooke shook her head even as she turned toward her own table. It was a sentiment she didn't necessarily disagree with, though she herself was usually more wary with Paula running the kitchen than Earl. *Either way, it'll be nice to get a solid routine going again.*

She was standing before her table, preparing to hand out the drinks, when she finally registered the sudden pit in her stomach. It felt as if someone were boring holes into her back, and she suddenly wanted to throw up. Still, she fought to keep her smile in place as she set down the drinks and pulled out her notepad to take their orders.

"Are you all right, Brooke?" Mrs. Buchannon asked after her order had been jotted down. She was sitting opposite her younger daughter, and both women were looking up at Brooke with concerned frowns.

"Yeah," Clarabelle said, her voice quiet, "you look a little pale."

Brooke swallowed and attempted another smile as she tucked away the notepad. "Oh, I'm fine." She paused, suddenly remembering a conversation she'd had with

Clarabelle once before, and lowered her own voice to ask, "Hey, Clare, have you learned anything more about … that guy?"

Clarabelle's eyes lit up instantly with realization and she slowly shook her head. "No, I haven't. I've only seen him in passing twice since you asked me, and no one I've talked to even knew who I was talking about."

Mrs. Buchannon was looking back and forth between them, before finally settling her gaze on her daughter and asking, "What are we talking about?"

Clarabelle leaned over the table so that she could stage-whisper, "The guy in the expensive shirt that's sitting in the booth behind Brooke."

"It's nothing, really," Brooke quickly insisted. "Just sort of a, um, passing curiosity. Anyway, thanks, Clare. I'll be back with your salads soon." She offered them one more slightly less strained smile and turned to make her exit. But she couldn't stop her eyes from flicking to the side, and she immediately regretted it.

Mystery Man was staring at her blatantly, and for the beat that their gazes met, his eyes narrowed and she could have sworn they sparked.

Best not to test that theory, she decided as she continued to the next table. She pulled her attention forward and did her best to ignore him, eternally grateful that he wasn't sitting at one of her tables.

****

Blake was walking downtown when he saw him—the older man that was somehow related to Brooke's 'Mystery Man'; the man they suspected was responsible for Nate's accident. He was exiting a shoe store less than a block ahead of Blake, and turning in the opposite direction.

Despite having only seen the man once, briefly, Blake was sure it was the same man, just as he'd been sure that the older man Logan had seen was the man who'd glared at him back in February. And he knew he'd never get a better chance to finally get a few answers. They were in the middle of Main Street, and though it wasn't particularly busy, there were plenty of people around. Blake doubted the old man would try anything with so many potential witnesses.

Decision made, he quickly increased his pace and began jogging after the man. He didn't care if a few people gave him odd looks for running down the sidewalk. If he could get even two answers out of the man, it would be worth it.

"Hey!" Blake called when he was close enough.

The man was taller up close than he'd remembered, though not by much. He wore a lightweight jacket, black dress shoes, and overly ironed black slacks. A single plastic bag hung from one hand, and his other hand was tucked away in his pocket. Up close, and from this different angle, Blake could see that the man still had traces of brown in his full head of gray hair.

The man in question stopped walking when Blake called out to him, and after a deliberate pause, he turned in place. He said nothing as he turned to face Blake, meeting Blake's eyes fearlessly. Blake noted, now that he was really looking, the man didn't actually appear as old as he'd first assumed. He bore notable lines across his face, proof of a hard life, but he didn't actually look much older than Blake's own parents. His expression was cold, detached, and his dark eyes betrayed nothing but hatred. His tone was demeaning as he said, "Blake Hawke, I suppose?"

Blake's eyes narrowed. He had honestly expected the man to play dumb. *Good,* he thought. *I wasn't in the mood for that game, anyway.* "And you would be?"

"Busy," the man replied shortly. "You should enjoy your final days, elemental." With a final sneer, he turned to resume walking.

"You don't really think I'm going to let you walk away without answering me, do you?" Blake challenged, taking a small step forward.

The man paused again, now sideways to Blake, and turned his head to glare at him once more. "Are you under the impression that because we're in *public* I'm not willing to strike you down? You fool. My family's entire purpose in life is to eradicate your family from existence. These ignorant human witnesses mean nothing to me."

Opting to ignore the man's blatant superiority complex, Blake said, "My family has done nothing to any of you. And if you really wanted to 'strike me down', you're missing a prime opportunity right now." *Okay, so goading the lightning-throwing enemy is probably stupid,* he reflected after the words had left his mouth. *Too late now. So let's see what he does with it.*

His dark eyes narrowed even more, and his hand curled around the handle of the plastic bag he still held. "I'm going to let you live today," he said in a tone that perfectly matched his expression. "Perhaps you should use the time to educate yourself, you insolent fool."

The man had already turned around, his back once more to Blake, by the time Blake said, "Are you talking about that old feud? The one that supposedly happened *centuries* ago? Because if you are, you need to realize that *my family* had nothing to do with that!"

The older man stopped walking once again, only a few feet away, and almost immediately, Blake could feel the increase in electrical energy swirling in the air around him. He had definitely ticked him off with that one.

"You know nothing," the man spat as he turned back around. He did not step closer, but there was a definite spark in his eyes. "The fact that my ancestors were nearly exterminated before my time does not mean you should be forgiven. Justice will not be achieved while even one elemental breathes!" He took a deep breath, and the crackle in the air receded slightly. His cold, calm edge returned when he opened his eyes again. "Your time is nearly up, Hawke."

Blake said nothing more as the man turned again and walked off. He really had thought the man would hold back, not wanting to risk exposure by using his powers in front of so many people. But he had clearly been wrong. And the surge of electricity in the air had caused Blake to break out in a cold sweat. He knew better than to pursue the man further, at least right in that moment, but he hated that he really hadn't learned anything at all.

He had hoped to at least get a name.

With a sigh, Blake turned and began walking in the opposite direction. As he walked, he reflected on the conversation once more. *Maybe I didn't really learn nothing,* he decided after a minute. *It's good to know that the enemy doesn't care about witnesses—and it's safe to assume they don't care about bystanders. And the way he talked about his family makes me think we're dealing with more than just him and the Mystery Man. But where are they hiding?*

For everything he might have gleaned from the man, he'd developed at least one new question. Still, a little contact was probably a step in the right direction. *And if he was shopping, that probably means he's— they're—staying somewhere local, right?* Darien wasn't that big, especially when you'd lived there your whole life. Blake knew most of the families, at least by name if not by face. It shouldn't be too hard to figure out who their enemy was if they were really living in town, right?

It's something, at least, he finally decided as he rounded the corner to the parking lot where his Mustang waited. *And in the meantime, I should make sure the others know not to try to corner them in public.* It was as much for their own sake as for the sake of everyone else. Their enemy might not care about the people around them, but Blake did, and he knew the rest of his family would feel the same. There was no sense in dragging innocent people into their mess.

The ringing of his phone pulled Blake out of his thoughts even as he unlocked his car. Brooke's obligatorily smiling face, from the picture she'd let him take near the beginning of the semester, greeted him when he looked at the display. Making a mental note to get a new picture, he said, "Hey."

"Hey." There was no underlying trace of discomfort or distress in her voice, and he hoped that meant she hadn't had yet another visit from her Mystery Man. "I'm off early… Are you busy, or do you think you can come get me?"

Lips curving in a smile, Blake angled into his car. "I'm always free for you. Be there in a few minutes."

As he drove, Blake called his mother and told her about his conversation with their enemy. "We definitely shouldn't approach them in public," he repeated when he was done. "He obviously didn't care about bystanders." Blake worried about some of his brothers in this regard. Mostly Dean, but both Dean and Nate were prone to impulse control issues. And then there was Dean's temper to consider.

Lillian, however, didn't seem to care so much for his choice of emphasis. "Blake, I'm surprised you would take such a risk. You could have been killed!" The anger in her voice was nearly overridden by the fear. And that combination tugged guiltily at his heart.

"I'm sorry, Mom," he said. "Really. I just … I thought it seemed like a safe risk. We need answers we're not getting from Uncle Nicholas." Or at least *he* wasn't. He'd spoken to Nicholas twice now—the second time asking his uncle to email over the documents he'd dug up—but neither call had yielded useful results. Although he hadn't finished going over the documents yet.

"Nicholas is telling us what he knows," Lillian said. "More importantly, *answers* to *questions* are not worth your life. I don't want you doing something so reckless again."

"Mom—"

"Promise," Lillian interrupted.

Blake released a breath as he pulled the car into a parking spot at the diner. He didn't want Brooke learning about his afternoon excitement by overhearing his conversation with his mother. "I promise."

"Good," Lillian said as Brooke stepped out of the diner. "I'll pass along the warning to your brothers."

Chapter Twenty-Three

Brooke shuffled into the diner bright and early Sunday morning, gathering with the rest of her coworkers in the dining area. She had been wrong, it turned out, about the day of their new cook's arrival, and Earl and Paula wanted all of their best (or at least most reliable) workers on shift that day to help break her in.

Georgia navigated her way to Brooke's side as Brooke came to a stop in the small crowd and, voice hushed, asked, "So, how was the car hunt?"

The day before Blake, Brooke, and Angela—riding along in order to decide what kind of car she wanted for her upcoming birthday—had gone into the next town over and spent several hours looking at vehicles. There were three dealerships in that town, it turned out, and they had hit each one. Angela had gushed over several options—all of which were out of Brooke's price-range.

In the end, Brooke had written down a few types and their associated prices, but she had not settled on any car in particular. Or, more accurately, the one she wanted was a little too much, and she was still trying to talk herself out of it.

Voice equally hushed, Brooke replied, "Unsuccessful."

Earl chose that moment to step through the door, followed immediately by a young woman dressed in a crisp chef's coat. The murmured conversations fell silent as they watched, everyone automatically assessing their newest addition.

The woman looked to be in her early twenties, and seemed to be several inches taller than Brooke. She had a lot of dark hair that was more auburn than brown rolled up into a messy bun on her head and bright, observant green eyes. The smile curving her lips was slow, careful, and somewhat awkward as she watched everyone watch her.

"Okay, okay," Paula said loudly, earning everyone's attention. Earl and the new girl moved to stand with her, in front of the doors that led to the back room, but stayed silent. "Thank you all for coming in a little early. Now, you've figured this out, I'm sure, but I'd like you all to meet Madison Price. She's a permanent addition to our staff, so I expect each of you to be nice. And as everyone's going to be feeling each other out today, I want everyone on their best behavior."

She paused, her gaze lingering on the gathered employees long enough for her to words to hit home, before turning a smile to Madison and saying, "Madison, meet your new family. I promise, by the day's end, you'll wonder why this was ever awkward to begin with. Is there anything you'd like to say?"

Madison shifted her attention from Paula, back to the group in front of her, and lifted one arm in a small wave. "Um, hi, everyone. I promise I know how to cook."

A few muted chuckles drifted forward, Madison's arm fell back to her side, and Paula took over once again. "All right, all right. Let's get everything set up and get those doors open, shall we?"

Just like that, the tension fled and the group began dispersing. Earl and the sous chefs took Madison into the kitchen, and Brooke, Georgia, and the other waiter on duty for the morning all made their way to the back.

As Georgia grabbed her apron, she said, "I kind of thought she'd be more my age."

Brooke shrugged. "I hadn't really thought about it at all, to tell you the truth."

Their coworker agreed with a nod, and the room fell silent again until he'd slipped through the door.

As soon as the door was properly closed again, Georgia asked, "What did you mean 'unsuccessful'? You didn't find *anything* you liked?"

Brooke sighed, not at all surprised by her friend's lack of satisfaction with her earlier answer. "No, I mean I didn't find anything I was willing to buy on the spot. It's hard justifying all that money in one place right now, since I still have so many things to try to replace."

"But a car is important," Georgia insisted. "Especially since you've got a roof over your head."

Tucking her notepad into her apron pocket, Brooke said, "I don't want Blake to think I'm taking advantage of his hospitality. We're dating, not married. I promised I would be out as soon as I could find a place."

Georgia's hand hovered over her hair, which she was adjusting unnecessarily. "What, are you trying to tell me you're actually looking around? I thought for sure you were just waiting for a ring."

Well, that'd be nice, her mind whispered. Ignoring that voice, Brooke hedged, "Um, well … yes and no. I mean, *no*, I'm not just waiting for a ring. But the actual apartment search hasn't really been my focus yet…" Saying it out loud suddenly made her feel guilty.

When she'd first moved in with Blake, she'd sworn to find another place as soon as possible. And though he'd told her not to pressure herself, she had honestly intended to do as she'd said. It was just that she'd gotten a little distracted with everything *else* that she needed, and everything else that was going on in general.

Oh God, what if he's irritated that I'm not really looking yet? She sincerely hoped that wasn't the case. And he certainly didn't seem at all bothered. In fact, he'd never once even mentioned her non-existent house hunt. *I don't think he'd stay so silent about it if he was bothered... Surely he'd at least mention it?*

"Well," Georgia began, oblivious to her friend's thoughts, "I think you shouldn't worry so much about finding a new place. I've got a sense for these things, you know."

Brooke pulled herself back to the moment and rolled her eyes. "Right." Georgia was as bad as Paula when it came to her matchmaking desires. Blake and Brooke were living together—circumstances be damned. In Georgia's mind they were probably soul mates. And the hopeless romantic living inside Brooke couldn't help but hope her friend was right.

As the duo turned toward the door, Georgia suddenly said, "Oh! You haven't forgotten about Tuesday, right?"

"Of course not," Brooke assured her. "I even already told Blake he'll have to live without me for a few hours."

"Good, because I called the rental place yesterday and reserved our boat," Georgia declared. "It'll just be the two of us, though. Emma can't come."

"That's too bad," Brooke replied with a brief frown.

Georgia shrugged as they neared the front of the diner. "Yeah, but it's her loss!"

Brooke laughed and nodded. "Very true. She'll just have to make sure to come with us the next time."

When they reached the front, where Shelly was setting up, they fell quiet again. The diner would open in the next handful of minutes, and if the small line out front was any indication, it was going to be a busy day.

****

Blake was smiling when Brooke walked through the door after Georgia had dropped her off later that afternoon. "How was work?" he asked, rising from his stretched out position on the couch to greet her.

Brooke let her purse land on the floor beside the couch as he wrapped his arms loosely around her and covered her lips with his in a sweet, chaste kiss. When he pulled back, she sighed. "You'd think Earl put an announcement in the paper for Madison's first day. *Your parents* even came in. I've *never* seen them there!"

Blake stepped back, one eyebrow lifted in surprise. "My parents really don't eat out that much. Maybe Earl handed out flyers or something."

Rolling her eyes, Brooke replied, "I doubt it. But we were *so* busy." She took a deep breath and narrowed her eyes suspiciously. "And what were you smiling about, anyway? Did you get to come home early?"

"I've only been home for an hour," Blake promised, holding up one hand as if he were swearing an oath. "But there is something I wanted to talk about."

It was Brooke's turn to lift an eyebrow. "Talk about what?"

Gesturing to the couch as he spoke, Blake said, "Well, remember how you told your parents you refused to let them buy you a new car?"

Immediately wary—it would be just like her family to ignore her wishes on something like that— Brooke lowered herself to the couch beside him as she said, "Yes…"

"I had this thought," Blake began, watching her carefully. "And in fact, I might have only gotten off the phone a few minutes ago." At Brooke's suspicious look, he pushed ahead. "I know how much you wanted that Accord, and I know you fully intend to talk yourself out of it. But since I—*we*—respect that you don't want to be some sort of burden on anyone, I was thinking: what if you put up the down-payment, like you wanted, and then your family and I *split* the difference? You can own it outright that way, and no one's out some outrageous, crippling, sum of money."

"Absolutely not! We're still talking *thousands* of dollars!" Brooke exclaimed without hesitation. "I can't, and won't, ask anyone to put up that kind of money for me. I don't know when I'd be able to pay it back."

Blake shook his head, obviously not at all surprised by her argument. Nor should he have been, as he'd heard most of it from her side of a phone conversation with her family on Friday. "We're offering, Brooke. That's different than you asking. And it'd be a gift, not a loan."

"No," Brooke insisted firmly. "I know you've got enough money, and I know my parents aren't poor, but I don't want anyone spending that kind of money on me. It wouldn't be right."

Frowning now, Blake asked, "How would it not be right? If we can afford it, then I don't see the problem."

"Because *I* can't afford it!" Brooke reiterated stubbornly. "I still only have half a wardrobe!" Tears suddenly clouded her eyes as the reality of her words hit her. *What was I thinking, assuming I could buy a car?*

Her bank account was already dangerously low from the few hundred dollars she'd spent on clothing and the various bills she still had to pay because she hadn't been bright enough to have had renter's insurance. It was near enough to the end of the semester that she was having to think about next semester's classes, and she would need money for those classes. A single semester's worth of tuition and books was more than she could realistically afford at the moment. Which meant she might have to skip a semester entirely. And soon enough she really would have to think about finding a new apartment, and then she'd have to budget for rent, too.

It was going to be a long time before she was properly back on her feet.

Releasing a heavy, defeated sigh, Brooke let her gaze land on the carpet and said, "Forget about it, please. It doesn't matter, anyway; I can't afford a car right now." *Oh God,* she thought as she realized she was going to cry. She doubted she could make it to the bathroom before the tears slipped free.

Before she could move, Blake reached out and pulled her into him. She tensed and braced a hand on his chest but didn't struggle to pull away. Quietly, Blake said, "I'm sorry, Brooke. I was trying to help, not upset you. The last thing I want to do is upset you."

Her hand curled, fist clenching the fabric beneath her palm, and Brooke let her head collapse against his shoulder. She still struggled to hold back her tears, but she relaxed into his embrace. A part of her felt bad for making him feel guilty. She *knew* he'd only been trying to help. But at the moment that part of her was small, and easily buried, as she couldn't focus past the reality of her situation.

Blake rubbed his hands lightly over her back and let his cheek rest against her head. He said nothing as he held her, and she offered nothing in return as she breathed deeply, fighting for control of her emotions.

****

"Brooke," Blake began on Monday night as he walked into the kitchen, where she was sifting through the fridge. She wasn't going to like what he had to say, but it needed to be said.

Brooke paused, her hand extended toward a row of bottled tea, and slowly stood up. It was obvious, as she eased the door shut, that she could sense his hesitation. She turned, her formerly raised hand landing on her hip, and asked, "Yeah?" Her tone was calm, non-accusatory, but her eyes were suspicious.

Blake swallowed and forcibly kept his arms at his sides. The last thing he needed was to send the wrong signal with his body language. "I've been thinking again about this boat thing you've got planned with Georgia tomorrow."

One slim eyebrow lifted curiously, but Brooke said nothing.

Biting the proverbial bullet, Blake said evenly, "I don't think you should go."

Both of her eyebrows rose then, and she shifted her weight. "And why not?" There was an undeniable edge to her tone.

"It's dangerous," Blake explained, hoping she would actually hear what he was saying. "I know you want to go, but now's a bad time to be isolating yourself like that. It's been over a week since they've made a real move. There's no way they'd ignore an opportunity like that."

"I'm not cancelling on Georgia over a hunch," Brooke argued stubbornly. "When they've come after me before, I was always alone. And besides, you'll be on lifeguard duty the entire time, so you'll be practically right there."

Blake's jaw clenched for a moment, but he forced himself to remain calm. She wasn't going to even consider his words if he got too pushy or lost his temper. "We already know they're willing to throw potential witnesses out the window, and I won't be able to see you from my tower. I won't have any idea what's going on out there."

Crossing her arms over her chest, Brooke replied, "But I think you'll see if our boat is followed out of the dock, and unless they follow us in their own boat, we'll be *fine*. I'm *not* cancelling."

"Brooke," Blake began again, more than willing to plead with her on the subject. "Please listen to me. It's *not safe* right now to be doing something like that. Not for any of us. You have to reschedule."

Brooke's eyes widened for a minute. She released a heavy breath and said, "We're meeting at the beach tomorrow morning. It's a little too late to cancel, and I'm not making Georgia eat the expense for no reason. You're being paranoid." She uncrossed her arms and turned toward the living room, but after taking a few steps, she paused. "And for the record, *I* decide what I do and don't *have* to do."

Cursing his choice of words, Blake followed after her, saying, "You know I didn't mean it like that. And you of all people should know I'm not just being paranoid. These people will take whatever advantage they can get!"

Brooke spun to face him, pointing her index finger in his direction as she argued, "Then why haven't they burnt down the diner during one of my shifts? I'm there all the time, it's not hard to figure out! And you said yourself they don't care about bystanders or witnesses." She dragged in a breath, dropped her arm to her side, and said firmly, "I refuse to let these bastards ruin my entire life. They'll make their move or they won't, and until that happens, I will be able to say 'at least I didn't cower inside this whole time'." But there was a flicker of hesitation in her eyes now, like she was starting to doubt her own argument.

"No one's asking you to cower, Brooke," Blake tried, fearing he'd already lost the argument. He hadn't expected her to react quite so angrily. He opened his mouth to say more, but Brooke beat him to it.

"And now that I'm thinking about it," Brooke said, "if you're so worried about them taking advantage of us, why have they never come after you when you're working? That'd be just as easy as coming after me, only you're more their target than I am, so really you'd *still* be the bigger target."

All good questions, Blake admitted silently. "I don't know the answers to those questions, Brooke," he said carefully. "I just know that … I have a bad feeling about Tuesday, all right?"

Brooke locked her jaw tight as she swallowed her initial response. Seconds ticked by before she finally took a deep breath. "I'm sorry. I shouldn't have gotten so upset. And I appreciate your concern, I really do. I'm not trying to worry you. But I'm also not cancelling on Georgia. If I had thought of it that way before she'd booked the boat, maybe I would have, but I didn't. I'll keep my eyes open for anything suspicious, okay? That's all I can promise."

Blake ground his teeth for a moment, not at all satisfied with her answer. But, all the same, he knew it was the best he was going to get. He could see her resolution in her eyes. So, finally, he nodded and said, "Fine. I don't like it, but short of tying you up and locking you in my parents' basement, I can't stop you. Just, *please*, be careful."

Brooke allowed the corners of her lips to tip up. "I will."

****

They were standing behind Blake's Mustang the following morning, Blake dressed for work in his lifeguard-red swim trunks, and Brooke dressed for fun in a loose white t-shirt and denim Capri's over her bikini.

Blake's eyes swept over the parking lot—which was mostly empty—as he said, "Remember—"

Brooke reached up and framed his face, cutting him off as she leaned up and pressed her lips to his. His hands found the exposed skin between her short shirt and her Capri's and settled over her sides. Their tongues met and dueled for an instant, sliding along the other sensuously before she pulled away and smiled up at him. "I'll be careful," she promised quietly.

Blake opened his mouth to respond, but a voice coming from behind him interrupted their moment, calling, "No matter how cute you two are, the 'no boyfriends allowed' rule still applies!"

The couple turned to face Georgia as she approached, Blake's nearest hand sliding around to the small of Brooke's back as he lifted his other hand to wave. "I'm wondering if I should be concerned," Blake said with a grin. "You're awfully insistent on that rule."

With a laugh, Georgia replied, "We're hoping to pick up a couple of mermen, and of course we can't do that with other types of men around!"

Brooke laughed, cutting a sideways glance up to her boyfriend. He met her gaze with a silently laughing expression of his own.

Turning her eyes forward again as Georgia came to a stop in front of them, Brooke said, "Good morning to you, too, Georgia."

"That was implied," Georgia assured them with a grin. She turned her attention back to Blake. "And not that it isn't great to see you, but your girlfriend and I have a very important date to keep. So I need to steal her now."

Chuckling, Blake turned toward Brooke one more time and pressed his lips to her forehead. When he pulled back, slowly retrieving his hand as well, he said softly, "Have fun."

Brooke smiled. "We will. And I'll see you when we get back."

Their gazes held a moment longer, his eyes silently reminding her of the need for her to be careful. She offered him another smile, this one promising to do exactly that, and a heartbeat later, Georgia had hooked her arm around Brooke's elbow and begun walking.

"We're off to talk about you behind your back! But I'll return her in one piece, promise!" Georgia called without looking back.

Brooke laughed, waving over her shoulder at Blake as she followed the eager, freshly dyed redhead.

Chapter Twenty-Four

"This is your boat," the rental-place employee stated as they approached the boat farthest out on the dock. It was a simple speedboat, like all of the other rental options, with a dark-green-and-ivory paint scheme. He turned and held the keys out for Georgia to take. "You said you don't need a driver?"

Georgia accepted the keys as she shook her head. "Oh, no. I rent boats all the time. I know what I'm doing."

He nodded again and turned to head back towards the shop. "Emergency frequencies are taped to the dash beside the radio. Otherwise, the boat's due back by four o'clock. Enjoy your trip."

Brooke's gaze followed him for a minute before she looked back to Georgia. "You *do* know what you're doing, right?"

Georgia scoffed and put loosely fisted hands on her hips. "Of course I do. I really do rent boats from this place a lot. I've been coming here since I was a kid."

"Okay, then," Brooke replied, accepting her answer. It was understandable, after all. She would certainly have been renting boats for years had she grown up near any large body of water.

"Okay," Georgia declared, turning and putting her back to the boat. "My car's in the rental lot, so I left the ice chest with the food and everything in it while I waited for you. All we have to do is go get it, bring it back, and we're good to go!"

True excitement began bubbling up inside Brooke as her gaze flicked back to the boat. *We're really getting to do this,* her mind whispered. She hadn't allowed herself to feel overly excited about it before, because in the back of her mind she'd believed that something would come up last-minute to make her cancel. And she was glad she'd been wrong. She really felt like she needed a few hours of strict girl-time.

Georgia was two full feet ahead of her as they made their way back down the dock, toward the small parking lot that was designated specifically for boat-renters. "When we get out there," she called over her shoulder as her feet landed in sand, "we're going to talk about you and Blake."

"Don't we do that practically every day?" Brooke asked with a laugh as she stepped off the dock after her.

"Yeah," Georgia allowed, "but we only get little snippets of conversation at work. And I really don't see you very often outside of work. This will give us a good opportunity to really talk! I need details, you know!"

Brooke laughed again even as she countered, "Do I get details about you?"

Georgia turned to throw a deliberate wink back at Brooke over her shoulder as she approached a large rock formation. "Absolutely! In fact, I intend—"

She was cut off as a fist came flying out from behind the rocks, catching her straight in the cheek and sending her head spinning around as far as it would allow. Georgia crumbled, crashing unceremoniously to the ground.

"Georgia!" Brooke cried in horrified shock as she watched. She instinctively sprinted forward in an effort to catch her fallen friend, but she didn't make it in time. "Georgia!" she called again as she dropped to her knees beside her friend, on the other side of the unconscious woman from the rocks.

Brooke's head snapped up again as she registered the sound of movement, and she found herself staring into the dark eyes of the Mystery Man. *Idiot!* Brooke berated herself as a dozen different reactions tore through her. *You should have cancelled!* But she hadn't, and now Georgia had gotten hurt.

Mystery Man altered course, clearly intending to walk around the unconscious redhead.

"Stay back!" Brooke demanded automatically, her hands hovering over Georgia's nearest shoulder. Her eyes staying locked on her enemy.

The man scowled at her as if he were irritated, but his feet paused anyway. And then he opened his mouth, addressing her for the second time. "Brooke Munroe, come with me."

"Not a chance," Brooke retorted, not moving. "You stay away from me, or I'll scream. The shop isn't that far behind us, they'll hear me."

His scowl turned into a sneer. "And if they come to investigate, they'll die. Alongside your friend. Or you could cooperate."

"What do you want with me?" Brooke asked, immediately switching to another topic. If he really didn't care how many people got dragged into this situation, then it was best to avoid bringing them in.

His eyes narrowed, and his feet started forward again. "You're a means to an end, nothing more."

"I can't do anything for you," Brooke insisted as he slowly, casually, walked around Georgia's head. *Too close,* her mind warned her. Reluctantly, Brooke shifted and scrambled backwards, away from him. When she was far enough, she pushed back to her feet, all the while keeping her eyes on him.

"You can," Mystery Man argued, his tone indifferent, "indirectly."

"Whatever it is that you're planning," Brooke began, taking a step backwards as he continued towards her, "it'll never work. Even if you kill me, they'll figure you out and stop you. You and that other guy."

The man's lips curved up in a faint, dark smirk. "Your threats might sound a bit more cultured if you actually had the information necessary to issue them."

"Yeah, well, I'm sorry," Brooke snapped, taking another step backwards. "You haven't exactly introduced yourselves. And by the way, was it you or him who burned down my apartment?"

A flicker of pride lit up his eyes for an instant, and the man replied, "That was Father. But it was me who attacked you before." He continued forward as he spoke, his pace ever casual, as if he had all the time in the world.

So the old guy's his father? It wasn't exactly a revelation, but even a confirmation of their suspicions was something to be grateful for. Or it would be, as soon as she was able to feel anything beyond fear. At the moment, all she could feel was the cold, unshakeable grip of terror around her heart and the squeezing grasp of panic on her lungs. She could barely swallow past the lump in her throat.

Without thinking, Brooke said, "So cowardice runs in your family, then? You wait to strike until you're covered by shadows and hidden by rocks. Tell me, do you do it because you know you and Daddy Dearest wouldn't last ten seconds against the Hawke family in a fair fight?"

His jaw tensed and his eyes darkened even more as an expression that could only be described as fury settled on his face. "Stupid woman," he snarled. "You know nothing of what you speak." As he spoke, his pace increased.

Brooke took two stumbled steps backwards, and her heel slammed into unforgiving rock before she could take a third. Her back met with the same rock before she'd even registered it. Her eyes widened when she realized that she'd let him back her into the same rock formation he'd hidden behind a minute ago. And she saw the moment he realized that she was well and truly trapped.

"You'll never get away with this," Brooke said. She cringed inwardly at the desperation in her voice.

"You're beginning to repeat yourself," Mystery Man declared as he stepped up to her. "Now, will you come willingly, or do I have to take you by force?"

Stalling blatantly, Brooke asked, "Come where?"

Without turning or looking away, the man swept his arm toward the dock. "To your rented boat, of course."

Brooke's eyes widened as a thousand scenarios raced through her head. She couldn't imagine why he'd want to isolate her in a boat on the Pacific Ocean. But, whatever his reason, she knew it wasn't one she'd like.

Only one choice, then, she decided as every internal organ she possessed clenched and swirled inside of her. Chances were good it wouldn't work, but what other choice did she have? Dragging in a deep breath, Brooke said, "Sorry, I get seasick." And then she threw herself forward, angled to shove him aside. She thrust her feet forward even as she stumbled, knowing she had only seconds to get as far away as possible.

One of the Mystery Man's hands shot out and grabbed on to her t-shirt, yanking her backwards. But he wasn't satisfied with simply stopping her, so he shifted his pull and tossed her towards the rock.

Brooke collided with the tall rock formation, barely managing to throw her arm up in time to protect her head. The rock tore into the flesh on her arm, and a sharp stinging sensation pierced through her. She cried out from the impact, too stunned to move right away.

That second was all her opponent needed to wrap his hand around her throat and hold her in place. His touch was scorching, and Brooke reflexively tried to recoil from him, but her head was pressed up against solid rock. There was nowhere she could go.

"Your efforts are in vain," Mystery Man snarled. His eyes crackled again as he glared at her. "You will die this day, in the name of vengeance—in the name of justice."

Brooke leveled her best glare at him and spat, "Your 'justice' is pretty screwed up, asshole."

"You say that only because of your unfortunate fate," he returned, his voice dark but calm once more.

"I won't go with you," Brooke reiterated. "And you'll look pretty suspicious dragging an unconscious woman to the boat dock."

His grip on her throat tightened, and the faintest little jolt of electricity surged through her. "I'll risk it," he replied plainly.

Brooke winced, trying and failing to suck in a deep breath as her body attempted to recover from the shock.

"First things first, though," Mystery Man declared even as his other hand reached forward. He calmly dipped his hand into Brooke's right pocket, ignoring her as she attempted to struggle against him, and extracted her phone. "This has to go."

As he spoke, his fingers sparked and the phone lit up, but an instant later, it made a strange, gurgled beeping sound and the lights snapped off. Smoke immediately began wafting off of it.

Dropping the phone carelessly to their feet, he returned his attention to Brooke and added, "Good night, Ms. Munroe."

His grip on her throat tightened again, and she knew he was trying to knock her out. And considering that she couldn't get a proper breath, he would probably succeed. But she wasn't willing to stand there limply and wait for it.

With one hand latched on to his, ignoring the immediate burning, she tried to loosen his grip on her throat. She lifted her other—injured—arm and shoved at him with all of the strength she could muster. Pain immediately shot through her, not because of the electricity crackling all around him, but because of her still-bleeding arm, but she did her best to push past it. *It won't matter if I fail,* she told herself, praying that motivation would be enough.

"Let ... go!" she gasped as she struggled. She braced one foot against the rock, ignoring the way the rough texture pushed against her sandal, and hoped the extra leverage would get him off of her.

"Your struggle is useless," he declared. He wasn't budging, and his hold on her throat wasn't lessening. "You are weak, and injured."

"Who," Brooke gasped on a shallow intake of breath even as her arm slackened against him. She was losing her strength, and her awareness. Still, she fought to keep herself conscious as she breathlessly demanded, "Who ... are ... you?"

The Mystery Man cocked an eyebrow at her nearly inaudible inquiry. As Brooke's eyes began to droop, her arms falling limply to her sides and her foot sliding awkwardly back to the sand, he said, "You may call me Jacob. I suppose you have earned that much."

Jacob... The name echoed through her mind in a haze, each syllable dragging as though she could barely remember how to pronounce it. His name was Jacob.

****

Blake was restless as he shifted again in his chair. He'd seen what he could only assume was Brooke and Georgia's boat heading off a couple of minutes prior, and had quickly lost all sight of it. In theory, she would be perfectly safe so far from shore. But something was still not sitting well with him.

Maybe I should call home and check on everyone else? Maybe this feeling has nothing to do with me or Brooke? It was possible, he supposed. And it was just as possible that the feeling was entirely in his head.

He was jerked from his musing as his phone went off, alerting him to an incoming text message. Sitting properly forward, he snatched the device off the small table that also held an unopened bottle of water. He frowned as Georgia's name appeared on his screen and quickly opened the message.

CAN'T TALK. BOAT DOCK. NOW.

Knowing—whether Georgia had actually been the one to send the text or not—that message couldn't mean anything good, Blake immediately moved to the ladder and dropped to the beach below his perch. He didn't worry about disturbing the few people who had already come out to enjoy the late morning, but he did wave to his coworker as he passed the tower. Whatever was going on, he didn't want the man to follow him.

As he ran, he sent a text of his own, letting Georgia—or whoever might have her phone—know he was one his way.

The swimming section of the beach was separated from the boat-dock section by a chest-high outcropping of rocks that trailed up the sand, almost reaching the parking lot. On the other side, they stretched out to sea far enough that the jagged rocks would provide the only available footing. However, there was a small area where the rocks didn't meet, a fair distance up the shore. It wasn't wide enough for an adult to run through, but if he slowed to a cautionary pace and turned sideways, he could fit.

He aimed for that break in the rock, knowing he was being watched by at least one of the civilians on the beach. When he reached it, he slowed and ducked behind the rock. The instant he was out of their sight, he liquefied, using his control of the water to drag his trunks along with him. It was risky, he knew, to come out as a puddle on the other side—but it was faster.

When he reached the other side he saw no one, at least from his limited vantage point, and so he quickly pulled himself back together. As soon as his body was solid, he sprinted toward the docks. His eyes immediately landed on the familiar redheaded figure of Brooke's best friend.

Georgia was leaning against the railing beside the steps that led to the dock, her shoulders shaking. Her back was turned to Blake as he ran up, but she didn't startle when he spoke.

"Where's Brooke?" Blake asked as soon as he was standing beside Georgia. It was obvious, though her face was aimed away from him, that she was crying. And any other day he would have taken a moment to ask her why—though he already suspected he knew the answer—but right now he was more concerned with why Brooke wasn't there with her.

Georgia sucked in a ragged breath and turned to face him.

Blake's eyes widened as he saw the dark bruise already mostly formed on the side of her face. Someone, or something, had hit her—and hit her hard. The eye above her bruised cheek was swollen partially shut. "What happened?" he asked, doing his best to take the edge out of his voice.

Sniffling, and cringing faintly, Georgia held out her smartphone without making an effort to speak. It didn't take a genius to figure out why, what with her already bruising cheek.

Blake took the phone, directing his attention to the screen, and realized that Georgia had typed out the story. She prefaced it by admitting that she was unconscious for most of it, having been blindsided by a man in shadow. But when she'd woken up, and been able to orient herself, she'd seen a male figure stepping into their rented boat, with Brooke in his arms. She hadn't gotten a good look at him, and by the time she'd pushed herself to her feet the boat was already speeding away, but she was sure she knew who he was.

... *MYSTERY MAN.*

Dread settled like a lead weight in Blake's stomach as he read the very words he'd been thinking. And knowing he'd been right about the danger of their trip didn't make him feel well at all.

Clenching his teeth, Blake handed the phone back to Georgia and said, "Thank you." He paused, pulling his own phone from his trunks pocket, and held it out to her before he added, "I need you to trust me now. Text my brother, Logan, and tell him that Brooke's been taken by the Mystery Man and that I've gone to get her back. Tell him to come meet you here. And please, don't call the police. There isn't much they can do right now."

Georgia had been nodding with each request, up until the last one. Confusion clouded her good eye, and her question was obvious.

"Logan, or someone he brings with him, can explain everything," Blake assured her even as he moved to the steps. "I have to go before they get farther away. *Please,* trust me." He didn't wait for her nod of confirmation before he turned and began sprinting down the wooden dock. And when he reached the end, he dove headfirst into the water without hesitation.

The moment Blake touched the water he shot forth in the direction he'd seen the boat go earlier. In the water, there was nothing that could touch him; he could swim faster than any speedboat. He knew he could catch them. He only hoped he wasn't too late.

Chapter Twenty-Five

"Are you awake?"

The voice that called to her was male, but not one she immediately recognized. Her mind was still too hazy to really process anything. But she knew, somehow, that she need to be awake, and she willed herself to open her eyes.

Brooke moaned and moved her arm, but her whole body winced with the motion, and she squeezed her eyes tightly shut.

"It is a shame," the voice declared. He reached out and grasped her upper arm. "You could have lived if you had only had the good sense to keep your distance from the Hawkes."

Mystery Man! The moment those words slipped across her mind, Brooke was awake, but her body still screamed at her every breath. She pried her eyes open anyway, finding herself unpleasantly close to his cold eyes. *Jacob.*

"Let ... go ..." she demanded weakly. Her eyes blinked rapidly as she forced them to stay open, but the glare she attempted to level at him was in vain as he tightened his hold and hauled her up from the bench seat. He held her upright almost entirely, as she was still too groggy to properly get her feet beneath her.

But the realization that the ground beneath her feet was wobbling and rolling, as if it weren't stable at all, had her eyes opening wide. And she realized that they were in the boat. *No ...*

"Why," she gasped, still struggling to regulate her breathing. Though now she suspected it was more because of the renewed terror that was squeezing her lungs. "Why did you take me out here?"

"To make a point," Jacob replied, stepping toward the bench seat he'd just hauled her off of. "You involved yourself with the first-born, the water elemental." He paused and looked back at her, his eyes boring into hers. "What better way for you to die, then, but by drowning?"

Brooke swallowed heavily as she realized his point. Disbelief numbed her aching body as she realized she had lost. She was too weak to fight and beat him. And she was too far from shore to make it back alive.

Another dark smirk curved his lips. "Unless, of course, the sharks get you first. You are still bleeding, after all."

Sharks…? Brooke's mind whispered, another wave of fear sweeping over her. She couldn't decide which would be worse—death by drowning, or being mauled to death by hungry sharks.

"I hope you've made your peace," Jacob stated plainly as he quite suddenly shifted and threw his weight forward, toward the rim of the boat.

When he moved, still holding her arm, he threw Brooke sharply to the side. She wasn't expecting the move; wobbly as she was on her feet at that moment, she toppled into the ledge and rolled right over. As soon as the rest of her body was over, he released her arm, letting her free-fall.

Brooke cried out as she flew forward, colliding roughly with the hard edge of the boat, before her momentum carried her the rest of the way over. Her mouth was still open, not quite screaming, when she crashed into the water.

The waves, and her terrible angle, slammed her solidly against the side of the boat even as she choked and gasped, trying to spit out the water she'd swallowed. But when her head collided with the boat a second time, everything went dark.

****

Blake could feel the boat now, resting in the water just ahead of him. And as soon as he registered that realization, he could see it, too. But almost immediately the boat turned back on, as if the Mystery Man knew he was there.

Blake paused in the water, preparing to stall the boat—he couldn't simply flip it if Brooke was on board—when he registered a sight that made his blood run cold.

Brooke was sinking, her body limp and her mouth partially open, several feet beneath the boat. And a slim trail of blood was floating up, off her arm.

He didn't need to think about his decision as he swam quickly forward again. At that point, he didn't particularly care if the boat—and its driver—got away. Brooke's life was more important.

Blake was beneath her in an instant, one strong arm curving around her and halting her descent. Simultaneously, he stopped the flow of the water from continuing to fill her lungs and, with a little focus, he carefully pulled out the water she'd already swallowed. Before she could choke and gasp for air she wouldn't find, he leaned forward and covered her lips solidly with his.

When she gasped, as he'd known she would, he breathed air into her, holding her lips firmly over his. He was suddenly glad he'd taken a deep breath before he'd hit the water.

Brooke, undoubtedly confused and aching, struggled when she realized someone was holding her. But then she seemed to realize what was happening—or at least who was holding her—and she relaxed into his touch.

Blake pulled away when she stopped fighting him, placing a finger over her lips to remind her to keep her mouth closed. She had barely nodded when he shifted his focus back to their surroundings. A single kick of his feet sent them rocketing up, and within seconds, they were above the surface once more.

Immediately, Brooke opened her mouth and sucked in ragged, gasping breaths.

"Where…?" she gasped, looking around.

"Shh," Blake said gently. "Just breathe. We'll be fine." Even as he spoke, he felt the water behind and beneath them slide over something large and moving in, but he bit back the curse. He didn't want to worry her over something he could handle.

Brooke let her head land in the crook of his neck as she focused on her breathing. But as she lowered her head, she must have seen something move in the water behind them. Her voice weak, but no longer choked, she said, "Blake!"

"It's fine," Blake said calmly. He easily redirected the water around them to swirl in a tight, controlled whirlpool, effectively shielding them from the first lunge of the approaching shark. As the hungry beast recoiled, preparing for a second attempt, Blake shot the swirling water toward it, forcing it back.

"How's your breathing?" he asked gently.

"Better," Brooke admitted.

Before she could ask any questions, and before the shark came in for a third strike, Blake said, "Keep your head on my shoulder, okay? And hold on to me if you can."

Brooke nodded and shifted, pulling her injured arm from the water and wrapping it around his shoulders as best she could.

Blake smiled faintly and angled their bodies forward without submerging them entirely. And then they were off, speeding toward shore.

He knew it was entirely possible that they would catch up with their enemy, but he wasn't concerned. Now that he knew Brooke wasn't on board, he wouldn't feel any qualms about sinking the boat with the Mystery Man in it.

His priority, however, was getting Brooke safely on dry land. And he really hoped Georgia had done as he'd asked and called his brother.

As they glided through the water, Blake kept his eyes peeled for their enemy, but even as they began approaching the dock, he saw no sign of the boat. *He must have docked somewhere else,* Blake realized. It wasn't overly surprising. Their enemies had been incredibly careful so far, and logically it would be too risky to return with the stolen rental boat and without the kidnapped woman.

His suspicions were confirmed when they got a little closer to the dock. One rental boat was still missing, just as there had been when he'd leapt off that very dock a short while before.

Blake automatically slowed their pace when they were close enough, moving one arm and kicking his feet a bit more than necessary, as if he were swimming normally. He didn't want to assume there wouldn't be a few too many witnesses.

Brooke lifted her head a bit when she realized they'd slowed down, but she kept her arm tightly around his shoulders. "Are we back?" she asked, her voice still softer than usual. She was still hurting.

"Just about," Blake assured her quietly. He relaxed when the only figures to run up to the end of the dock were Nate, Logan, and Christopher. Their speed increased marginally, quickly closing the gap between them and the dock, and Blake said, "Take Brooke."

Nate knelt down and held out his arms. "I've got her," he promised even as the air around them swirled and began gently curling around Brooke.

"It's okay," Blake said, aiming a reassuring smile to her. "He won't drop you."

Brooke slowly nodded and released his shoulders. Almost immediately, she was pulled up in a controlled vortex, before the air began carrying her towards the trio on the dock.

The swirling air gently lowered Brooke into Logan's arms, and it wasn't until she was settled that she gasped, "Georgia! Where's Georgia?"

"She's fine," Christopher assured her quickly as he and Nate helped pull Blake out of the water. "Dean and Angela are with her. Angela just finished healing her."

As Blake pushed to his feet, he asked, "You got Ange out of class already?"

"Of course we did," Christopher replied. "It's a legitimate family emergency, after all."

Logan stepped up to Blake, and Blake scooped Brooke back into his arms carefully.

"Come on," Christopher said, gesturing toward the beach. "Angela's waiting to heal Brooke." He paused, his concerned gaze sweeping over his eldest son, and he asked, "Are you hurt?"

Blake shook his head as the group began walking back down the dock. "No, I'm fine. But Brooke definitely needs healing."

"Brooke can still hear you," Brooke said quietly, the humor she'd probably intended falling flat.

"Good," Blake said, smiling down at her faintly. After a minute, as they neared the steps, he asked, "Did you see where the boat went?"

"It drove past the dock," Logan declared.

"I thought about flying after it," Nate added, an uncharacteristic weight to his words, "but it was too risky. And we didn't know where you and Brooke were."

"Blake! Brooke!" Angela exclaimed from where she knelt on the sand beside Georgia. Georgia was resting, her body fully engulfed in the deep, rejuvenating slumber that accompanied Angela's healing.

Dean was in the process of rolling out another beach towel, on Angela's other side, but he paused to look up and ascertain that his brother was all right.

When Dean stepped back, Blake moved and knelt beside the towel, helping Brooke to stretch out. "Just relax," Blake instructed softly. Once she was supported by the sand beneath the towel, he reached up and carefully, lightly, brushed back a strand of wet hair from her forehead.

Brooke offered him a weak smile, before her gaze shifted to look around at the gathered family. Her attention was pulled away from them, though, as Angela knelt on her other side.

"You'll feel better when you wake up," Angela promised as she reached out and covered Brooke's forehead with one hand. Her other hand hovered, not quite touching, over Brooke's injured forearm.

As the familiar golden glow formed over Angela's hands—and the associated areas of Brooke's body—Brooke returned her gaze to Blake and whispered, "Thank you."

Blake's smile was tight, and he swallowed heavily before he managed, "You're welcome. Now rest."

No one said anything until Brooke's eyes had drifted shut and her breathing had evened out. The golden glow of Angela's power was surrounding her entire body now, faintly pulsating as the younger girl concentrated on the task at hand.

Blake dragged in a deep breath and lifted his eyes from Brooke's face until they settled on Angela's. "Angie," he called softly. His sister lifted her gaze from her patient in silent curiosity, and he said, "Thank you."

Angela smiled reassuringly. "She's family, right?" She said nothing more as her eyes returned to Brooke.

A hand landed on Blake's shoulder and Blake turned, seeing that the hand belonged to his father. Taking the hint, Blake leaned back and pushed to his feet before stepping slightly away and turning to face his family.

"You're sure you're all right?" Christopher asked quietly.

Blake nodded. "I am. I just wish I'd been able to stop the bastard while I'd been out there."

"Don't beat yourself up," Logan said. "You did what you had to, and you kept Brooke alive."

"Yeah," Nate added. "We all know those jerks will show up again—and when they do, we'll give 'em hell for this."

Blake took a deep breath and nodded again. "I know," he said. Something occurred to him then, and as his gaze flicked over to the seemingly closed rental shop, he asked, "What happened to the employees?"

Dean laughed even as Christopher grinned and offered a shrug, saying, "I might have mentioned that the girls' boat had been stolen, and I'd seen it take off toward that boat dock a few miles south of here. Then I offered to pay for the rest of the boats for the day so that the shop wouldn't be out any money, and when he ran off to catch up with the stolen boat, he never looked over, so he didn't see Angela or Georgia."

"And he just believed you?" Blake asked, arching one eyebrow curiously. He certainly didn't think *he* would have believed that story.

"Turns out our old man's a pretty convincing liar," Dean explained with a grin.

With a mock-lecturing voice, Christopher replied, "Which is entirely acceptable and forgivable, provided I only use that talent when it's necessary. Situations like this, for instance."

"I don't know why I ever thought you weren't cool," Dean joked.

"You were a teenager," Christopher said calmly. "It happens to the best of us."

Short, strained laughter followed the declaration, and the group fell silent again.

It was Nate who eventually spoke up, his eyes having strayed over to Georgia's still-sleeping form. "So … we're going to have to tell her everything, aren't we?"

Four other sets of eyes followed his, and Christopher sighed. "I suppose we are."

"It's too bad we can't just convince her that she slipped, hit her head on a rock, and dreamt the whole thing," Dean said with a frown.

"That doesn't work in the real world, Dean," Blake replied. Despite his words, he agreed with his brother. It was better with fewer people knowing their secret—especially with dangerous enemies running around. And Georgia wasn't known for her ability to *avoid* gossip. So they would just have to hope she could keep this secret.

****

"She'll be fine," Brooke declared as they turned back toward town and Blake's house. The family had explained everything to Georgia, who had insisted on staying with Brooke until she'd woken up. Brooke hadn't been surprised to learn that they'd told Georgia the truth, and in turn she told them what she'd learned—the Mystery Man's name.

After all the information had been shared, Georgia had asked to be driven back to her car, which was still in the parking lot at the beach. So Blake, Brooke, and Georgia had piled into his Mustang, and Blake had taken them back to the beach. Georgia departed with the promise to call Brooke later, and the couple watched in silence as she fast-walked to her car.

Brooke felt horrible. She was berating herself for not listening to Blake's warning the night before, and for not thinking of it on her own before she'd even agreed to the trip. Because of her thoughtless stubbornness, she had gotten her best friend hurt and nearly gotten herself killed. And now her best friend was understandably freaked out, not having any sort of clue how to react to the situation.

The only thing Brooke could use to console herself with was the fact that, despite the danger, Blake hadn't gotten hurt, too. For whatever reason, Jacob hadn't seen fit to stick around. *Maybe he never even knew Blake was there*. But it didn't matter. So much damage had already been done.

"I'm sorry," Blake said quietly. His voice was tight, matching the grip he had on his steering wheel, and he kept his eyes on the road.

Brooke let him pull her out of her thoughts and turned her head in his direction. She knew what he was apologizing for, so she didn't ask. Instead, she said, "You don't have to apologize. If it weren't for you I'd be dead right now. *I'm* the one who needs to apologize." She paused, intending to do just that, when Blake interrupted what she was about to say.

"It's my fault you've gotten dragged into this in the first place," he insisted. One hand released the wheel, and he reached over to pull one of Brooke's hands into his. "I nearly lost you today." The words were low and filled with a kind of pain Brooke wished she couldn't recognize.

She squeezed his hand reassuringly, her other hand covering his as she held his hand in her lap. Softly, Brooke said, "I knew what I was getting myself into, remember? And that means none of this is your fault."

Blake said nothing, but he let her keep his hand sandwiched between hers as he turned onto his street. He didn't agree with her—she knew that. It wasn't the first time they'd had this argument.

Taking his hint, Brooke fell silent once more. She knew he was upset, she was pretty sure she knew why, and there was nothing she could do to make him feel better. So she watched quietly as he pulled into his garage, and she made no attempt to move until the door rolled shut behind them.

They remained silent as they eased out of the car and Blake led the way into the house.

Relief washed over Brooke when she stepped through the door. Her eyes swept over the familiar space as she finally allowed herself to realize just how close she'd come to never seeing it again. To never seeing her family or friends again. Never telling Blake exactly how much he meant to her. *And why not? What am I waiting for?*

"Brooke…?" Blake asked carefully when he realized she wasn't still walking behind him. He was facing her, concern clouding his eyes as he searched her expression.

Brooke took a deep, shaky breath and smiled. "I'm okay," she said. "I'm just ... happy to be here."

Blake opened his mouth to say something, a flicker of relief in his eyes, when he was interrupted by the ringing of his telephone.

They both jumped at the unexpected noise, their heads immediately swiveling toward the kitchen, where the phone was mounted on the wall above the counter.

Frowning suspiciously, Blake quickly strode to the kitchen and lifted the device from its cradle. "Hello?" He paused, listening to the caller, before saying, "Yeah, just a second." Then he pulled the phone from his ear, placed his free palm over the mouthpiece, and stage-whispered, "It's for you."

Confusion settled on Brooke's face, and she stepped up, taking the phone from him as he moved back to give her breathing room. "Yes?"

****

Blake watched as she listened to her former landlord. She had already received all the money she was due as a result of the fire, so he was curious as to why the man was calling. He shifted and leaned against the counter a few feet away, crossing his arms as Brooke finally spoke.

"Oh," she said, clearly surprised. Her eyes flicked over to Blake, but she looked away quickly and said, "Um, thank you. I do appreciate you calling, but, is it all right if I take the day to think it over? I promise I can give you an answer by tomorrow morning."

Answer to what? Blake wondered as his lips curved in a frown. A potential answer popped into place in his head, seeming like the most realistic reason for the call, and Blake's stomach clenched. He didn't want to be right. And more importantly, he didn't want Brooke to accept the offer if he was.

Then he remembered something else, and before he could second-guess himself, he pushed from the counter and turned to the hall. He could hear Brooke ending the conversation in the kitchen, but he kept going.

"Blake?" Brooke called, her voice coming from the kitchen. She must have ended her call already.

"I'll be right there," Blake called back without breaking stride. He'd made it to the bedroom, and a couple of quick steps more took him to his destination. Once he had what he needed, he turned and quickly moved back toward the kitchen and Brooke, curious to know if his guess was correct. And more than a little curious—among other things—to know what the answer to *his* question would be.

"So," Blake began as he walked back into the kitchen. "What did he want to talk to you about?" He did his best to keep his nerves from showing. The last thing he wanted was to worry her or tip his hand.

Brooke released a breath. "He, um … he said that one of his tenants is going to be out by the end of the month. He offered to hold the unit for me."

Then I was right, Blake thought as he nodded slowly in understanding. Carefully, he asked, "And … do you want him to?"

Brooke swallowed as though she were nervous, but her answer wasn't long in coming. "No," she admitted. "But I promised to find a new place as soon as I could. I don't want you to think I'm taking advantage of you."

Blake frowned and stepped up to her, framing her face with one hand. "I don't think that." He paused, his thumb caressing her cheek gently for a moment, and then he pulled his hand away, taking a step backwards. "The choice is yours, but, before you make your decision … let me make a counter-offer."

"A counter-offer?" Brooke repeated. She watched, confusion mounting in her eyes, as he took another step backwards.

"This might seem crazy," he warned as one hand dipped into his jeans pocket. "But I can't figure out why I haven't told you this before. Brooke, I love you."

Brooke's eyes widened at his confession, and her mouth fell open just a bit when he pulled his hand from his pocket and knelt on the kitchen tile.

Blake swallowed again, fighting against the sudden, unusual dryness of his mouth, as he held up the ring that he'd been hiding in his palm. He'd only purchased it a handful of days prior, and he'd honestly thought it would be a little while before he found the right time to use it, but now he couldn't think of a better time. He could only hope she would feel the same.

Clearing his throat quickly, Blake forced out those all-important words. "Nearly losing you today has made me realize that 'the right time' is never guaranteed. So I'm asking now … Brooke, will you marry me?"

****

Brooke could barely breathe as she absorbed the scene before her. His words washed over her, caressing her ears and warming her heart. And she couldn't help but stare at the diamond he was offering her. Never in her life had she imagined owning a ring like that. It was beautiful, yet simple and elegant. It was perfect.

And her family hadn't met him yet—they'd only heard a few stories in emails and phone calls. And there was the one time he'd actually talked to her mother on the phone. They were definitely going to accuse her of rushing into things, or demand a test just to prove she really wasn't pregnant.

But none of that mattered, because he was still waiting for an answer. So she took a deep breath and dragged her eyes to his as a smile curved her lips. "Yes," she said.

The nerves in Blake's eyes vanished as he allowed himself to smile and pushed to his feet in one fluid motion. They each took a step forward, and Blake slipped the perfectly sized ring on her finger. For a moment, they both stared at her hand, admiring the way the main diamond sparkled in the kitchen light.

And then their eyes met again, his hand came up, beneath hers, and wrapped around it gently.

"My family is going to have questions," Brooke stated quietly.

"Probably," Blake allowed. "But at least they can't ask me about my intentions."

Brooke laughed and curled her fingers around his wrist. "I should call my old landlord back," she said, her voice softer than before.

Blake leaned in until their noses were almost touching. "You can call him in the morning," he mumbled, his voice thick.

Brooke tilted her head and let her lips brush just barely over his. "I love you."

Blake's lips sealed over hers an instant later, and he kissed her with every ounce of desperation and passion that had built within her throughout the day. And she felt the rumble against her lips when she returned his kiss.

They both knew their new engagement didn't solve all of their problems, but it didn't matter. Jacob and his father weren't going away any time soon, but that was no reason to put their lives on hold. Whatever happened next, they would deal with it together.

The kiss broke for a moment, and Blake quietly asked, "Does this mean you'll at least let me buy you a new cell phone?"

Breathless laughter slipped past her lips, and Brooke said, "Sure." She curled her hands in the collar of his shirt and tugged him back to her lips. "Now stop talking."

Blake obliged her willingly, his arms wrapping tightly around her and pulling her close as their lips met again.

The End

www.rosewulf.weebly.com

Evernight Publishing

www.evernightpublishing.com

www.ingramcontent.com/pod-product-compliance
Lightning Source LLC
Chambersburg PA
CBHW020257200626
46816CB00001BA/332